"You're certainly a tease now, aren't you? Bold and uninhibited. Beautiful and enticing. The most desirable woman I've ever known, but no longer shy about her sexuality. I don't know if I can handle that, Shannon."

"I don't either, but I can't wait to find out."

Wasting no time, she removed his shirt, her mouth leaving wet trails down his chest.

S0-AAZ-685

# Separate Dreams

**Joan Early**

Genesis Press, Inc.

# INDIGO LOVE STORIES

An imprint of Genesis Press, Inc.
Publishing Company

Genesis Press, Inc.
P.O. Box 101
Columbus, MS 39703

All rights reserved. Except for use in any review, the reproduction or utilization of this work in whole or in part in any form by any electronic, mechanical, or other means, not known or hereafter invented, including xerography, photocopying, and recording, or in any information storage or retrieval system, is forbidden without written permission of the publisher, Genesis Press, Inc. For information write Genesis Press, Inc., P.O. Box 101, Columbus, MS 39703.

All characters in this book have no existence outside the imagination of the author and have no relation whatsoever to anyone bearing the same name or names. They are not even distantly inspired by any individual known or unknown to the author and all incidents are pure invention.

Copyright © 2011 Joan Early

ISBN: 13 DIGIT : 978-1-58571-434-6
ISBN: 10 DIGIT : 1-58571-434-8
Manufactured in the United States of America

First Edition

Visit us at www.genesis-press.com
or call at 1-888-Indigo-1-4-0

# Dedication

To my beautiful, fascinating granddaughter, Devon.

# Acknowledgements

I am grateful to Genesis Press for publishing my work and to the readers for their support. I'm especially grateful for a grandmother who taught me to believe in myself and never give up.

# Chapter 1

Announcements of flight delays boomed in three languages around the crowded terminals at Charles de Gaulle airport. Shannon Travers looked out at the Paris lights. In the maze of historic elegance, she could almost see the heavily guarded Palais de l'Elysee and the mansion where Thierry lived. It was all there. The lights. The glory. She had come and she had conquered, but the grimace on her face was a bitter contrast to the joy she'd felt upon arrival almost two years earlier. The price of fame had been staggering.

"Ms. Travers, can we have your autograph?" a bright-faced young woman in a Paul Lager coat asked, alerting the other bystanders to her identity. The crowd, especially the younger ones, quickly surrounded her. A freckle-faced woman in hiking boots tried to corral a group of students, all yelling Shannon's name. Several young men tugged on her arm. A group of persistent gawkers climbed on chairs for a better look.

Shannon smiled politely. They were her fans, her adoring public. Placing her purse and carry-on between her feet, she repeatedly signed her name on slips of paper, airline stubs, and the back of a few hands. Thierry had advised her to carry lots of photographs and pens, which she normally did, but this was not a normal outing. She was going home to her mother's funeral.

Before the first crowd had dispersed, others hurried over from nearby terminals, all stranded because of cancelled flights. They were not as persistent as American fans, yet anyone who suffered claustrophobia would find their intrusion overwhelming. Thierry had said her fans were diverse, and so was the crowd that gathered around her. The last time she'd faced a crowd at close range, Thierry had rescued her just before her world went black. She really needed him now.

She could feel sweat forming on her face and under her sweater. Her head pounded and her throat threatened to close. Her hands trembled. Her signature became one long, indistinguishable line. She answered questions with as much of a smile as she could muster. Thierry's brother, Henri, had asked how she was able to walk on stage under blinding lights and perform before a crowd of strangers. That was easy. The stage was her forum. On stage, alone but secure, she felt safe rather than smothered.

Someone asked her her destination. Feeling tears gather in her eyes, she said, "I'm flying to New York and on to my hometown in Mississippi. It's in the South. No, I'm not married. I'm traveling alone. No, I'm not performing there." She tried to back away as she murmured. "My mother just died. That's why I'm going home."

They responded to the tears in her voice. The leader of the first crowd, looking quite motherly in spite of her boots and backpack, stretched her arms in front of Shannon. "Okay, let's give her room to breathe. She just lost her mother."

"Thank you." Shannon mouthed the words, then continued signing their luggage, their newspapers, or whatever they held out to her. Fame was wonderful, but for someone with severe claustrophobia, it could sometimes be more frightening than boos or jeers.

"I love you, Shannon!" someone yelled.

"Thank you. I love all of you."

More declarations of affection followed until the crowd began to scatter. After returning the last young girl's pen and her smile, Shannon moved closer to the window and opened a copy of *Musique* magazine. Feeling the presence of someone close by, she glared down at the magazine, hoping they would go away.

"Excuse me."

She looked up and saw a robed man wearing a heavy crucifix. "Yes, Father?"

"I'm Father Bertoniere. Father Bert, for short. Would you allow me to sit next to you? My frock will keep most of them at bay." His English was wobbly, but his kindly smile restored her calm.

"Yes, Father. Please, have a seat."

"That is a little bit frightening, no?"

"Yes, it is frightening."

He told her the weather had caused his flight to Switzerland to abort before takeoff. He could not leave for six hours. She told him she was scheduled to leave in two hours, though she knew she had missed her connecting flight. Then, feeling overcome with emotion, she told him her life story.

When the weather cleared enough for takeoff, Shannon thanked Father Bert, boarded and scrunched down in seat 2B. As the glamour of Paris faded into darkness, the pain in her chest became overwhelming. Turbulence jostled the large 747 as if it were a child's toy. The snoring passenger next to her sat up in alarm. Two rowdy children behind her quit kicking the back of her seat, but she knew she would not rest.

She flipped through the pages of *Musique*, though she had little interest in stories of new recording artists and their expected rise to the top of the music charts. Growing up in Shepherd, Mississippi, she could never have imagined being one of them. In fact, most events in her twenty-nine years of living had been unexpected.

She had studied hard to get exceptional scholarship offers to major universities, yet had relinquished all of them for four years in Grambling, Louisiana. She had made that choice for Edison because she had wanted him more than anything else. She'd never dreamed a singing career would spoil their love and end the marriage she'd thought would last forever.

She certainly had not expected her mother to die suddenly and at such a young age. She saw her mother's face before her, still vibrant and happy. She felt her arms, heard her voice and remembered their last conversation three days ago. Between Paris and New York, each word of caution, love, and praise her mother had uttered came alive in her thoughts. Her pain was greater than any she could have imagined.

~

Shannon moved easily through the crowd at La-Guardia without much recognition. Her music was popular in the States, but with only two U.S. magazine interviews, her face was not overly familiar. Conversely, Thierry had plastered her posters across Europe. He had arranged interviews with every news source, even the smallest pamphlet-style papers. He had even planted words that painted a better image than any camera could capture.

Every description he had used would also fit her mother. Shannon was tall and willowy like her father, but her large, brandy-brown eyes, skin the color of perfect toast, and legs that were glamorized by her trademark four-inch heels, were all inherited from her mother. She even had the same tiny mole on the right side of her nose. Knowing she would never again see her mother's smile caused more sorrow than she felt able to handle.

There were no direct flights from New York City to Jackson, Mississippi, but Shannon was grateful to find an available seat on the next flight to Jackson out of Atlanta. Physically and emotionally exhausted, she made the hurried connection in Atlanta and felt her burdens grow as the small plane neared Jackson.

Returning home to the most painful event of her life meant she also had to face Edison and the ruins of a marriage she had cherished. She thought of her daughter and tried to smile. Leila was now a pawn, the one thing Edison could use to make her miserable. She didn't blame him. His scrutiny of the choices she had made could never be as severe as her own.

He was dating Jeannie Stanberry, his best friend's older sister. She had wondered why he had chosen Jeannie, but knowing the pain she had caused him gave her little room to question his choice. In her absence, Edison had been elected as Shepherd's new sheriff, a position he had coveted since childhood. She hoped he was happy.

When the plane landed, she made her way down the stairs. She immediately spotted her father pacing the gray tile in front of the baggage carousel. Even from behind, the profile of John Patrick "J.P." Travers was easily distinguishable. The staggering pain in her chest had not blinded Shannon to the fact that her father's grief was even greater—he had lost his companion of over thirty-eight years and the only woman he had ever loved.

Tears welled in her eyes. She quickly detoured to the ladies' room. There was no disguising her red, puffy eyes, but a splash of water and a dab of lipstick restored the glow to her face.

"Daddy." She walked into her father's arms.

"Baby. I'm so glad you made it. I was beginning to worry. I've called the airlines so many times I'm sure I'll be placed on that no-fly list." Holding her at arm's length, he gazed at her face. "Other than the delay, how was your flight from Paris?"

"Not as bad as the one from New York to Atlanta." She breathed deeply and stifled her tears. "I can't believe it, Daddy. It seems so unreal."

"I know, baby, but we have to be strong. She wouldn't want us to grieve ourselves sick."

"She wouldn't. Mom was the most selfless person I know."

He took her bags from the carousel and led the way through the freshly striped parking lot. When he slowed and pressed his keyless entry remote, she looked around for the white Cadillac; instead, she saw the trunk open on a shiny Chrysler with temporary tags.

"You have a new car? No one told me."

"We just got it four days ago. The Cadillac needed work and your mother fell in love with this model, the 300M. She..." His voice broke. "Champagne was her favorite color."

After he loaded her bags in the trunk, they talked of everything but their shared agony. The air was muggy. Ribbons of russet slashed through the autumn landscape. Shannon's heart lurched when they passed the high school. She had matured and fell in love there, but more than anything, it held memories of her mother's unending devotion to the profession she had loved.

Everything had changed greatly since she first left for college. Boarded windows attested to the many failed businesses in the area. Main Street and the once tidy town square were now pocked with desolation and decay. She had loved Shepherd. Now she saw it as a wasteland of broken dreams. Memories chafed her soul like wet grains of sand. Though her future was uncertain, she doubted she could ever live in Shepherd again.

"I have to go to Wells' Funeral Home and make the final arrangements," J.P. said. "If you want, I'll drive you home and come back later."

A fist of fear tightened around her heart. She had never sat through a funeral without becoming hysterical. "No, I'm going with you."

"Are you sure?" J.P. asked. "I don't mind taking you home and coming back. I have a few other things to do in town as well."

"Don't worry about me. I'll be fine, Daddy." She gazed in silence at her wonderful father, the stern but loving disciplinarian. She had not noticed his age until now. Silver threads ran through a receding patch of black. The sparkle was gone from his eyes. She remembered her aunt saying that her mother was the only one who could humble him, because no man had ever loved a woman more.

He stopped in front of the gray building that even an array of colorful zinnias could not brighten. Her despair heightened. The interior was as she remembered. Box-like windows framed by heavy green drapes that were faded white around the edges from years of intense Mississippi sun. The reception area, like the chapel behind it, was filled with chairs upholstered in the same green material. Multiple stains and frayed cushions evidenced frequent use.

The owner hurried to greet them, offering his personal services to make arrangements for her mother's final journey. She wondered if she could get through it without breaking down. She looked at the series of caskets, still holding her father's hand. Next came a selection of interiors and floral sprays. She took a deep breath and prepared for the part she knew would be hardest. Her grandmother had always said death was as much a part of life as birth. She knew she had to be strong. This situation was final. Irreversible. There was nothing she could do.

The owner assured them he would bring in the same hairstylist her mother used, and asked if they had brought the dress. J.P. offered Shannon the car keys.

"Honey, why don't you just wait for me? Sit in the car or wait out in the garden."

"I'll wait in the garden." She rushed away, knowing he did not want her to see his tears.

❧

The conversation was pleasant as the crowd gathered in Shepherd's courthouse assembly hall. When the gavel came down and the meeting was called to order, the friendly exchange of words quickly turned to accusations and innuendos.

"I want to know how a little town like Shepherd is having a robbery darn near every week." Alistair "Red" Calhoun rested his hat on his knee and looked around the room. "If it's drugs like everybody says, I want to know how they're getting in and why we can't stop them." He turned to face the sheriff. "Have you arrested anybody yet?"

Edison had expected the questions, but his mind was elsewhere. "No, we haven't arrested anyone yet. We have three suspects, but not enough evidence to hold them."

"Then maybe you're not trying hard enough," a voice yelled from the back of the room. "Maybe you're not looking in the right places, like right under your own nose. Bettis was robbed for the third time. They took cigarettes, beer, and money from the cash register. Carl Bettis is damn near eighty years old. It's a wonder it didn't give him a heart attack."

"We know all about the problems," Mayor Townsend said. "We know what they did. We even know what they look like. We just can't catch them doing it."

David Ennis, president of the school board, stood and looked around the room. "Drugs are coming into the schools faster than we can haul them out. Maybe you're too close to the problem." His eyes were focused on Edison. "It breaks my heart to see the young people, even the older ones, strung out on that stuff. Just look at your best friend, Bobby Joe Stanberry. It hurts when it's so close to home. You have to take a stand, not just close your eyes and just let it happen."

"If you're implying I'm not doing my job in order to protect a friend, you're dead wrong. Bobby Joe is a drunk as far as I know. He's been arrested for public intoxication several times. I'm not the one who imposes the sentences, and I've never asked anyone to go easy on him in court." Edison's patience was already worn dime-thin. "Most of you have been looking over my shoulder. You've seen exactly what I've seen. If you think I've missed something, point it out now. If you have enough evidence to indict Bobby Joe or anyone else, please come forward."

"The sheriff and his deputies have been working 'round the clock," the mayor added. "We all have thoughts on this, but without evidence, we can't do a thing. It's up to all of us to keep our eyes and ears open. Get as much information as you can before you come down here naming names. Even when we know someone is guilty, we need proof in a court of law."

"Too bad *they* don't know about that court of law," the voice called again from the back of the room.

"They obviously do know," Edison answered. "That's why they're always one step ahead of us."

"We need to see something positive happen in Shepherd." Edith Bloomfield spoke on behalf of the Women's League. "Mayor, what progress has been made on the state bringing that prison here? I don't really want more of the criminal element around us, but this town needs the business."

The discussion shifted to Shepherd's financial needs. Edison's anger abated and his mind strayed. He desperately wanted to rid Shepherd of its criminals, and he would. But today, his concentration was shattered by the loss of someone dear, and by knowing the woman who still meant the world to him was coming home.

"I know that bunch attacked you pretty good," Mayor Townsend said after the meeting had ended. "I hope you know they were gunning for me, not you. This is election year, and there's a whole bunch of folks hoping I'm not in this chair when it's over. Oliver Prince is the most vocal of all, but the old goat stayed hidden in the back of the room."

"I know it's mostly political, but it stings when you're doing all you can."

"I do want to ask one question." Mayor Townsend turned to Edison. "How well do you trust your deputies?"

Edison met and held his gaze. "I trust them with my life. Why?"

"I just wanted to hear you say it. It does seem these thieves and crooks know what we're going to do before we do it."

"I know, but there's not one man on my staff that I doubt. Vance is the only one who didn't grow up in Shepherd, but I've known him since college. He spent a lot to time with…" He left the remembrance unfinished.

"Is Shannon home yet?" Mayor Townsend asked.

"She's coming today. I saw J.P. heading into Jackson when I came here."

"Then I'd better let you go. I'm sure you'll want to be there when she gets home."

Startled for a second, Edison shook his head. "I hadn't planned to be there."

"Shannon is your little girl's mother, and she just lost her mother. One of the true ladies in this town, I might add. You're family."

"I *was* family."

Mayor Townsend's bushy eyebrows came together in a frown. "I don't know all the details of your divorce, but did you divorce J.P. and his wife as well?"

Edison stood. "I love J.P. and Miss Doris, and I never talk to anyone about my problems with Shannon. The town does enough talking as it is. It's just hard to be around her without feeling things I don't want to feel." He looked at Mayor Townsend. "I'm still angry."

"And hurt. You know, Shannon is hurting something awful herself right about now."

Edison stood in the doorway for a second before answering. "I need to follow up on something." He turned. "Thanks."

Edison drove to the diner, not to see Jeannie, but because it was the place he had always gone when his world was falling apart. He parked and sat in the squad car, his body slumped over the steering wheel. His heart was beating wildly. He wanted to hate Shannon, and sometimes he hated himself because he could not.

He had talked to J.P. earlier and knew her plane was delayed. He wanted to see her. He just didn't think it was a good idea.

He thought of the beginning. Everyone said Miss Doris got him through high school, but that was only partially true. Her tutoring sessions had been the highlight of his life back then. He would sit in the room filled with sewing machines, desks, and books, hoping for a chance to talk to Shannon. When he got it, he was too tongue-tied to speak. He had loved her from afar since eighth grade. She was more than pretty. She was cool and refined. Nothing seemed to ruffle her, in class or at home. He had ached to hold her and finally had that chance at the homecoming dance of their junior year. Even then, he'd stammered a preamble of the invitation to her mother.

"Uh, Mrs. Travis, do you think Shannon would go to the dance with me?"

Miss Doris had smiled slightly. "She might, but you'll have to ask her first."

Two days later, she had given him $50 for removing a wasp nest from her carport. When he tried to protest, she said it was worth it not to have to face those horrible wasps. Edison had taken the money because he knew she wanted him to have it. He also knew that both mother and daughter were afraid of very little, and certainly not wasps. Water gathered in his eyes.

Doris Travers had been a mother in every sense of the word.

He saw eyes staring from the diner window and wondered why he hadn't waited on the highway. J.P. had said they had to finalize the funeral arrangements, so he knew where they would stop. Did he dare go there? Did he dare not?

He took his hat from the seat and went inside. Jeannie pretended to be busy wiping the counter.

"Hey. Business okay today?" he asked.

"Not really." She rolled her eyes up to meet his face. "Why were you sitting out in the squad car all that time? Got one of those big personal problems you can't talk about?"

"I have a big problem. It's not personal. I've already talked about it, and talked, and talked. Didn't I tell you about the meeting this morning?"

She dropped her stare. "Oh."

He slumped into the booth and took her hand. "Sit down a minute. We need to talk."

She slid in opposite him and leaned forward, straining the fabric of her pink-and-white- checked uniform. "Now, that is the conversation I expected when I saw that look on your face. Anything that begins with 'we need to talk' is bad news."

"It's not bad news. The look on my face should be expected. I just had my head handed to me on a platter in that meeting. I'm doing all I can, and it's not enough. On top of that, a woman who meant the world to me just died. She also happens to be my baby's grandmother. I can't do a banjo solo right now, and it shouldn't be expected. Why don't you tell me the reason you've been acting so irritable? We both know, so you might as well say it."

"I don't have to say it because we both know what happened the last time Shannon came home."

"The last time Shannon came home, she was still my wife. Shannon is coming home now to bury her mother. I'm directly affected, not because Shannon was my wife, but because she is Leila's mother. Miss Doris was Leila's grandmother. My baby doesn't understand everything, but she knows her grandmother is gone. She's hurting, and so am I. That shouldn't be hard for you to grasp."

"Have it your way." She scooted from the booth and pulled her uniform in place. "Shannon left Leila here with her mother, and now her mother is gone. I think that's why you're so worried. You were messed up when Leila was over there with Shannon for three months. You can't hop on a plane and fly to Paris. She wanted to flaunt her money by having that child come over there, not once or twice, but three times."

"We have shared custody. I work and so does Shannon, which means we divide the time as best we can, with our parents filling in when needed. Whenever Shannon is not touring or doesn't have lengthy engagements, I give my permission for her parents or her sister-in-law, Donna, to take Leila to Paris. It's important for Leila to spend time with her mother. If we have to divide the six months into several trips, and Shannon can afford the travel expense, I'm fine with it. Shannon can't take Leila out of the country without my permission. I gladly gave it when Shannon's parents took Leila over there, and when Donna made the trip. I have never given my permission for Shannon to take her to Paris permanently, and I never will."

"I don't want to argue. Shannon has money and fame. If she wants to take Leila away permanently, she'll get a judge to jump through hoops just like she does you. I'm just worried about what will happen to you when she does it." She walked away and he followed.

"I don't want to argue, either. I want you to stop questioning my moods and trying to read something shady into everything I do. I don't think Shannon will take Leila away from her family, but I need to be able to make a home for her. We need to make a home for her. That's the one thing you don't seem to want to talk about."

"Did you find out when she's coming home?"

He sighed. "J.P. said she would leave on the first available flight, but there's been a lot of bad weather in Europe. I hope she didn't have any problems getting out of Paris."

"I'm surprised she was available on such short notice." She toyed with the buttons on her uniform. "Maybe her career isn't doing so hot. I did hear someone say that recently, and I don't see all of those commercials for her music as much as I used to. From what I hear, her music is not happening anymore."

He knew it was bait, but took it anyway. "She's only been recording a year, Jeannie. Who said that?"

"Oh, I don't remember. Somebody was talking about it in here not long ago. I don't speak French and I don't listen to Shannon's kind of music."

"How do you define Shannon's kind of music? Most of her recordings are in English. Her style is quite versatile."

She angrily swiped a coffee mug from the table. "I don't know her style. I just know it isn't mine. You play that stuff; I don't."

"Shannon has a great voice no matter what she sings. I play it mainly for Leila. As far as I know, Shannon's career is doing quite well. Of course, I don't think a busy schedule could keep her from coming home. Her mother just died, Jeannie."

"Don't get defensive. I didn't mean anything negative. I was just repeating what I heard." She flipped the dishtowel over her shoulder.

From the corner of his eye, Edison saw the champagne blur coming down the road and stood to leave.

"Whatever. I'm going back into town. I'll see you later."

He sat in the squad car and checked his messages, but started the engine when he saw Jeannie peeping from the window. A small photograph of his daughter on the dashboard reminded him of a different time. A happy time. Merging with traffic, he drove into Shepherd and down Main Street listening to the lilting voice he loved, and to the pounding of his heart.

Shannon walked out to the park-like setting and sat on a stone bench beneath a flowering crepe myrtle. Staring at the biblical inscriptions on the table before her, she suddenly became aware that she wasn't alone. The air, even the smell, had changed. The flip-flop of her heart was quite familiar. It happened every time he was near. He called her name but his voice seemed distant and arid. She waited.

"Shannon?"

She stood and turned slowly, her eyes downcast until she saw the spit-shined brown boots. She lifted her gaze past his ironed khakis and the holster that rested on his hip. Memories cascaded over her. She glanced past the barrel chest that once held her head in passion. Seeing the hardness in his eyes, she fixed her stare on the cleft chin he found hard to shave. It was all there, standing before her, a memory, engraved for life.

"Hello, Edison."

He half smiled and shifted restlessly from one leg to the other. "I was on my way in to pay my respects." He cleared his throat. "You have my deepest sympathy. The entire town is feeling the loss of your wonderful mother."

"Thank you." The scratch in his voice was not unexpected, but still hard to take. "How is Leila?"

"Fine. Getting sassier every day. She asked why you didn't call last night. I told her you were on your way home, but with the horrible weather conditions over there, I wasn't sure when you would arrive."

"The weather was bad. It was a bumpy flight."

"Your father didn't say if you were flying from Paris or somewhere else. I keep hearing about your busy schedule."

Each time she had Leila flown to Paris, he had asked why she could not spend time with her in Shepard. He had asked if it was commitments or her lack of concern for their child. That swipe of bile always hit hard, but she had refused to react, focusing instead on Leila. "I came as soon as I could get a flight. Right now, I just want to see my baby." She smiled. "She hates it when I call her that. She's maturing too quickly. Can you bring her over, please?"

"Sure, but it may be tomorrow. I know you're tired, and I think Leila is busy this evening. She and Jeannie have plans—"

"Oh?" she interrupted, wondering how so much disdain could have developed between two people who could not have been more in love. "When did Leila start spending time with Jeannie? She told me you never take her to Jeannie's house and the three of you never do things together."

She watched him fidget and continued her offensive. "I know Leila is left with your mother when you're with Jeannie. Our daughter doesn't seem too fond of the woman you're about to marry."

"I'm not engaged to anyone at this time, and I don't take Leila on my dates. I'm sure you don't take her out with you and Thierry. I spend a lot of time with my daughter." He clinched his jaw.

"I know you spend time with *our* daughter, and I'm happy for that. I'm glad you were here for her. I know this is your time with her, but I would like to see her tonight if that's not too much to ask. Leila spent most of her time with my mother, so I'm sure she's very upset. Daddy said she became hysterical when you tried to explain why she would never see Grandmommy. She should be home with me and Daddy right now."

His attempt at a smile faded. Harshness was reflected in his sarcasm. "Of course, your highness." He made a mock bow.

Shannon had not heard her father approach, but all at once his strained voice sounded behind her.

"Hello, Edison. Is everything okay?"

"Yes. Yes, sir." His head fell forward. Embarrassment shaded his face. "I'll bring Leila over this evening. Please let me know when the arrangements are finalized. I've already asked for deputies to lead the procession. Everyone wanted to volunteer. They all loved Miss Doris."

"Thank you." He took Shannon's arm. "We'll see you at the house."

She had not expected much. Edison had been devastated when she had accepted offers that would prevent her from returning home as planned. She had hurt him. His resentment was understandable, but she had hoped he would contain it, if not for her sake, at least out of respect for her parents.

# Chapter 2

The relentless sun beamed down on the roof of the patrol car, but the heat Edison felt came from within. Filled with shame and frustration, he dropped his head into his hands.

The mayor had told him he should have been a judge because he was fair, level headed, and always considerate of others. If he ever disobeyed as a child, he was punished, not spared. If he participated in childhood mischief, he was the one who got caught. He was not good at being the bad guy. His conscience was enormous and always kept him on the right path.

Everything was different where Shannon was involved. He seemed to lose all sense of reason. Why had he thought he could see her and not feel the pain that still consumed him? Their divorce was final but the ache was fresh. His minister said the pain was so great because he'd let pride drive him to break up his family. He wondered if today he had purposely tried to make her feel bad. If so, he was the one suffering.

He had accepted her decision to take advantage of a once-in-a-lifetime opportunity. He hadn't wanted her to go, maybe because he knew her talent could explode into a career in Paris. Maybe it was because of the way

Thierry had looked at her. His wife was not only beautiful, she was bright, talented, and sexy without having to try. What man would not be tempted?

She had at first said no to Thierry's invitation to cut a demo in Paris. She was part of a group, she had told him. Their talk took place after Thierry followed them back to Shepherd and presented a contract that even Edison knew was legitimate. She had said she only wanted to try her wings and told him how much she loved him. She would cut the demo and return home. For two months, he had believed she would.

The weekend she was supposed to return, he had shopped for candles, flowers, and all of her favorite foods. Her mother had made her favorite cake. When she called to say her return was delayed, his heart began to doubt that she would ever come home again. Thierry had planned an audition with a club in the Latin Quarter that could lead to concerts all over Europe.

"Leila stays with Mom most of the time and she sees you every day. I talked to her earlier. I know this is taking longer than planned, but Thierry—"

"Damn Thierry!" he had yelled.

He had wanted her home with him and with their daughter. She had no right to leave her child, and he had told her so. "You're a married woman with a child. You can't go gallivanting all over Europe with another man. You say he's your business manager, producer, whatever. I want my wife back home."

Two weeks later, she had been booked for shows in France, Germany, England, and Italy. It was Thierry's way of maximizing her public exposure before the CD was released.

"I don't care what Thierry is planning. You said you were coming home. If you're not here by the end of next week, I'll know that your husband and your child no longer matter."

Two weeks later the divorce papers were drawn and served. She came home three days later.

"How can you do this? Have you counseled with Pastor Tim? What grounds can you use for divorce, Edison? Why can't you believe that I love you?"

"Okay, stay home with me and Leila. I'll tear up the papers."

"Baby, I wish I could. I've got scheduled engagements. Thierry said—"

"Then go back to Thierry. That's where you want to be."

She had talked and cried. Lying in bed with Leila between them, he had believed her. She was hungry for him and spent a great deal of time proving it, but when Thierry called, she left.

She had not wanted a divorce, but refused to return home. She was in Paris with Thierry, living life in the fast lane. He could not accept that. She had left him. She had left Leila. What choice did he have?

He adjusted the rearview mirror and saw her holding her father's arm while walking down the steps of the mortuary. She moved with style and poise, even in her time of sorrow.

"What on earth is wrong with me?" he muttered. He had heard his voice, had heard the venom, had heard himself repeat Jeannie's unfounded and stupid remarks, but could not stop. Hurting Shannon, especially now, made him feel lower than he already did.

"How could I be so cruel?" he asked himself. The answer was obvious, and he saw no end to his dilemma. Standing next to her, looking into her eyes, inhaling that familiar scent had completely reopened wounds that had scarcely begun to heal.

He knew Shannon's sorrow was great. He had wanted to reach out, not lash out. He watched her cross the street, head bowed, still holding her father's arm. Always in awe of her beauty, he was most fascinated by her calmness. She had been unflappable, even in times of extreme pressure. It was as if she could remove herself from stressful situations…except funerals. He remembered holding her tightly against his body to calm her shakes at her grandfather's funeral. She had needed him then, and feeling needed had been wonderful.

When they were younger, he'd thought she had superior knowledge. He still thought she possessed emotional strength that was hers exclusively. Her calmness still made him feel inadequate and small.

27

The other feeling he could not deny was the desire that pierced his body like a lightning bolt. He ached to hold her, to touch her, to feel her softness. There was no truth in the cruelty he had displayed. He knew it. Maybe she did, too.

He headed back to the diner, but quickly changed his mind and turned in the middle of the street. The only person who could comfort him now was the precious gift Shannon had given him. Stopping the patrol car beside the freshly painted white gate of his parents' home, he sat for a second, hoping to discard the telltale look of frustration.

A smaller version of Shannon bounced down the steps and into his arms when he walked into the yard. Tears stung his eyes. She had her mother's face and her mother's smile. Even after his worst day, she made him feel ten feet tall, just as Shannon's first smile in the morning had kept him floating through his work days when they were married.

"How's daddy's girl?" He lifted her into his arms and kissed her cheek. "What have you and Granny been doing all day?"

"I was waiting for you." Her voice was small but confident. "Did my mommy come home yet?"

His mother, who had been watering plants on the front porch, stopped, placed the watering can next to a big pot of geraniums, stood akimbo, and gave him a stern, inquisitive stare. "You saw her, didn't you?" Etta

Page wiped her brow with the back of her hand. "I can tell by that powerful load of grief I see in your eyes."

"Yes, she's here. I saw her with her father at the funeral home. I'm taking Leila out to the house, so would you please comb her hair and change her dress?"

"Don't surprise me none," she muttered before kicking the watering can from her path.

"Mama! This is not the time."

He walked away, but, as he'd feared, his mother followed.

"I asked Jeannie to come by for dinner this evenin', but she's shorthanded at the diner. Two of them people she had over there quit yesterday. The only ones left are Hazel and Dot. Young folks just don't want to work these days."

"I saw Jeannie today, Mama."

"Did you tell her where you was goin' this evening?"

"No. I haven't spoken to her since I saw Shannon." He knew his mother and Jeannie kept in constant touch. His brother Raymond and his sisters had managed to keep their private lives away from her scrutiny, but she had full access to his, mostly because of Leila.

"Well, don't forget the woman who was there for you when you needed her. You just need to set a date and get married. Go find your daddy and tell him to come inside for dinner. I need time to get this child ready."

Edison sighed. She knew his feelings for Shannon were still alive. Jeannie suspected it, and he was infinitely ashamed of it. Time and distance had not squelched his overwhelming desire to have Shannon in arms and in his life. His feelings for Jeannie and his anger did not matter when he was close to Shannon. Fear of rejection was the only thing holding him back.

"Come on, Leila. Let's find Papa so we can eat. I think he's in the garage. We're going to see your mommy after dinner. Won't that be fun?"

She smiled and took his hand, but held back once they were in the yard and pulled on his arm until he stopped. "Is Mommy bad?"

Her question was not surprising. She was too perceptive to ignore his mother's veiled comments. "Your mother is a wonderful person. She's beautiful and talented, and she loves you very much."

"Why does she live in Paris instead of here in Shepherd?"

He knelt beside her and took her small hands in his. "Your mommy is very talented. You know that, don't you?"

She nodded.

"She had a chance to sing, but she had to go to Paris to make her music. You know they love her over there. You've been there with her."

"Does Mommy love me?"

He lifted her in his arms and held her head to his shoulder. Leila had always asked more questions than most kids, but they were usually thought-provoking or filled with self-doubt. They also twisted his heart.

"Your mother has always loved you. Didn't you tell me how much you enjoyed being in Paris? You said your mother had told everyone about you. That's because she's proud of you and she loves you very much."

"Does she love you, too?"

That question was not expected. "Your mother and I had some wonderful times together. We were very much in love, but your mother needed more than she could get here in Shepherd. She's talented and very special."

"Did you love her?"

He wanted to say he loved her with all of his heart. Then and now. "I loved your mother very much. She will always be special to me."

"I don't understand. Are you angry with her?"

"That's all very hard to explain, honey. We'll discuss it when you're older."

"I hope so, because you always say that when I ask questions."

She strutted ahead of him, her head cocked defiantly to the side, her mother's image. Seeing Shannon and hearing his daughter's questions dredged back every second of joy associated with falling in love. Lingering not far behind were the heartaches of a failed marriage.

He sat at the kitchen table in a home that exemplified rural living: blue wooden shutters rested on white boards, print wallpaper that was beginning to peel at the seams, furniture that had survived two generations, and potted plants in every room. After several renovations and additions, it was still a home that lacked sophistication. It was filled with love, but little understanding. He picked at his food in silence, stealing glances at his daughter's youthful frowns. More than ever, she reminded him of Shannon. He cringed when his mother continued her inquisition.

"What time you plan to have this child back home?"

"We won't be late."

"Make sure o' that. Jeannie will be lookin' for you."

"Can you please cool it, Etta?" His father, James, Tito to family and friends, looked up and spoke for the first time since the meal began. "Is it too much to ask for a little peace and quiet when I'm trying to eat? As soon as Shannon's mother died, I knowed we would have World War III around here. Edison done told you, I done told you, but you still keep harping. I thought even you would cut the girl some slack now. Just drop it."

"I don't care what you say. Edison ain't supposed to be running after anyone but Jeannie. She's a fine woman."

"I don't care who runs or who gets caught. I just want to eat my food in peace. I'm surprised all of us don't have ulcers the way you keep rattling on like a tin lizzie, yakking your head off about something that, frankly, ain't your business. Edison is a man. If he can run that sheriff's office, I think he can run his own life. You ain't helping any, you know."

Edison pressed his hand against the ache in his head. "Jeannie and I are not married, Mama. There's no twenty-four-hour tracker on either of us." Noticing that Leila had also stopped eating, he took his plate and hers to the sink. "Come on, Leila. Let's get you ready to go."

"How come the child can't finish her food?"

"Papa isn't the only one who needs peace and quiet to digest his meal. It appears Leila has lost her appetite, and so have I. I'll get her dressed and take her to see her mother and grandfather. I'm sure J.P. misses her and needs her right now."

"Fine. I'll get her ready. You can't comb her hair worth nothin'."

Edison sat next to his father and watched them leave the room. "Now that Mrs. Travers is gone, I'll have to make a home for my child. Mama keeps talking, but if Jeannie really wanted to help, now is the time."

"Your mama ain't satisfied 'less she's fussin 'bout somethin'. I swear I saw that plant over there shrink up when she started runnin' her mouth. Every living creature in this county lost their appetite."

Edison smiled and they talked until Leila came bouncing into the room. "Excuse me, young lady. Do I know you?" He stood and scooped her into his arms.

"You're beautiful. Do you have the picture you drew for your mother?"

"It's in my room."

He kissed her cheek and lowered her to the floor. "Well, get your picture so we can go." Watching until she left the room, he turned a stern stare on his mother's frowning face. "Mama, I've asked you to please not say certain things in front of Leila. You should have heard the questions she asked this evening. You have her thinking her mother doesn't love her. That will just make her feel she's not worthy of being loved. Is that what you want?"

"What I want don't matter none. If it did, you wudda married somebody else." Etta plowed her hands through the soapy water in the sink, and rinsed the dishes before placing them in the dishwasher. "You're too pigheaded to listen to anythin' I said."

The past came rushing back with enough force to knock him to his knees. Advice had come from all corners when Shannon did not return as scheduled. "That's not exactly true, Mama. I listened to you plenty. I listened when you…forget it. Some things are better left unsaid."

His father stood in the doorway, looking from one to the other. No one spoke.

Leila ran in and broke the silence. "I found it! Can we go now, Daddy?"

"We'll be home early, Pop." He paused next to his mother, gathered his emotions, smiled, and took his daughter's hand.

Just as he walked outside, Jeannie's car careened down the gravel drive, stopping just short of his father's pickup. Knowing his mother had alerted her of Shannon's arrival, he gripped Leila's hand and prepared to face another indictment.

He had known Jeannie all of his life. For as long as he could remember, the diner had been a social gathering place for all ages. Because of his friendship with Jeannie's younger brother, he had spent most of his free time there during high school. Jeannie, seven years his senior, was usually behind the counter. She had taken over after her father's death. During the peak of his despair, she had offered kindness and understanding. When she offered more, he had accepted. Their relationship had grown, but in the process, he had learned that her understanding was limited, just like his mother's.

He stared at her face, which was drawn and twisted in anger. She was still wearing her uniform with the words 'Crossroads Diner' stitched across the left breast. Her hair was pulled tightly back in a wrap, and the indentation of the elastic band on her hairnet was still visible across her forehead.

She stopped at the bottom of the steps, anchored her hands on her hips, and rolled her eyes up to meet his.

"I guess I don't have to ask where you're going. I heard the princess has arrived. Why didn't she come and pick Leila up herself?" She stood on the bottom step, looking up at him. "I asked a question, Edison."

He hesitated. If only Shannon were standing there. If only her arms were open and he could walk into her warmth. The thought almost brought a smile to his lips. He released Leila's hand. "Wait for me inside, honey. I need to speak with Jeannie."

When she hesitated, he leaned down and offered assurance. "It's okay, honey. We're going to see your mother. This will only take a few minutes."

After the door closed behind her, Edison walked down the steps. "You should see yourself standing there like that."

"What are you taking about?"

He laughed. "Your hands on your hips, fire in your eyes." The laughter turned serious. "Talking to me as if I were a child. I know I'm tolerant, but my patience is wearing pretty damn thin."

"You think this is funny?"

"Only the way you look right now. Isn't there a better way to deal with this, Jeannie? I have a child with my ex-wife. Shannon will be in my life until Leila grows up, and beyond that. We'll interact when she marries, has children…" He stopped. The thoughts were getting too heavy. "Let's not get all worked up over this."

"If your mother hadn't had the forethought to call me, I would have spent hours wondering where you were. Are you going to allow Shannon to come between us?"

"Will you listen to yourself? Has the fact that Doris Travers just died escaped your mind?"

"And my question was, why can't Shannon come here and pick Leila up? Why do you have to go over there?"

"I don't think a woman who just lost her mother, who traveled here from Paris, should have to face the woman in that house." He pointed to the door. "Mama hates Shannon, and you know it."

"Your mother's feelings are what they should be. Shannon deserted her family for a career in Paris. Why do you feel you have to run over there and take the child she left behind?"

Placing one foot on the step, Edison leaned forward, his face now filled with frustration. "Don't ever say that again. Ever. I don't want my child to hear it, though I'm afraid it may be too late for that. Shannon didn't run off and leave Leila to fend for herself. She's never been without good care and people to love her. She's brighter than most, and she has a hefty savings account, courtesy of Shannon. We have joint custody. Leila is with her mother part of the year. She's not deserted."

"So it's okay to leave your child as long as you send money. She's—"

"Daddy?" Leila peeped out the cracked door. "Can we go now?"

Edison looked back at Jeannie. "Yes, honey, we're leaving now, and Jeannie is coming with us."

Jeannie walked backwards to the gate. "No, I'm not. I have better things to do with my time." She ran to her car and drove away.

Leila looked up at her father and back to Etta, who stood in the door behind them. "Everyone in Paris likes my mommy."

"Lots of people like your mommy. You know that."

"I like it over there. Why can't I stay there all the time? Why can't you stay there, too?"

Divorce was so wrong, he thought. Especially for the children involved.

❧

Shannon had not spoken much after her father drove away from the funeral home and from the bowed head in the patrol car parked across the street.

"I don't know how to handle this, Daddy. I know I hurt Edison, but I'm not prepared to deal with his anger, especially now. Should I try and reason with him?"

"I didn't always take your side in your battles with Edison, but you're not to blame for this. I saw him back there with his head down. He feels like dirt because he just acted like dirt. He had no right starting in on you, and I'm sure he knows it."

"Do you think he hates me that much?" She didn't want Edison's opinion of her to matter, but it clearly did.

"Honey, it's easy to avoid people you hate. Edison was very hurt and angry when you left, but he doesn't hate you. Quite the contrary. What he feels right now is eating him alive. For a man who's always in control, knowing he can't get over his ex-wife could make him mighty frustrated. He waited here because he wanted to see you. Once he did, his emotions overpowered him, and he took it out on you. It happens to most of us at one time or another."

She was silent. Everyone they knew had told her over and over how broken Edison had been after the divorce, and how much he still loved her. He had told her so himself until anger and frustration made him lash out as he had just done.

"He and Jeannie are supposed to marry. Why would he do that if he still loves me?"

"He doesn't have you, honey. You're not even here in the United States, and, by the way, why didn't you marry Thierry?"

That was a question she had hoped he would not ask.

When she didn't answer right away, her father added his own conjecture. "Could it be that you also haven't released the past? You and Edison were madly in love. That kind of feeling doesn't just die, no matter how far apart you are, and that includes ideals as well as distance. You have a child together. If only for her sake, please try and reach amicable ground."

A fantasy played through her pain like liquid shadows. Edison was there, holding her, loving her. Just knowing he cared eased her anguish.

She squeezed her eyes shut and remembered him as he was in the beginning. Tall, handsome, and wonderfully virile, he was the first man to stir her feminine cravings and the last to completely satisfy them.

"Let me try and explain my relationship with Thierry." She wanted to answer her father's question, but struggled for words that would convey her feelings without making both of them feel uncomfortable. "Even after the divorce, I was too in love with Edison to see Thierry as anything but a dedicated manager, producer, and friend. I moved into his guest wing because it was the practical thing to do, and because I hated living alone in a strange city. Thierry was always busy with other clients and business matters, so our paths seldom crossed unless it concerned work."

"You did make friends, didn't you?"

"A few, eventually. Most of them are industry people. When I wasn't recording or touring, I rehearsed or practiced, had long conversations with the help, read, and enjoyed the city. I'm sure you remember my bouts of claustrophobia when I was a kid. What you don't know is that I still have them."

"I've wondered about that. So did your mother. Did you have problems in Paris?"

"Twice, actually. One happened on my may home as people at the airport mobbed me. A kindly priest was my saving grace. He noticed how upset I was and sat next to me. The time before that was the cause of Thierry and I having a relationship. We were in Brussels for a concert. Thierry left me in the limo and went inside to see if we could get a layout of the stage. He was gone so long, I started out to find him and a mob of people hurried toward me. I felt so overwhelmed; I just knew I would pass out. Thierry came out of the facility just in time. He put his arm around me, trying to calm me down. I had not touched or been touched by anyone since I'd been there. We were together a lot more after that, in public and in private. I really care for him, and he for me."

She thought of a comparison, decided against using it, and then changed her mind. "Think of the love in your heart for Mom. The great memories that will always be with you, sometimes so strong, you'll feel she's right by your side. But you're a young man, Dad. Sometimes your arms will ache because Mom isn't home to fill them. You'll reach out for the comfort a woman's arms can bring. They won't be the arms of the woman who will always hold your heart, but you'll be thankful for the comfort. It wasn't just sex, I can assure you. Thierry is a wonderful man, a good person. He's helped me in so many ways, and I love him dearly. He's just not Edison."

She changed the subject, hoping she had not added to his pain. "Where are we going now, Dad?"

"I need to stop at the store, but I can take you home now if you prefer."

She settled back in the seat. "No, I'll go with you."

Even under tragic circumstances she was happy to be home where she was just Shannon, not a popular recording star. She became lost in thought as her father drove slowly through the streets of Shepherd.

A small speck on the map along Highway 61, Shepherd had been a hotbed of unrest during the civil rights movement. White citizens had fought court-ordered desegregation as vigorously as their ancestors had fought the Civil War. Likewise, victory and defeat were muddled in the painful aftermath.

"Mom said Shepherd is a totally different place, even compared to the way it was when I visited at Christmas. It seems like a ghost town. Is it that terrible?"

Remembering the headlines on old newspapers her parents had kept, Shannon shuddered. Shepherd had gained national prominence in 1968 when a team of federal agents sent to investigate the alleged use of government funds to construct private schools had disappeared. County marshals, Shepherd's sheriff's department, and hoards of FBI agents had combed the area for a missing white Ford bearing a government plate. The car and the men were never found.

"That depends on who you talk to, honey. Most blacks feel things are better. In my opinion, we went from having a little of something to having all of nothing. This nation soon forgot Shepherd's ten minutes of infamy, but we've had to live with the aftermath."

"So you think this is related to things that happened back then?"

"I know it is. The wealth of this town belonged to whites. They left and took it with them. Back in the '60s we had a sawmill, paper mill, and a canning plant. They're all closed now. The state is planning to build a new prison on Highway 61. Can you imagine that? A stone building filled with hardened criminals right here in the midst of decent citizens."

Shannon was born too late to remember the appalling revelations of a continuing national shame, but the stories she'd heard had struck her hard. "Did the town fight to keep it out?"

"How could they? Most of them need the jobs this prison will provide. And the school is now a disgrace. Shepherd High is nothing like it was when you were there. The older teachers have retired and the younger ones simply don't give a damn. Some did when they first came in, but the apathy of the majority soon prevailed. I spend most of my time trying to ride herd. Some days

I have to teach three or four classes myself because of no-shows."

"That's awful. I've never thought of living here again, but I didn't think it would come to this."

"It's worse than I can describe. Drugs are a pandemic among youths, and I strongly suspect they're getting them from the adults. Edison and his deputies try, but it's bigger than all of us. This is election year. Edison is under a ton of pressure. I don't think the mayor will make it back for another term. We've got problems with illegal immigrants, crime of all kinds, and a don't-give-a-damn attitude by a good many of the young people. I worry about Edison right now. He drives around all hours of the night, just trying to keep his eyes on things. I do the same thing at school."

Shannon knew how much the school meant to her family. J.P. had been principal for as long as she could remember. Her mother had taught English and math, and now her brother was athletic director. Feeling more depressed, she reached for her purse and checked her makeup in the compact mirror. She applied ginger-snap lipstick and changed the subject to one that was also dear to her heart—her older brother. "How is John holding up? He was so close to Mom."

"He's holding up remarkably well. Too well, in fact. Donna and the kids have been crying since it happened, but, according to her, John hasn't shed a tear. That bothers me."

It bothered Shannon as well. Her brother was highly emotional and sensitive, as well as an admitted 'mama's boy.' "I think he's a lot stronger than we know, and he has Donna. She's a good wife and companion."

"And God knows every man needs that."

Emptiness filled his voice and Shannon's tears overflowed. It was autumn. All around her burnished gold leaves and chilly air boldly announced the change of seasons. It was her mother's favorite time of the year.

J.P. reached over and patted her hand. "She had just taken the Halloween decorations down from the hall closet and put them in a box to take to school. Last Saturday I helped her repot plants that she said would soon be filled with winter blooms." He smiled. "Do you know how she made the house smell so good during the holidays?"

"Common kitchen spices mostly, and lots of pine and lemon. I'll never forget that aroma. She placed bowls of apples around the kitchen with bundles of cinnamon sticks stuck between them. No packaged potpourri can compare." She wiped her eyes.

"I don't know how I'm going to get through this season without her."

"Neither do I, but we'll make it. When we spoke last week, I told her I was planning to spend the entire holiday season—Thanksgiving through the end of the year—here at home. Thierry scheduled a few press functions during that time, but the only real commitment I have is a New Year's Eve concert. I've asked him to cancel all of it."

"Your mother told me you were coming home for the holidays. She was looking forward to it. Said you were concerned about Leila, and you have every right to be. I love Edison, but that mother of his is something else. I've never seen a woman so intent on living in misery and making life miserable for everyone around her. Edison loves Leila. I'm not sure he realizes just how much it bothers her."

"Mom told me." She thought of her little girl and her mother. "Mom always supported me, even when she disagreed with my choices. Thierry said I should get counseling or join one of those survivors' groups. I can't see doing that." She saw her mother's face. The familiar smile. "Did she suffer, Daddy?"

"No. The doctor said that such a massive heart attack would...no, she didn't suffer. I left her in the kitchen, doing what she normally did after dinner, and went back to the living room. I heard the thud, but thought she had dropped something. I called out and went in there when she didn't answer. She never regained consciousness."

She watched him fight for composure, and visualized her mother's last hours.

"I'm glad she didn't suffer, but I wish she had opened her eyes for just a second," J.P. said. "I...I never said goodbye."

Her tears flowed freely. She knew her parents had married later in life than most, meeting and falling in love at the high school after her father's military stint. Her mother said she simply hadn't found anyone worth marrying until then. They had been inseparable for as far back as she could remember. "Tell me about the store. Mom said it was doing quite well."

"Oh, it is. Did she tell you I changed the name to Family Supermarket?"

"Yes, she did. I'm glad you have John and Donna to help out."

"Couldn't do it without them. John loves athletics and spends much of his time with school activities, but he still helps out a great deal. Donna is really my saving grace. She manages the kids and runs that store like a pro."

"How's Mama Lou?"

"Physically well, but her mind is slipping fast. The doctor confirmed what we already knew. Alzheimer's. Your mother and I had just finished discussing Mama's care. Now I'll have to talk to Rosie and see what we can come up with. Leaving Mama alone is becoming more risky by the day."

Shannon felt another weight added to an already heart-wrenching load. Louisa Mae Branford Travers had been a rock in her life. She dreaded witnessing her grandmother's mental demise. "Is Savannah still living there?"

"Where else would she go? That girl is about the most worthless soul God ever breathed life into, but for the time being, we need her there with Mama. She's good at handling her, that is, if she's around. I know all families have dysfunctional members, but I think mine got a few extra helpings. Seems everything went to hell in a hand basket after Daddy died. Mama was never as stern as she should have been. Now, I think she's just afraid."

Shannon listened to the details of everything that had gone wrong in her family, and wished there was something she could do. "That's all families. Being part of one is great, but it comes with a price."

When they arrived at Family Supermarket, she was happy to see her sister-in-law's smiling face.

"I'm so glad you're home," Donna whispered when they were alone. "I'm worried about John, and about your father."

"I am, too." She hugged the strong, erect shoulders, thankful that her brother had married a woman who made him happy. "We'll get through it together."

Donna pulled from the embrace and looked at Shannon. "How long do you plan to stay?"

"As long as I'm needed."

"In that case, send for the rest of your things. Your father needs you, your brother and I need you, but your little girl needs you most of all."

# Chapter 3

After the visit, Shannon rode with her father on the most painful leg of the trip home. The car stopped and she stared at the house where happiness was usually plentiful. The large oak tree where her swing had been, the row of potted plants under her window, and her mother's prized roses were all still there. Nothing had changed, but everything was different.

She saw a fresh coat of paint and knew her mother had continued her ritual. She had the house painted every four years, whether it needed painting or not. Fall was a time for "turning over the turf" in the flower garden. Her mother would mark the calendar at the beginning of each year, giving everyone fair warning of the changes she planned to make or the maintenance she expected to complete. Shannon had made her own notes once she was in high school. She had helped with the spring and fall changes, and in the process, had learned to sew. She had not liked the meticulous manner in which she was forced to live growing up, especially since most of her friends' rooms were always messy.

"I'm not raising them; I'm raising you," her mother would say. "When you grow up and have your own house, you're free to make whatever mess you feel comfortable living in."

"This house is so special to me. I remember bringing my friends here when I was a kid because they didn't believe I lived in the red brick house at the end of Maple Street."

"That was because they considered this house off limits to blacks. Your mother and I were the first ones to move in here. An old Jewish couple, the Steins, owned this property back then. Two generations. When Abe Stein died, his wife, Adie, said she wanted someone to come in and take care of it the way she had. Your mother had made drapes for her one time and she came to our home to get them. That woman just raved over the way your mother kept house, and the way she had it decorated. Doris went over there and helped her rearrange her furniture. I guess you could say they became friends."

Shannon listened with interest. "I don't remember this story. Was there opposition to you and Mom buying the house?"

"Not a lot, to the best of my knowledge. Adie Stein remembered that your mother had said she wanted to buy a house in town. We were living way back across the tracks at that time. Adie called and asked if we wanted to buy her house. She said she would make it easy for us by having her nephew draw up the papers. I used my GI benefits and went through a loan company up in

Jackson. By the time folks around here found out about it, your mother and I were already in the house, and Adie Stein had moved to New York with her daughter."

Shannon looked at the satin drapes in the living room as if seeing them for the first time. The house was special, not because it was large or nice, but because her mother had made it so. The living room still looked like something from a decorator's magazine. Her mother had said the house was on a ten-year plan. They would travel to New Orleans during the summer and shop for fabric every ten years. The drapes and matching pillows were just four years old.

Photographs dotted the antique table that sat between two high back chairs. Shannon stared at the ornately framed photograph of her parents on their wedding day. She had thought that same love was hers when she married Edison. Now she wondered if she would ever feel what she saw in her parents' eyes.

The kitchen was spotless, just as her mother kept it. Containers of all shapes and sizes were neatly stacked on the counter. Shannon knew the neighbors and townspeople would bring food, but had not expected so much so soon. She started the coffeemaker before taking her bag to the guestroom. The lavender wallpaper along the hallway was almost hidden under framed poses, a chronological collage of Shannon's career. Her mother never made a fuss over her celebrity, but it had obviously meant a lot. She sat on the window seat and wept softly.

Careful not to place her bag on the expertly made bed, she inspected the furniture, which was new, even the lamps and rugs. Her mother had decorated the room after she left and had given her old room to Leila. Gripping a white chintz pillow to her chest, she inhaled the newness of her surroundings. Tears fell on her folded arms. She had not thought of losing her mother or father—not this soon. There had been little illness in their home when she was a child and longevity prevailed on both sides of the family. Her mother had left much too soon.

Pulling away from her thoughts, she walked through the rest of the house. Stopping in the back room that had been a combination sewing room and classroom, she could hear her mother's voice. She had spent her free time there, sewing and tutoring. The consummate teacher, she had refused to lose any child who had a desire to learn.

Leaning against the paneled walls, Shannon drifted back to the image of a tall young man sitting at the old oak desk in the corner, rubbing his chin, and pretending not to notice when she walked past the door. Interested, but not wanting to make him more nervous than he already appeared, she would stand behind the door and peep through the crack. Her mother had patiently repeated questions, each time giving him more clues while he fidgeted and squirmed until he got the answer. She also watched when he was alone and saw him stare at her photographs. Standing in the shadows, watching his admiration, she had fallen in love. She smiled in remembrance of the talk she and her mother had in that room, just after Edison asked her to the homecoming dance.

"Edison asked my permission to invite you to the dance," her mother had told her. "Did you agree to go?"

She had nodded, holding back the desire to scream. After the usual pep talk, her mother added an observation.

"I'm very proud of Edison. His family is poor, so don't expect anything special. He wants desperately to attend college and he hopes to return here to work in law enforcement. It's a long story, but it has to do with his grandfather losing an eye back when he was a young man. Instead of carrying a chip on his shoulder and becoming consumed with hatred, Edison wants to take an active role in law enforcement."

Shannon could not remember how she felt after hearing that story. She had been so excited that the boy she had secretly admired from her position behind the door had actually asked her out. She had turned down two invitations already, waiting for the one she really wanted. She had watched him on the football field, always screaming louder than the other cheerleaders when he carried the ball or made a great play. She found Edison Page fascinating and arousing. Now she would have the chance to learn more, to dance in his arms. The things she had thought of before the night arrived still made her shiver.

Closing her eyes, she saw him just as he looked that night, walking to the door with a little box in his hand. She felt him tremble when she tried to pin the rosebud on his lapel without puncturing his chest. With her arms wrapped tightly around her shoulders, she swayed the way she remembered doing that night, close to him, lightheaded, floating on a cloud. It was the first time a boy's touch had brought such excitement and terror.

The first date had been a memorable beginning. Instead of waiting for him to build enough nerve to kiss her, she had taken the initiative. She found him staring when she opened her eyes, and figured he had been too surprised to close his. Being close to him brought warmth and comfort. When he kissed her back, the warmth turned to heat.

They saw each other at school, but she still fussed over him when he attended her mother's tutoring sessions. She made lemonade, hot cocoa, cookies, and even baked a chocolate cake with nuts, just the way he liked it. Her mother had questioned her after one of Edison's tutoring sessions.

"Honey, do you think you're moving a little fast? Don't overwhelm the poor boy."

She had smiled. That was exactly what she had wanted to do. Knowing she had fallen in love, she curbed her enthusiasm when the scholarship offers started pouring in. She wanted to be with Edison. He had hurried over the evening he received his offer from Grambling, bursting with joy.

"I've always wanted to play football there." Edison held the letter in his hand. "Have you heard about Coach Eddie Robinson? That man is great."

Without mentioning her own offers, Shannon had stuffed the letters back in her keepsake box and applied to Grambling. When talk of her many offers circulated around campus, Edison had come to her in a state of panic.

"I'm going to be in Louisiana and you're going to… wherever. How do you think that'll work?"

"I've applied to Grambling. I want to be with you."

A mile-wide smile had crossed his face. He had spent the next half-hour telling her how much he loved her.

"What are you thinking about?" her father asked, calling her back to the present.

"Nothing in particular. I remembered Mom here in this room, tutoring so many students, including Edison."

"I remember that, too. That's when he fell in love with you and was almost too nervous to drive the first time he came to take you out." He chuckled. "I didn't think the boy would make it out the door without faint-

55

ing." His eyes became misty. "I also remember how beautiful you were that night."

"I remember the dress I wore. I also remember your reaction when we told you and Mom that we had to get married. I thought you were going to kill both of us before we had a chance to explain."

"I remember that more than anything. Your mother and I let out a yell and you said 'Oh no! It's not what you think.' That boy was so embarrassed. I could see the color drain from his face."

"Well, I had to make you understand why it was so important for us to get married so soon. Edison knew I was a virgin, but I wasn't sure about him. We did wait, you know."

"I don't think I've ever been as proud of you as I was at that moment. Your mother was, too. We talked about it later and decided to give you the biggest wedding this side of town had ever seen."

"And you did. I remember Miss Etta standing around, her hands on her hip, asking how much everything cost. You said, 'None of your business, Etta. This is my only daughter.'"

"She sure wasn't afraid to touch the food. When she couldn't eat anymore, she started stuffing it in her purse."

J.P. laughed before his eyes turned somber. "Honey, you need to give some serious thought to what you're going to do about Leila."

"I thought about that on the plane. The last time Mom and I talked, she said Leila was not being properly cared for when she was over there, and that would not change when Edison got married. The word is that Jeannie has no plans for Leila to live with them, even if they do marry. I'm not sure Edison knows."

"I know how much your career means to you, but you've been to the top. Now it's time to be a mother to your little girl."

"I know that, Daddy. It usually took a few days for her to warm up to me on her visits, even when you and Mom brought her to Paris, but the last time was much worse. She was moody. Kept staring as if she didn't know me."

"Young minds don't retain much, but they can hold onto bad experiences like a rich man holds his money. I didn't tell you, but she cried herself to sleep on the plane when we left Paris. She wants to be with you."

The front door opened and John rushed in and hugged his sister. Donna herded the kids in next to them. Just as Shannon was about to break down, Donna lightened the mood.

"I didn't have to tell him you had arrived. One of the checkers said she saw Daddy with a 'beautiful, well-dressed, sophisticated woman,' and we don't have many of those around here."

They laughed and Donna followed Shannon into the kitchen.

J.P. shouted out. "There's plenty of food in there. Neighbors and friends have brought over hams, cakes, and pies, and all kinds of casseroles and meats. I grouped them in terms of the cooks. Everything that I feel safe eating is on the left counter by the coffeemaker."

Shannon found one of her mother's aprons to cover her navy pants suit. "I'm glad you're here. I didn't want to go into this at the store, but I need someone to talk to." She told Donna about Edison. "After saying how badly he felt about Mom, he acted as if he wanted to slap me. He was never that way before."

Donna shook her head. "Edison is still suffering from the divorce. I'm sure his mother's evil comments don't help. Etta Page is the devil's flunkey. Every time someone compliments Leila she takes the opportunity to talk about how you abandoned your family. John said the next time he hears her use that word he's going to wring her neck. He hates Etta."

"I've heard it so much I'm numb to it all." Shannon sighed. "Actually, I'm now saying it to myself. I've walked through this house and felt agony like I've never known. Losing someone you love is always hard, but losing your mother is devastating. Mom didn't have a choice, but I did. I shouldn't have gone to Paris. I just hope Leila will forgive me."

"That little girl loves you. She just doesn't understand how to balance her feelings. Edison wants to spend all the time he has with Leila, but he also loves to come here. It was not unusual for him to spend Sunday evenings here with your parents, or to stay until Leila went to bed. She loves for him to tuck her in. It was an almost perfect setup. I've noticed Leila's mood after she returns from Etta's. Your mother noticed it, too."

"I know. There's nothing I can do to change the way Edison feels, but I have a lot of making up to do with Leila."

"Oh, I'm sure his mother started preaching to him as soon as she knew you were coming home. I used to try and tell John to forgive her, but he was right all along. She's a damn witch."

"I didn't know John felt this strongly about it one way or the other."

"He's hated her for years. You do know about John and Carol, Edison's older sister? She and John were the same age. They dated in high school and college."

"You're kidding. I didn't know that. All I remember about Carol is that she married Harold Turner and he killed her."

"And John blames Miss Etta for that."

Donna took a seat on a stool next to the counter filled with dishes of food, while Shannon made trips back and forth to the pantry.

"That's how John and I met. Well, not met, but that's when we started dating. It was Carol's birthday and her mother gave her a party. I was dating Peter, the only one in the family as good looking as Edison." She stopped and looked at the cooking ingredients Shannon had placed on the counter.

"Why are you cooking? There's enough food here to feed Coxey's army, as your mother used to say."

Shannon laughed. "I remember spending an entire evening searching the encyclopedia, thinking Coxey was one of the great generals in American history." She surveyed the containers of food. "I'm making spaghetti for Leila. Edison is bringing her over this evening, and spaghetti is her favorite—my spaghetti."

Donna nodded. "You're a good cook. As I was saying, we all went to Carol's party and John was her date, or at least that's what he thought. That old woman came in the living room wearing one of those old faded print dresses with her boobs hanging down to her waist and started raising all kinds of hell. First, she told me I needed to go home and change. My skirt was too short, and she didn't want me giving Peter any ideas. Can you imagine that? Peter was as horny as a toad without any help from me."

"I think he still is. What's he on now, wife number four?" Shannon asked.

"Four or five. I've lost count, but he's still the same. I'm sure old lady Etta will say they all tempted him with short dresses and slack morals. Well, after she finished with me, she started in on John. I don't think I've ever seen him as embarrassed as he was that night. She told him that her daughters were raised properly, and if he tried anything ugly with Carol, Mr. Page would straighten him out but good.

"After she had made her rounds, she came back in and saw John give Carol a happy birthday kiss on the cheek. We thought that woman was going to have a fit. Before it was over, most of the kids had left, including John and me. We went for hamburgers afterwards and started dating after that."

"I wonder if Edison knows any of this."

"He knows. He was there. I guess I should thank the old bat. I can't imagine what my life would have been like married to her son, who can't keep his pants zipped long enough to cross the street. John and I talk about that sometimes, but it makes him sad. He never said it, but I know he loved Carol."

"It must have been a big secret. I certainly didn't know about it."

"You know we traveled in packs back then. We were in college and afraid our parents would raise the roof if they thought we were getting serious. Miss Etta didn't know about John and Carol until she saw them holding hands, and saw him kiss her cheek. I doubt she said a word when Carol married Harold Turner because he was older and had a reasonably good job. Within two months after they married he started beating her, and then killed her when she tried to leave."

"I remember finding Edison in the back yard one day, just sitting on the grass. I think he had been crying," Shannon said. "Turned out it was Carol's birthday. That night we discussed the whole issue of domestic violence and he told me once again how much he had always wanted to be a cop. That was one of the things that made me give in. I hated the whole idea. Still do. I want my daughter to grow up with two parents, even if they are divorced." Shannon stopped chopping onions and turned to face her sister-in-law. "I made a big mistake leaving her and Edison. If I've caused her as much pain as I feel now, I doubt that she will ever forgive me, or that I'll forgive myself."

"Don't be so hard on yourself. It's easy for others to say you should have stayed home; they haven't been in that position. You didn't leave Leila in harm's way. She was with your mother and with Edison. Of course, Edison thinks you left to be with Thierry, but I know that's not the case."

"It doesn't matter. I had a responsibility to my child. Nothing should have swayed me. I hurt the people I love most, and that's just wrong. Now that I know the pain of losing someone close, someone you love, I know just how deeply I hurt Edison. I don't blame him for hating me." She held onto Donna and sobbed.

Donna went to check on the kids and Shannon felt the past creeping back. She and Edison had lived their lives in the same small town, but were still worlds apart.

With both parents in the school system and her father's outside businesses, she and John had been privileged.

Edison's dad augmented his income as a farmer with his mechanical skills, but the family had too many mouths to feed. Tito, as he was called, expected his children to help in the field, and college was not high on anyone's list of priorities. Edison's older brother continued his education on grants and loans while Edison depended on his athletic abilities to further his studies. Only one of his sisters, the youngest, graduated college. Shannon remembered Edison's early struggles.

She also remembered comments he had made during their marriage. One, in particular, had stayed with her. He'd first said it after they made love on their wedding night, then after Leila was born. He had sometimes whispered it in her ear when they snuggled together, even in a crowd. Hearing it now in her head added to her anguish. "I'm really happy for the first time in my life."

Hearing a car, and bright conversation, Shannon opened the kitchen door and felt her heart leap. It had been less than two months since Leila had been with her in Paris, but her daughter had changed a great deal. Long legs, large, dark eyes. She resembled the black porcelain dolls Shannon had admired in store windows along Des Champs-Elysées. She wore a blue dress with a white pinafore, red buttons, and long red socks. Her eyes were now more downcast than when Shannon last saw her, and she held steadfast to her father's hand.

"Hello, sweetheart." She gathered her baby in her arms. "You get prettier every time I see you. Turn around and let Mommy have a good look at you."

Leila rolled her eyes, but obeyed.

"I can't believe how fast you're growing. Soon my little girl will be a young lady." She hugged and kissed her again.

Appearing none too happy about the attention, Leila pulled away in the direction of John and Donna's children.

Donna stepped in. "My boys think their cousin Leila is the prettiest girl in town. Robert socked a little boy one day for pulling her pigtails." She bent to give Leila a hug. "Of course, sometimes Robert and Trey think she should be as tough as they are."

"So what? She beats Trey at video games," Robert chimed in before taking his cousin's hand and heading toward the family room J.P. had added to the back of the house.

Leila spent the evening staring at her mother as if she thought Shannon would disappear. She answered questions in one-word replies, and came to life only in the presence of her father.

Instead of setting the breakfast table for the children as they usually did, Shannon and Donna placed extension leaves in the dining room table so they could all dine together. They selected a variety of foods from the dishes and containers. Shannon placed the large serving bowl of spaghetti on one end of the table, along with a tray of sandwiches and a bowl of chips. Leila had a second helping of spaghetti, and so did her father.

Leila continued staring at her mother until it was time to leave. Shannon held her close and kissed her over and over. "Did you like the spaghetti? Mommy made it especially for you."

"I knew that was your spaghetti," Edison said in a voice Shannon had almost forgotten—the one that had made her fall in love with him. "I would recognize your cooking anywhere."

"It was good," Leila said solemnly. Without looking at Shannon she asked, "When are you leaving again?"

Tension mounted in the room.

"I'm not sure when I'll leave, honey, but it won't be soon." Shannon looked at her daughter's sad expression and knew it was time to make a decision. "I've been thinking about that a lot since I've been home. I miss you so much. I miss my family. I'm even thinking of staying here permanently. Would you like that?"

Leila's face lit up. "I want to stay with you. Can I come back to Paris with you? Me and Daddy, too?"

Shannon stared at Edison, who had not said anything since the spaghetti remark. "Edison, you and I have to talk."

"Of course, but not now. Leila, didn't you bring something for your mommy? I think you left it in the car. Let's go find it so you can give it to her."

"She looks more like you every time I see her," John said after Edison and Leila left the room.

"And Edison looks more lost every time I see him," Donna added.

Leila came back holding the folded paper and gave it to Shannon.

"What is this, honey? Oh, how beautiful! I didn't know you were such a great artist." She passed it around. "Did you do that just for me? I'm such a lucky mother."

Shannon was finally rewarded with a big smile. She brought out the gifts she had packed for Leila and her nephews, and for Donna and John's baby girl. Watching them tear into the boxes, she tapped Edison's shoulder. "This might be a good time for us to have that talk."

"Actually, it's getting late and I've still got to patrol before turning in. Besides, I'm sure you're tired. You can spend time with Leila tomorrow."

He said an arid goodbye and she watched them drive away. Telling herself to remain calm, she felt her heart turn sideways. She had heard his harsh words and had seen his gruff exterior, but knowing him as she did, she saw down to the depth of his suffering.

When everyone had gone and the dishes were done, Shannon and her father sat at the kitchen table for one last cup of coffee. After they rehashed the events of the evening, J.P. became reflective and sad.

"You know your mother was very proud of you. She was proud of your accomplishments. I feel it made up for the things she never had a chance to do."

"Don't say that, Daddy. Mom was happy, very happy. She loved you and the life you had together. I know because she told me so many times. She was fulfilled."

"I know she loved me. She loved the two of you, but she had dreams, just as you did. She wanted to leave here, to go into interior design. It still bothers me that her talent was wasted."

"So Mom never went to New York and worked in the fashion industry. Look in any number of homes in Shepherd, including the most expensive ones, and you'll find traces of Doris Travers. This isn't New York, but Mom's work is well known, from wedding gowns to draperies and bedspreads. I remember women coming here when school first let out to place their Christmas orders. And think of all the kids she helped. Kids like Edison, who otherwise would have dropped out of school. She had two fulfilling careers, and she was the best mother in the world."

"As much as I hated to see you leave here, leave us, leave Edison and Leila, I kept thinking that you deserved to go where your heart and your talent took you. I've always felt bad that your mother didn't go to New

York. The Steins' daughter offered to host and even help pay for it. That would have meant so much to her."

"You meant so much to her. Mom was happy, not bitter like Etta Page."

"Speaking of Etta, I noticed how reticent Leila was tonight. Everyone thinks Tito is weird because he spends most of his time out in that shed in back of the house. He's just trying to stay away from Etta, and I don't blame him."

"Since we're talking about Mom not going away, I'm sure she's glad she didn't, not after John and I were born. It was selfish of me to leave my child. I know that. I'll never do it again. If I go back to Paris, Leila goes with me."

J.P. took her hand. "I've never heard you say that before."

"Losing Mom has made me see a lot of things. I truly didn't intend to stay in Paris when I first left, and I never should have. I'm long overdue with apologies I owe. I doubt they will help, but I hope God and my little girl forgive me."

"God forgives and Leila loves you. She's very young and, I think, very confused. I would love for you to stay here, but you were given a rare gift and an opportunity to use it. Take Leila with you. Marry Thierry. You've explained your relationship with him, but I don't think that's a good example for Leila. You're not married or bound by any conventional ties, but you enjoy a married relationship. Make a commitment. Get married."

Shannon sank into the chair. "Thierry is too much of a free spirit to marry. I guess he realized that after his prior commitments."

"I think you're selling Thierry short. He's done a fine job of managing your career. You say he was there for you when you really needed someone. I've seen you two together, honey. I may not understand or agree with modern lifestyles, but I think I know love when I see it, and I saw it on his face. Maybe he hasn't reached out that way because you've placed yourself beyond his grasp. Would you marry him if he asked?"

She pondered his question.

"Are you still in love with Edison?" J.P. asked.

"Thierry and I are intimate, but we don't sleep together. I know you and Mom thought I moved to a different bedroom when you came to visit, but I didn't. Thierry and I never lived together as husband and wife. I'm not evading your questions, Dad. There's just so much uncertainty in my heart."

"About your feelings for Thierry or for Edison?"

"Both. When I left home I was in so much pain and still very much in love with Edison. My heart barely stopped aching long enough for me to go on stage and sing or spend time in a recording studio. The pain was almost unbearable. I was far from home, in an unfamiliar world with a broken heart. Thierry helped me through it. I came to depend on him. I do love him, but I still have unresolved feelings for Edison."

"Do you see that changing? After all, Edison is engaged to Jeannie."

"This time here with Edison and my beautiful little girl will help me decide. Life is so different over there, Dad. When I was first introduced to the Paris lifestyle, I was shocked speechless. I hate to imagine how life would have been without Thierry. He's so kind and attentive, and he exposed me to more culture than I knew existed. The United States is one big country. You can drive for days and you're still in the U.S. The countries in Europe are small and close together. My life became a whirlwind of traveling and performing. We also took pleasure trips to help me wind down. We would go to Switzerland to ski or to London or the coast for the weekend. It wasn't love for Thierry that helped me forget. I was too busy to dwell on the sadness. Now, I have to think things through and make the best decision I can for Leila."

"Thierry seemed devoted to you when we were there. Was that just an act?"

"Thierry loves me. I'm his big star of the moment. It's easy for him to heap affection and attention on the person who's making him tons of money. When my popularity ebbs and there's a new star on the horizon, I doubt he will be as dedicated."

"That doesn't seem like a basis for marriage. You think you're just another meal ticket for Thierry?"

"Honestly Dad, I'm still too hurt to want marriage. It may appear that I shrugged off the fact that my husband divorced me, but it hurt—deeply. Maybe Thierry could be a good husband, and maybe he does love me enough to remain faithful. When we're together I feel loved and wanted, but when he's out with other clients, I just feel he hangs his hat, or in this case his pants, wherever his latest project takes him."

"That's awful!" J.P. vigorously shook his head. "That will not be a good atmosphere for your child. Not at all."

"When Leila was with me, she and I stayed in my wing of the house. Thierry's sister and daughter were also there, and relatives and professional friends were in and out. Leila never saw us as a couple, except at dinner or when we went out together, which, by the way, she adored. You should have heard her asking Thierry if we could take a cruise on the Seine. She was very happy there. Everything could change now. In fact, it has to change. If Leila goes to Paris with me, now or later, Thierry and I will have to define our relationship.

"I'm concerned about what she sees here with Edison and Jeannie. I know she doesn't spend time with them together. He says they're not engaged, but if his mother has anything to say about it, and I'm sure she's saying plenty, they will marry. Leila will be okay."

"Tell me about Thierry's family. You said they accepted your relationship. Do you think they would object to your marriage because of your race?"

"Thierry's folks don't care who he marries as long as he continues taking care of them. In our time together, there's been only one uncomfortable incident, and that came from his aunt."

"What happened?"

"Nothing major. She knew I was American but when she saw that I'm black, she asked if I was from an American ghetto. She asked in French, and I shocked her by answering in French. I suppose that's the image she had of American blacks."

J.P. chuckled. "And what did you say?"

"Not nearly as much as I wanted to, and she can thank you and Mom for that."

"Your mother and I taught you and your brother to always be polite, but we never said you had to allow yourself to be stepped on. I feel the same way about this situation with Leila. If you have to fight, then do it. If you have to fight dirty, do that as well. I don't care whose toes you step on, as long as that child doesn't have to spend her formative years with that crazy old woman. I know you have your dreams, but you have a child, too."

"Dreams change, Daddy. We grow up, mature, our focus changes. Just like Mom was happy without going to New York, I'll be happy, even if I never see Paris again. Of course, I have to return to get my things, close out bank accounts, and I have at least one more engagement I have to fulfill." She hugged J.P. "I've lived my dream. Mom lived her dream right here in Shepherd with the man she loved."

"I guess you're right. She was happy that you pursued your dream, and so am I. It's what you wanted and deserved."

The house was quiet. Shannon's thoughts were scrambled. She knew her mother had been happy with her life in spite of the dreams she deferred to raise her family. Shannon knew she could have been happy being a wife and mother. She had been happy before Thierry offered her another route.

"I was talking to your brother about your grandmother. He feels I should get the rest of the family together and get them to take turns caring for her. That way no one will be worked to a frazzle. I'll do that after…" His face turned ashen.

"I'll help, Daddy. Since I don't live here anymore, I'm unaware of the available facilities to care for Alzheimer's patients. Does that nursing home out on the highway have adequate staff to offer the comprehensive care Mama Lou needs?"

"I don't really know. They put Donna's uncle out there, and he didn't live a year."

They talked about the needs of elderly family members, but Shannon was thinking of her mother. She had been the caregiver. Maybe the stress of having so much responsibility had been too great a strain on her heart. *Why didn't I think of this before?*

She looked at the worry lines on her father's face. "Try and get some sleep tonight, Daddy. I'll go visit Mama Lou tomorrow and we'll make plans later."

"Yes. I suppose you're very tired. It's almost eleven. What time is it in Paris? Is it six or seven hours ahead?"

"Seven hours. So right now it's 5 a.m., which means I've been up for twenty-four hours."

Shannon kissed him goodnight, went into the guest room, and closed the door. After removing her shoes, she rubbed the deep rings in her swollen skin, showered, cleansed her face, and dressed for bed.

Home had been a fun place. Now it was filled with too many painful memories. Losing her mother also made her long for the comfort of Edison's arms. Most of all, she wanted her child to love her, and to be happy. She knew tough decisions had to be made. Her marriage had ended badly and now she had to make a decision that would surely cause another major blow-up.

"Sorry, Edison," she mumbled. "Our daughter must come first."

# Chapter 4

Edison could not relax. When he tried to concentrate, his mind wandered, always stopping at the same junction. He had loved a woman with every fiber of his being, loved her so completely, so deeply, that nothing could extract those feeling from his heart.

The old wallet he had in high school was still packed with photographs of Shannon. He kept it in a box with his high school and college diplomas, the highlights of his life. When he felt especially lonely, he would look at them and remember how it all started.

He had loved her for as long as he could remember. Even as a little girl, she had more charm than anyone around. He wasn't the only one who found her irresistible. Back then, he had felt he was the least likely to win her heart and didn't even try. She was the best student in school, which was no mystery. Her mother was certainly the best teacher. She had everything: a great voice, a fantastic body, and eyes that seemed to dance when she spoke. He would pretend not to notice when other boys spoke about her, but found it hard not to punch them for daring to dream his dream.

He had felt clumsy in her presence back then. In some ways, he still did, but he knew none of that was her fault.

His mother had felt Shannon only wanted to date him because he was an athlete, and would break his heart. She'd even asked if Shannon's mother had put him up to asking her daughter out because she felt his athletic ability brought great earning potential. He knew better. Shannon was less interested in money than most of the girls he knew. He had been shattered when a knee injury dashed all hopes of a professional football career. Shannon's big concern had been cheering him through therapy, and she had. Even that had not convinced his mother.

"That girl is stuck on herself," she had said. "She won't do nothin' but break your heart."

His mother had seemed almost gleeful when Shannon proved her right.

Thinking back, he realized that first date with Shannon had done more to boost his ego than anything he had done on the football field or in the classroom.

He had begged for a new suit, which had fueled his mother's objections.

"See! It's already started. You trying to impress that girl and her folks."

When his father saw his arms sticking out the sleeves of his old suit, pride sent them on a shopping trip for a new one. *I was on top of the world that night.*

*There was no doubt in my mind that the prettiest girl at that dance was on my arm.*

He had stopped when they neared her house and thanked her for a great evening. Before he could gather enough courage to try for a kiss, she had taken his face in her hands and sealed her lips over his. Breathless and trembling, he was still fumbling for words when she leaned over and did it again and again, until his body was weak and his mind too flustered to speak. Later, after they were married, she had teased him about the way he trembled through those first kisses.

He still trembled in her presence.

His life had been simple before Shannon. As a young black boy growing up in the rural South, many of his dreams and ambitions were shaped by the times in which he lived. Like all young boys, he watched cop shows on television, played with toy pistols, and had make-believe gun battles with his friends. In that pretend world, the sheriff was always the good guy, the defender of justice, and paladin to the weak. Reality proved a woeful contrast. He had witnessed brutality, indifference, and inequality at the hands of local whites, and in most cases, with the full knowledge, if not participation, of the sheriff.

Placing his holster on the night table, he shuddered in remembrance of the eye patch his grandfather had worn, and the fear he had felt upon learning it had been no accident.

"You boys better keep your eyes in your head," his grandfather had warned Edison and Ray when two white girls walked past. "That's how I lost my eye."

The story had stayed with him and strengthened his desire for equality in law enforcement. Shannon had been elated when he had applied for a position with the Mississippi Highway Commission, but protested vigorously when he had accepted an offer from the local sheriff instead.

"How can you accept this job?" Shannon had asked. "They have no intention of allowing you full authority unless they appoint you the black people's deputy. Arrest one white person and they'll get rid of you in a flash—maybe permanently. They just need a black face to quiet the crowd."

Shannon's world had been different, even then. Her family was royalty in Shepherd. He had noticed her when they were six years old and she sang in the children's choir at church. Everyone had talked about her mastery of the French language, her great singing voice, and her proficiency in music. She wrote and arranged her own songs, even before high school. Everyone in Shepherd had been amazed at her talent. He had wanted only to love her and have her love him back.

Their marriage had alleviated most of his fears. He had felt almost completely secure when Leila Rose Page was born. Shannon had been a good mother and a wonderful wife, always thoughtful of his needs. He lay across the bed and closed his eyes. His world had been perfect back then.

He remembered the nights of tucking the baby in and watching her fall asleep and then going to the bedroom with his wife. Motherhood had unleashed a torrent of passion in Shannon, and he had found her more desirable than ever.

Pride was all he felt when the group accepted local gigs, but his fear grew when they started traveling. He knew she was good, and, given the right chance, would be discovered. Her father had advised him to explain his feeling and apprehensions, and he did as soon as she arrived home from a gig in Biloxi.

"Maybe I'm being selfish, and if so I'm sorry, but I thought you married me because you wanted to be a wife and mother."

When she mentioned that Jackie, one of the singers in their group, had two kids, he had become more insistent. "That's two more reasons not to go parading around in nightclubs. Good mothers don't go off and leave their babies."

"Edison! I can't believe you're being so ridiculous. Leila is just a baby. Think of your dream to be a lawman, the dream you're living in spite of my objections. Do I not have the same right?"

"I don't like the idea of my wife parading around on stage with a bunch of men drooling over her. If that makes me some kind of control freak, then so be it."

"And I don't like the idea of my husband parading around with a gun strapped to his hip, an open target for all the crazies in Mississippi, but I didn't forbid you to do it."

"My job doesn't take me away from my family. It allows me to stop in during the day and to have breakfast and dinner at home—lunch, too, if you're here to have it with me. And your place is here, not traipsing around in Biloxi or New Orleans or anywhere else. I want my wife at home."

"And what about what I want? Does that count for anything, Edison?" She had sat in his lap, taking his face in her hands, as if she knew that made him helpless. "You're a bright person with limitless potential, yet you've chosen a career in law enforcement. You are here in Shepherd, but you're often out in the middle of the night, leaving me to worry about your safety. I don't pout when you come home. I'm here for you, to love you, and that's all I'm asking. I love you and Leila with all my heart, and if you love me half as much, you'll understand."

They made up, and he tried to be supportive, even accompanying her to New Orleans when her group was invited to sing at Grambling's big game. Her parents joined them, keeping the baby in their room to give them time alone. It was a second honeymoon with champagne and late-night lovemaking. His heart swelled as her voice rang out in the stadium.

The family agreed that a voice as sweet as Shannon's deserved to be heard, and he tried to feel good about her talent. Over the following months, the group traveled to New Orleans to perform at several functions, the last being a New Year's Eve party in the Convention Center. Shannon's group, Smoke, was one of several performers that night, and Edison had accompanied his wife on the trip.

Had he not been present, he would have found the events of the evening hard to believe. He was sitting in the dressing room, waiting, when a group of well-dressed men came backstage asking to speak with the manager of the lead singer of Smoke. With their limited mastery of English and his few words of French, he tried to make them leave, but they insisted on waiting for Shannon.

Thierry Doussaud, suave and cosmopolitan, had looked at his wife in a way that made Edison see fire. Kissing her hand and gushing over her performance meant only one thing to Edison. This man wanted his wife.

And now he had her. There was nothing in Shepherd, not even her child, to compete with the glamour of Paris.

He was up the next morning long before anyone else stirred. He found Leila in almost the same position he had left her in the night before. She was the only bright spot in his world.

&

Shannon had been tired enough to fall asleep as soon as her head hit the pillow, but she awakened well before the sun was up, slipped into the kitchen, and started the coffeemaker. She was on her second cup when John arrived. He hugged her tight and they sat together by the breakfast room window.

"I haven't had a chance to speak with you alone, but I want you to know that Daddy is going to need all of us to support him through this. We loved Mom and we're going to miss her, but she was his life. He doted on her, depended on her, and I know he's going to have a hard time adjusting."

"I know. I don't have anything pressing in Paris right now, just some publicity events that Thierry can easily cancel. I'm concerned about Daddy right now, so I'm not leaving. Losing Leila so soon after Mom's death would crush him. I'm staying here for now, but if I do feel comfortable leaving Daddy, I'll take Leila with me."

"And do you think Edison is going to let you take Leila to Paris?"

"I'll fight Edison if I have to."

John stood with his hands on his hip. "I'm not trying to debase you, sis, but you should have stood up to Edison a long time ago."

J.P. came into the kitchen and began talking about the arrangements for the memorial service. "This town really loved your mother. I just talked to Mr. Wells and he said there have never been so many flowers and plants delivered for a service since he's owned that place."

J.P. looked at Shannon's glum face and stopped talking. Halfway through breakfast, he broke down in tears.

"We'll make it, Daddy," Shannon said, flanking his left while John rushed to the other side. "We'll make it together." Choking back her own tears and watching their faces, she knew she was needed at home far more than she was in Paris.

Shannon drove out of town, headed west on the highway, and almost missed the exit to her grandmother's house. She smiled when the tarpapered roof came into view. The old house stood as it had when she was child, on top of a steep hill, surrounded by trees. There were still dogs lying on the front steps. Her cousin recognized the car and ran down the steps to the front gate.

"Shannon!" Savannah screamed her name. "It's really you." She took Shannon's hands and squeezed them. "I'm sorry. I just have to touch you and make sure you're real. It's been a long time. I'm so sorry about Aunt Doris. I loved her. I just can't tell you how sad it makes me."

Shannon picked up a whiff of cannabis. Crinkling her nose, she stood back from her cousin. "Let me look at you. Girl, you've changed, even since the last time I saw you."

"I look bad, huh?"

"You look different." She stared at the unkempt hair and weight gain. "You know you're the prettiest one in the family."

She followed Savannah inside, becoming more unsettled as she walked through the house. Clothing, empty fast food containers, newspapers, and magazines covered every surface. The entire house was in disarray. Shannon was fearful of what she would find in the kitchen where Savannah said their grandmother was eating a late breakfast.

"I know the house is a little messy right now. Taking care of Mama Lou is a full-time job. I don't have the time or the strength to do everything."

Shannon stepped over a pile of towels and bed linen in the doorway. "We'll have to do something about that. Does anyone help at all?"

"Just Uncle J.P. and Aunt Doris. The others criticize, but they don't do a thing to help."

Shannon cautiously walked through the doorway to the kitchen and saw her grandmother sitting at the head of the table. "Mama Lou?"

The infirmities she expected were nowhere to be found. Her grandmother's movements were swift, as she stood and stretched out her arms.

"My baby, Shannon! My little heartstring! I was hoping to see you before the funeral." A bright smile covered her face. "You're as beautiful as ever."

Shannon was also surprised at her grandmother's appearance. Her silvery hair was pulled back in a neat bun. She wore a yellow and white dress, freshly pressed. She smelled of fresh citrus as she hugged Shannon tightly against her shoulder.

"It's so good to see you, Mama Lou. You look wonderful." Tears ran down her face and met under her chin. "Why don't you finish your breakfast and let me take you home with me. I'm sure your other granddaughter has a lot of things she needs to do, and Daddy would love to see you there when he gets back today."

"Thanks, Shannon." Savannah started clearing the table. "I'll get this place cleaned up. It's not as bad as it looks. I would like to have my hair done if I can get an appointment, so I won't look ratty at the funeral."

"Why don't we keep Mama Lou with us and give you a little break? I'll bring her home tomorrow morning so she can dress for the memorial service. Is there anything else I can do? Do you need money?"

"I could…no." She shook her head. "I'm just glad you're home. How is Edison? I hear everybody's coming down on him because of all the drugs here in Shepherd. They even think Bobby Joe Stanberry is involved. You know that's ridiculous."

"Daddy mentioned the problem. That stuff may have been going on when I was still here, but I sure didn't know about it."

"Well, I know Bobby Joe doesn't know anything about it. He's clean. I'm so glad you're here. I can't tell you how much I envy you—but in a good way. You've done it all."

"Thank you. I had a strong foundation." After promising to relieve Savannah as often as possible, Shannon chatted with her grandmother on the drive home.

"I can't believe how well you look, Mama Lou. I guess Savannah takes good care of you."

"She tries. She has her problems, and she's just about the laziest person God ever breathed breath into, but she tries. She won't keep the house clean and she can't cook worth nothing. I know she smokes that stuff. My nose still works fine. Then she sits around and stares into space, like a zombie or something. She takes money from my purse if I leave it lying around—

been doing that since high school. She's intelligent and creative, just lazy."

When Mama Lou asked how long she planned to stay in Shepherd, Shannon thought of Donna's advice. "I'll be here for a while."

She took her grandmother's things to the guest room and ran back downstairs when she heard the doorbell.

The woman standing on the stoop was vaguely familiar. She was tall, not unattractive but not beautiful, quite shapely, and dressed better than most women in Shepherd. Shannon was searching through her memories for a name when Mama Lou came in the hallway.

"Valerie!"

Shannon looked on as they embraced.

"Shannon, I don't know if you remember Valerie Brooks. She's a nurse down at the hospital. Her family lived next door to ours when your father was growing up. Val, this is my granddaughter."

"Hello, Shannon. I remember you well. I worked at the doctor's office when you were a little girl. I was the one who gave you shots and took care of you when you were ill. I'm so sorry about your mother."

"Thank you. Come in, please."

"Thank you, but first I have to get a few things from my car. I'm sure you have plenty of food already, but I know all the things J.P. likes. I made his favorites."

Shannon walked out to help her with the four baskets of food. "This was very generous of you, Miss Brooks. You must love to cook."

"I do when I'm cooking for someone else. I live alone, so I don't cook very much for just me. Your father loves my potato salad. I baked a Virginia ham, too, and made all of his favorite pies. He loves chocolate and pecan, so I made one of each."

Shannon followed her back inside. She only vaguely remembered Miss Brooks from the doctor's office. Being ill was not a pleasant memory.

Miss Brooks took the apron from the peg on the door and tied it around her waist. "Now you go in there and spend some time with your grandmother, Shannon. I know you two must have a lot to talk about. I'll tidy up and make sure food is served when company comes over."

"Thanks, Miss Brooks, but you're a guest. I'll take care of the kitchen."

"Nonsense. Neighbors and friends help out in times like these. And I want you to go on out and do your errands or visit with friends. I'll stay here with Mrs. Travers. I'm a nurse. I want to do this."

Shannon stayed home until after her grandmother's nap, and then went to visit Donna at the store. Surprised at the continuous stream of shoppers, she marveled that Donna was able to handle things with so little help.

"It's hard to find good help around here. I've been looking for part-timers to do inventory, but these kids don't want to work. We had Bobby Joe here helping out until I caught him stealing. I wanted to have his butt arrested, but J.P. wouldn't hear of it."

"I'll help out as much as I can. I'll also try and relieve Savannah. It must be hard to stay out in those woods all of the time. I think I'd go crazy. I know Savannah has problems, but she seems to take good care of Mama Lou."

"That's right, you said you brought her back to the house. Did you leave her alone?"

"No, Miss Brooks is there with her. I don't remember her very well, but Mama Lou said it was okay, and she seemed fine."

"Miss Brooks? Valerie Brooks?" Donna seemed surprised.

"Yes. Why? Is something wrong with her?"

"Uh, no. She's a sweet lady. She's a nurse, so I'm sure she can handle Mama Lou."

Shannon wondered about Donna's reaction, but did not question her any further. Her heart and mind were already crowded with problems and situations.

There was no need to cook when she returned home, and Mama Lou did have a lot of questions about her travels. J.P. joined them on the back porch and they talked for hours. Feeling more jet lag than the day before, Shannon slept well.

❧

The family huddled together at the service, which was brief, as J.P. had requested. Everything spoke of the elegant tradition Doris Travers had left behind. Doris's only brother, Bill, and his family sat on one end of the first pew, and their two sisters sat with their families on the other. Shannon's head remained bowed most of the time. When she did lift her eyes, they focused on Edison, with Leila at his side.

J.P. had carefully chosen the speakers for the eulogy. Most of them were fellow teachers or former students, all claiming to have been inspired by Doris's benevolent character.

Shannon had heard Edison sob when one of the women mentioned how many students had gathered "around Doris's knee to learn what they had not been able to get in the classroom." Shannon knew he had loved her mother, just as she knew he once loved her.

Later, when everyone convened at the Travers' home, Shannon cornered Edison. "You've been avoiding the conversation we need to have, so let's do it now. Believe me, it's as hard for me to say as it might be for you to hear."

His eyes clouded with emotion. "Okay. Say what you have to say."

They walked to the back of the house and sat on a bench next to the barbeque pit her father had built. "I've been trying to find the best way to say this, because it's very important to me. Edison, I married you because I loved you. We started a family because we both wanted one. I couldn't have loved Leila more. The plan I had back then was to raise our baby, teach, maybe have two or three more children and spend the rest of my life loving you and raising our family.

"I never dreamed someone would offer me a chance to sing, certainly not in Paris. Think about it. Things like this rarely happen, especially to anyone from our part of the country. When I left for Paris, I meant to stay just long enough to see if I had the talent Thierry was raving about. Like everything else, the best-laid plans often take different directions. But I was a wife and a mother. My responsibilities were here with you and Leila. I shouldn't have gone to Paris in the first place, and I certainly shouldn't have allowed anything to keep me long enough to destroy our marriage." She watched his expression change.

"As you can imagine, my heart is in a million pieces right now. I didn't expect to lose my mother. I'm sure that's similar to what you felt when I went away. I'm so sorry, Edison. I can't go back and undo the hurt I've caused, but I hope you can find it in your heart to forgive me. I hope I can make it up to our little girl."

"Wow." His voice was barely audible. "And I didn't expect this."

"You deserve an apology and a lot more. I just don't know what else to say or do."

"But things are different now, aren't they? You have Thierry."

"And you have Jeannie. I'm not suggesting you abandon your plans, or that we could repair our relationship enough to get back together. I'm just admitting that I was wrong. Very wrong."

He stood and walked around the bench.

"Please know that I never meant for any of this to happen. I'm glad you've found someone to make you happy. I hope she will be the kind of wife you need."

"And I'm glad you have Thierry. Are you getting married? Is that why you're telling me all of this?"

"No." She shook her head vigorously. "This has nothing to do with Thierry. Nothing that's happened between us had to do with Thierry. We have no plans to marry or anything else at this time."

He looked puzzled. "But you're together."

"Thierry is first my producer and manager. I'm happy for the success I've had. Right now, my career and my personal relationship take a backseat to my responsibility to Leila. I might go back to Paris later, after Daddy is better and things have calmed down, but I'll be here as long as I'm needed, and I will never leave my daughter with anyone again."

"Are you saying you're taking Leila with you? You know the decision on that. She stays here. Neither one of us can move her out of this state."

"I'm not talking Leila from you, Edison, but we have to face facts. My mom took care of her. You work, Dad works, and Leila needs her mother. She needs me."

"So that's what your little speech was all about? A set-up for the big punch line? Well, let me tell you something, Shannon, I don't believe a damn word you just said about being sorry for what you did. I also will never approve you taking my baby away from Shepherd. If you live here, Leila can spend equal time with both of us. If you don't, the arrangement we have will stay in effect."

"I can't argue with you right now, Edison. I had to say I'm sorry, and whether you believe me or not, I am. Whether I'm here in Shepherd or not, you can't provide any kind of home life for Leila, and I can. I will."

"That's not true. Jeannie and I are getting married. We'll have a home for Leila. You can go on back to Paris, California, to the ends of the earth if you choose. My baby will be here with me, and with the rest of her family. How can you even think of taking Leila away from J.P.? Oh, I'm sorry. I forgot. The princess gets to do whatever is convenient for her. How stupid of me to forget."

Her face flamed in anger, but her voice was calm. "As I said, I don't want to argue. Not today."

"But you chose today to talk about it, probably thinking I'd feel sorry for you. Well, it's not happening, so cancel your show."

"I've tried to tell you before, but you were too busy hating me to listen. The last thing I want is pity. Not today, not ever. Not from you or anyone in your family. Your mother didn't even come to the memorial service. I also noticed your future wife wasn't there for Leila or for you."

She held up her hand when he opened his mouth to speak. "Don't. You brought Jeannie into the discussion, not me."

"And you need to listen to what I have to say. Jeannie doesn't spend a lot of time with Leila and me because Leila is jealous. She gets upset when I'm with Jeannie. That will change once we're married."

"Good. I have to go inside now. Maybe this wasn't the best time to talk. I'm sorry for all that's happened. I'm sorry you don't believe me, but thanks for listening."

❧

"I tried to apologize to Edison," she confided to J.P. when they were alone. "It didn't go well."

"Edison is being defensive because he's afraid of losing Leila. Maybe you should try and reassure him that he'll always be part of his daughter's life."

"I know you and Mom were both against me going to Paris, but you never really said so, and that meant a lot to me. Mom said you both raised me to think for myself. I was an adult, and it was my decision to make. Even adults don't think clearly sometimes. That's all I was trying to say to Edison."

"You did what you thought was best at the time. Don't try and second-guess your decision, just take it from here. Leila was a happy child when she was younger. The time she spent with Etta didn't bother her that we could see, but it does now."

"I'm sure the first word out of Miss Etta's mouth after I left was 'abandoned.' I'm not saying she was wrong, but there's nothing I can do to change the past. I'll fight for Leila now. I'm never leaving her again."

"As much as I would have missed your mother, I would have gladly granted her time to fulfill a dream. That part is understandable. I didn't condemn you leaving Leila for so long and neither did your mother. We were happy to have her here. Your mother made breakfast for us every day. Most of the time, it was very simple, but a warm meal on a cold morning is great for kids and adults. We usually rode in separate cars, which gave your mother longer to get Leila dressed."

"You were both great with her. I never would have left unless I knew she was in good hands. She really loves that day-school."

"She does, and it's right across the road from our school. We both stopped in there to check on her, especially if she wasn't feeling well. She's happy there with her cousins. Donna usually picks all of them up and takes them to the store after school. It worked out well, but everything has changed. Our lives, certainly mine, will never be right again."

⮞

The following day was even more chaotic with relatives coming from out of town and friends trying to help, but mostly getting in the way. Miss Brooks arrived before Shannon had finished breakfast, with a platter of bacon, sliced ham, biscuits, and an egg and cheese casserole. J.P. said food was not just a means of helping, but also an attempt to comfort. Shannon just wanted to be alone with her family.

She found John alone upstairs, looking sad but composed. Sitting next to him, she slipped her fingers through his the way she had done when they were kids. "Why do you think Daddy arranged to have a memorial service and a funeral? He's the one who always said the two services put too much strain on the family?"

"When he said that, he was not referring to his wife. I think prolonging this is Daddy's way of holding on. I wish there had been only one service. Trey and Robert insisted on saying goodbye. Shelby is with Donna's sister."

He embraced her. "I have never felt this empty and sad in my life. I feel part of me is missing, and I know I'll never have it back. She was so much more than a mother to me, to us." He squeezed her fingers. "Let's just stiffen up and brave the day."

Once inside the church, Shannon glanced around at the people with whom she had shared her life. She had attended school and parties with the younger ones. The older ones had dished out wisdom and love. Clutching her father's hand, she tried to smile as Leila looked up from her place at Edison's side.

The funeral was brief. John sat with his head held high, staring straight into the distance. Shannon felt she had no tears left, but wept uncontrollably at the gravesite. She also felt she was being watched closely because of her previous behavior at funerals. This time, she would hold up, no matter how great the pain. No fainting. No hysterics.

John's arms went around her and they wept together in the limousine. The finality of the moment was overwhelming. She understood her father's reluctance to say goodbye.

John left her to go check on J.P. and Shannon tried to regain her composure. What happened next pleased her immensely. The door opened slowly and Leila poked her tear-stained face inside. Shannon held her, dripping tears on the frilly black and white plaid dress she had sent from Paris. Edison joined them and they cried together. She still loved him and knew only his anger kept him from admitting the same. With their daughter between them, they were a family. That fact had not been changed by divorce.

"Losing a loved one is the greatest pain of all," Edison said, dabbing his daughter's eyes and then Shannon's. "But we haven't lost the love she left with us. She had a unique way of inspiring those around her. I wanted to say that at the memorial service but didn't trust myself to speak."

Shannon cuddled her daughter and reached over to hug Edison's shoulder. The love in her heart had not changed at all.

# Chapter 5

The scene back at the house was a repeat of the previous day.

"Miss Brooks is certainly keeping a vigil over Daddy," Shannon remarked to Donna. "I know she's just trying to help, but it's starting to seem kind of creepy."

"You know how people are at times like this. Most of them don't know what to say, so they end up saying and doing something stupid."

Leila stayed close to Shannon, seldom letting go of her hand. When Shannon sat down, she climbed on her lap and stayed there for most of the evening.

"Come on, honey. It's time to go home now." Edison came in and bent down to take her in his arms. "Say goodbye to your mother."

"Why can't I stay with Mommy?" She clutched Shannon's shoulders.

Donna stared, and Shannon held her daughter closer.

"You'll see mommy tomorrow. She's not leaving just yet." Edison took Leila 's arms and tried to lift her up, but she clutched Shannon's dress and began sobbing.

"It's okay, sweetheart." Shannon flashed a stern look up at Edison. "You can stay here with me tonight. You have lots of nightclothes here." When Leila nodded, she continued, "You can spend the night in your room or you can sleep with me." She spoke without looking up. "Tell her it's okay, Edison."

"It's okay, baby. Stay with your mother. I'll pick you up tomorrow."

Leila sat up, but did not loosen her grip. "I have lots of things here. Did you go in my room?"

She had, but wanted to give Leila the pleasure of giving the tour. "You can show it to me."

Leila nodded. "I will if you promise not to say I have too many toys. That's what everyone else says when they see my room."

"I promise I won't say that." Just knowing Leila was with her because she wanted to be was more wonderful than she could have imagined. Donna helped Miss Brooks with kitchen duties and Leila led Shannon upstairs, but not before she offered Edison a chance to share. "Why don't you wait here until we conduct our upstairs tour? Have a cup of coffee with the family before you leave."

His smile and nod made her feel much better.

"Oh, honey. It's so beautiful." She smiled as Leila showed off her grandmother's handiwork. Shannon's old desk had been freshly painted and the shelves of the hutch were lined with Barbie dolls, including a special section for the ones from Paris.

"I have never seen so many Barbie dolls, and you keep them so neat."

"I keep them here because my cousins break them. One time, Mattie Jean cut my doll's hair. Granny said I have to share, but I don't want to. They're mean to me sometimes."

"I'm glad you take such good care of your toys. That makes me very proud. I agree with your grandmother that one should share, but not if the other children destroy things that are yours." She smiled with pride. "You are so mature and poised for your age." She looked around. "I just love this room."

The room was decorated with rag dolls in many colors and designs, all undeniably made by Doris, including a bedspread with small doll faces sewn around the bottom. Other dolls were used as curtain tiebacks and four dolls' faces adorning the walls had long braids that were used to hold Leila's hair barrettes. Overcome by her mother's presence, Shannon cried softly.

"Are you thinking of Grandmommy?"

She nodded. "She made a pretty room here for you. This was my old room. Did you know that?"

"Grandmommy told me. She said you were a happy little girl when you stayed in here. I'm happy here, too. I don't know why people have to die."

"Your grandmother loved you, and you have so many things to help you remember her."

"She told me stories at night. Granny never tells stories. Daddy says I have to stay with Granny and Papa now, but I don't want to."

She silently rearranged the toys on her shelves before asking the question that caused Shannon to grip her chest in fear her heart would burst through.

"Mommy, why did you leave?"

She took her daughter on her lap and wiped the tear tracks from her face. "I went to Paris to sing. It was very exciting, but you know what? I'm here with you now and I'm never leaving you. If I go back to Paris, you're going with me."

"Thierry says I'm pretty and special, just like you."

"You are, baby. You're very special."

Leila was still clutching her hand when they went back to the kitchen. She let go and sat on one end of the counter with her cousins and Edison joined John at the table nearby. Shannon gathered mugs from the cabinet and slices from three of the many cakes they received.

"Let's join the guys for a cup of coffee," she told Donna. "Or whatever everyone would like to drink."

"Just coffee for me," Edison said. "I'm nowhere near catching these…" He looked at the kids. "I haven't finished rounding up the bad guys."

"A lot has changed in Shepherd." Shannon sat next to him. "It was such a nice place when we were growing up."

Leila walked over and climbed on Edison's lap. "I want to grow up in Paris. They have so many pretty things. I love the Jardins des Champs-Elysees."

"Did you hear that?" Donna exclaimed. "She is good. How the heck does she remember those names?"

"I can't believe she can pronounce them so well," Edison said. "I had to look up this Jardins place online. Leila kept talking about kids under an umbrella. The word statue didn't quite make the translation."

"She loved the gardens." Shannon felt good for having asked Edison to stay. "We went out every day. Leila couldn't wait to see the sights. We went to Marche d'Aligre, this large open marketplace with everything from fruit and vegetables to art and clothing. We had a routine when I wasn't rehearsing. Breakfast and a tour in the mornings. Leila loves the theatre, so we attended all of the matinee performances at Gymnase-Marie Belle, Porte St-Martin, and the Café d'Edgar on Saturdays and Wednesdays."

"Don't forget l'Arpège," Leila said with perfect diction. "I loved that."

"That was her favorite restaurant. It's close to the Musée Rodin." Shannon shook her head. "She does not like Rodin."

"I want to go to Paris," Trey said. "The only place we go is Disney World."

Everyone laughed, except Edison. "Was all of this just you and Mommy?" he asked.

"Sometimes," Leila answered. "Thierry went sometimes, but he was gone a lot. When Chrissie was there, we all went together."

"Chrissie?" Donna asked.

"Thierry's daughter. We had several routines. If we had adult functions at night, we would have a children's version earlier in the evening." Shannon stole glances at Edison.

"We got all dressed up for dinner," Leila said. "Thierry would hold my chair. He called me…I can't remember, but it means 'little lamb'. That's because he called Mommy lamb, too."

Shannon tried to change the subject. "Trey, we didn't have a movie theatre when I was growing up here in Shepherd. It was closed for a long time."

"Mommy bought me long dresses to wear to dinner," Leila said, continuing to share her Paris experiences. "Chrissie said she was too old to wear long dresses—she's thirteen. She wanted short, short dresses, but I like the long ones. Mommy wore long ones, too."

"Paris is a beautiful place," John said. "I've only been the one time Mom and Dad took us to celebrate the new millennium. What I remember most is that after the big fireworks display at the Eiffel Tower, there were no cabs anywhere. We walked for hours. We'll all go together one summer when you kids are older."

"Are you going, too, Daddy?" Leila asked Edison.

"Of course he is," Shannon said quickly. "Your father would love it. I thought of him every time I went to Parc de la Villette. That's the other theme park in Paris. Disneyland Paris is much like the ones here, but Parc de la Villette had so much natural beauty. There's a little area with a gazebo on a hill overlooking the water. It's fabulous."

"Yeah, she probably thought I'd pull out my rod and reel and try and catch all the fish," Edison said to the children. He looked at Shannon. "I'm glad Leila had a chance to experience so much culture."

After a discussion of politics and the results of the local primary election, John and Donna left with the kids, and Edison helped tuck Leila in. When Shannon walked him to the door, he kissed her forehead. "You're a good mother, no matter what."

The night was long and bitter with regret. *I'm a good mother. That always should have come first.*

❧

Edison wearily climbed out of his patrol car after parking in front of his mother's house. Jeannie's car was in the driveway and all the lights were on inside. He hesitated, trying to hold onto the bittersweet feelings of holding his daughter and her mother in his arms.

"You been gone a long time." Etta looked up as he walked inside. "Jeannie was 'bout to leave. I said…Edison, where's Leila?"

"With her mother for the night."

"Don't tell me you let that woman talk you into leavin' that baby with her."

It was not a conversation he wanted to have with either of them. "She clung to Shannon and begged to stay. What was I supposed to do, rip her from her mother's arms?" He looked at Jeannie. "I'm glad you're still here. We need to talk, and this time, we need to finish the conversation."

He followed Jeannie to her house, his mind racing feverishly. His daughter had bonded with her mother, something he had known would happen if they spent time together, and now he had to make sure he protected his place in Leila's life.

He remembered the night his marriage dissolved and he sat, devastated, drinking beer and trying to understand why he was alone. Jeannie had offered a shoulder and he'd begun to lean.

She was not beautiful, but had a certain quality that made him feel comfortable in her presence. She could never take Shannon's place. No woman could. Parking the patrol car behind her car, he followed her inside.

"Come on in and tell me what Miss Shannon has convinced you to do now. I've been waiting for one of your earth-shattering disclosures ever since she came to town. You go over there and spend the entire evening with her, so why are you here? To end our relationship?"

"Where would you get a damn fool idea like that? Don't tell me. You got it from my mother. I've never understood why she hates Shannon so much, but I loved Doris Travers, and she was Leila's grandmother. Now, that's the last time I plan to repeat that."

He slammed his hat on the coffee table and stretched out on the sofa. "You were right about one thing, I do want to talk about our relationship, not calling it off, but setting a firm date to be married. We've played with this long enough. It's important for me to have a home for my daughter, especially now."

"We talked about it in the beginning, but you didn't seem ready, so I backed off."

"And I've been trying to revisit the subject lately, but you seem reluctant to do so. Please tell me why."

"Marriage shouldn't be a matter of convenience. You want to do it now because you're afraid Shannon will take Leila. It's unfair to ask me to inconvenience my life. This house is too small for all of us. That extra bedroom is filled with things that I can't throw away and—"

"I didn't say anything about staying in this house. You can sell it, keep it, or do whatever you want. I plan to take the front six acres of our property and build a house for the three of us. I didn't know Doris Travers was going to die two months ago when I tried to get you to discuss marriage. You were anxious to do it until then, so tell me what changed your mind. And please don't drag Shannon into this. It's between the two of us."

"Actually, it's between the three of us. Does Leila want to stay with us? She doesn't seem to like me very much."

"Could that have something to do with your reaction to her? When I hesitated before, I was hoping to give the two of you time to bond. Instead, you rarely agree to do things with the two us. I have a child. You've known this all along. I enjoy the way things are, but I can only be truly happy if my daughter is part of my home."

"And this has nothing to do with your fear that Shannon will take Leila to Paris? I know you, Edison. I saw the way you were each time Leila was gone for a couple of months. I'm sorry, but I need to know I'm marrying for something other than being a convenient nanny for Shannon Travers's daughter."

He sprang from the sofa. "When did Leila become just Shannon's daughter? If you thought that was my motive, why the hell have we been together all this time?"

When she didn't answer, he grabbed his hat. "Did you pick my uniforms up from the cleaners?"

"They're in the closet, but I hope you don't think you're leaving here to spend the night with her."

"After what you just said, I don't think you give a damn where I sleep, as long as my child is no bother to you. Does your feeling about my daughter have to do with the fact that she's not yours or that she's Shannon's?"

She shrugged and turned away.

"Answer me, Jeannie."

"Let Shannon take Leila to Paris. If you had a child with no one to care for her, I would accept the responsibility. Is keeping Leila your way of punishing Shannon for leaving you?" She rolled her eyes up at him. "Or maybe you can't let go of Shannon."

Fury swept over him. "I want my child with me. I always have. But you're right, she is my responsibility, not yours. Thanks for pointing that out."

He gathered a stack of clothes from the drawer and stuffed them in a laundry bag. Jeannie came into the bedroom.

"I've been staying here sometimes and at my parents' house whenever I have Leila. About two months ago, I told you I was starting to feel like a nomad. I said I wanted to marry you and start living as a family. I will have my child with me when the court permits and we will live like a family, with or without you."

Instead of going to his parents' house, he drove aimlessly down the highway. The dull ache in his chest became a sharp pain when he drove by the house he had shared with Shannon. He wanted to believe she had missed the love they once shared. She had apologized, but was she sincere? "Hell no!" He pressed the gas pedal. "She didn't miss me. She had Thierry."

The stores along Main Street were closing earlier because everyone wanted to be home before dark. He checked the back alley behind Hayes' Furniture Emporium and Shepherd Dollar Store.

Thirsty and angry, he parked on the side of Grady's Café and went inside. Most of the men gathered there were still dressed in the suits they had worn to the funeral. He spoke, calling each of them by name. There were few strangers in Shepherd, but the most familiar face in the crowd was that of his friend since second grade.

"I've been looking for you, Bobby Joe."

"Hey, man." His face mirrored Jeannie's but was marked with serious neglect. "It's a sad day in Shepherd. Mrs. Travers was a remarkable woman. We were just talking about how many of us she taught at one time or another. Just about everybody here."

"She was a great lady," Edison answered, amazed that he and Bobby Joe were the same age and yet his friend's face was that of a weathered old man. "What have you been doing with yourself, man?"

"Just tryin' to live, bro. You know how it goes. What you drinkin'?"

"A soda." He turned to the woman behind the counter. "Root beer, Mandy, and whatever Bobby Joe is drinking."

"Another beer for me, and I'm paying." He pulled a roll of rumpled bills from his pocket. "I'm sorry for the circumstances, but it was good to see Shannon again. We keep getting older and she keeps getting prettier. She hasn't changed since high school."

"No, she hasn't." He drank the soda and went for another one, this time treating Bobby Joe to a beer.

"Thanks, man." Bobby Joe moved closer, bringing the distinctive odor of alcohol and stale smoke. "Look, I know you and Shannon's folks are still tight, so I'm wondering if you'll do me a little favor. See, I got this chance to make some money, but first I have to have money. Know what I mean?"

"So what's the favor?" Edison asked.

"They're looking for help down at the store. Donna's been hiring. I think they're doing inventory or something like that. Think you can get me on down there?"

Edison hated that Bobby Joe was living in such a manner, but knew there was little he could do. "Didn't I get you a job at the grocery once before, man? If I'm not mistaken, Donna let you go with good cause."

The unshaven face fell forward. "I was messed up, Edison. I was in bad shape back then, but I'm cool now. Other than an occasional beer, I ain't doing nothing

I could go to jail for, and that ain't no lie. I just need some kind of legitimate hustle so I can make a little money to invest. That's all."

"Tell me what you're investing in, and I'll see what I can do."

Bobby Joe's face brightened. "Yeah? Thanks, man. The hustle is good, man. These dudes from over in Falcon go on buying trips to Mexico all the time. They get designer knock-off handbags for almost nothing and sell them here for something like a 300 percent profit. They've been looking for investors to buy a big stash for the holidays. All I need is some start-up cash. I went over to the diner yesterday to ask my sister. She started screaming before I could get the words out, talking 'bout how she already bought me out of the diner and I wasn't entitled to anything. I wasn't seeking entitlement."

"Man, I hate to ask you this, but I have to know. Are you using?"

"Hell no. I just told you, I don't use nothing I can't buy in the liquor store. Never did."

"There are a lot of drugs moving through Shepherd. I need to find out how they get here. You help me with that and I'll find you a job."

"Man, I ain't got nothing to do with that." He held his hand up in a gesture of surrender.

"Yeah, but you know where it's coming from. Keep your mouth shut and every time some young person gets high and wraps his vehicle around a tree, robs or murders, you're an accessory."

"You don't know nothing about the people doing this stuff. They're crazy, man. They don't give a damn about blowing your head off if you get in the way. Besides, ain't nothing here in Shepherd but the little pushers. You can't stop them. Arrest one and two will take his place. You need to get the big man, and you can't do that."

Edison wanted to believe him, but didn't. "So who is this big man?"

"He ain't local is all I know."

"So who are the middlemen? Surely the local dealers don't go to the big man directly. Tell me what you know, big, little or whatever, before someone gets killed."

Bobby Joe ground the toe of his shoe against the concrete floor and looked around. "If I say something and you arrest them, I'll have to testify. Then they'll have me killed."

"I won't let that happen."

"Come on, man. We both know you can't do that."

Edison figured there was no one in Shepherd with money invested in drugs, but it was likely someone in the town was bringing it in. "I tell you what. Just give me the names, man. Let me worry about the rest. We don't have money in our budget to pay for information, but I'll make sure you get something, and get a job."

"I don't want you to pay me." He chugged the rest of the beer and set the empty bottle on the counter. "Of course, if you get me enough to make a payday on this handbag thing, I'll find out what I can."

"See what you can get."

He looked at his friend's unsavory appearance. Enveloped by disappointment, he finished his root beer and left. He did not want to go to his parents' home, but it was the lesser of two evils. He was turning into the driveway when Jeannie called.

"I'm waiting for you, baby. I was selfish earlier. I'm sorry. I want to make it up to you."

He quickly turned around. "I'm on my way."

Seeing the windows dark when he parked under the carport, he thought Jeannie had rented one of his favorite movies, but when he opened the door, the sound that greeted him was a raunchy blues number that left little to the imagination. "Jeannie? Where are you?"

"In the bedroom, baby. Waiting for you."

With everything that had happened the past five days, sex had not been at the forefront of his mind. He stopped in the doorway where candles cast eerie shadows on the walls. Blinking to adjust to the dimness, he saw Jeannie lying across the bed, her skin glistening in the candlelight.

"Come on over here, baby. Let me show you how sorry I am for what happened earlier. Let me show you how much I love you. How much I want you."

He was startled. Jeannie had made him great dinners before. She had held his face between her massive breasts and spoken softly when she knew he was upset, but she had never been sexually aggressive. Days would sometimes pass before he realized they had not even kissed, except for hello and goodbye pecks on the cheek or forehead. She had been willing, but never eager.

"Wow. Candles. Nice."

"There's chilled wine on the table." She draped the sheet across her chest, leaving most of her breasts exposed. "Pour yourself a glass. I started without you. Just lying here thinking about us. Our future. Holding you in my arms."

He tried to think of an appropriate response but nothing came to mind. "Smells good in here. What scent is that?"

"It's called sex on the beach, except in our case it's sex on the sheets. Put that gun on the table, take off those clothes, and come on over here. Don't let me lie here all hot and bothered by myself."

He started to undress, anxious and curious. "I wouldn't do that."

"Just take off the gun and get out of those boots. I'm sure you're tired, so I'll do all the work."

Now he really was anxious. Maybe she was a demon in bed and he had not been able to excite her. He removed his boots and socks, placed the holster on the chair, and stretched out next to her. She removed his belt and unzipped his pants.

"Looks like you're ready for me. I like that."

She stroked the ridge under his shorts before pulling them down and closing her hand around him. In spite of being aroused, he could not relax. Her behavior was unnatural.

She moved up on the bed, squeezed her breasts together, and leaned close to his mouth. "I know you like these. Go ahead, use them any way you want."

Without wanting to, he thought of Shannon. Making love by candlelight was routine before Leila was born. The music had been soft and romantic. Everything was natural, sweet and wonderful.

"What's wrong?" Jeannie was asking. "You deflated like a popped balloon. That's never happened before." She moved swiftly, turning on lights and wrapping herself in a terrycloth robe. "She's here. She's in our bed. Have you been with her already or were you just thinking about her? And don't bother lying."

He sat up and covered with the sheet. "I'm not going to lie. Yes, I was distracted. You asked if I wanted to get married so Shannon wouldn't take Leila. I'm wondering if you're doing all of this because you're trying to make sure I don't—"

"Hold it right there. I was doing all of this, as you say, because I was sorry for the way I reacted earlier. You've been under a lot of stress. I know you loved Shannon's mother, and I know these people in Shepherd have been giving you a hard time about this crime wave. I was just trying to relieve your tension. I wanted you to know how much I care." She twisted her hands around the belt of her robe. "I can't do anything right." Tears streamed down her face.

"Now I'm the one who's sorry. Come here, baby. It's just that this is so unlike you. You can't blame me for being surprised. I appreciate you wanting to help me lose some of this tension. Now I am relaxed."

He kissed her and wrapped his arms around her body. "That's all I wanted. You don't have to try so hard. I'm glad to be here with you." Feeling tears on her face, he held her away from him. "I don't think I've ever seen you cry. I'm sorry."

"I seldom cry, but I've also never turned a man off before. I'm not Shannon and I never will be. Your mother said you married her because the two of you were practically living together in college. I guess she put something heavy on you and threatened to take it away if you didn't marry her."

Her words did not immediately sink in and when they did, he stood abruptly, almost dumping her on the floor. "You and my mother actually discussed my sex life with the woman I married? That's sick, Jeannie."

"That's not what I meant," she said quickly. "Anyway, I didn't say it, your mother did. You didn't even have an engagement period. Your mother said you came home ranting about wanting to marry right away. That was her interpretation, since Shannon wasn't pregnant."

"I married Shannon because I loved her." He hurried into his clothes. "For the record, Shannon was a virgin when we married. Tell that to my mother next time the subject comes up."

"I'm sorry. I didn't mean for it to come out that way. Your mother was just speculating on why you married someone who seemed so wrong for you, that's all." She started crying again. "I just wanted to relax you. To take your mind off everything. I thought it would make you happy."

"I doubt a hooker could make me happy, Jeannie, but thanks for the insight."

"A hooker? That's a terrible thing to say!"

By the time he finished speaking, he was halfway out of the door. Slamming it hard enough to jar the windowpanes, he hurried to the patrol car and sped off. Dejected and feeling suddenly alone, he drove back to the station and paced the floor. When his legs refused to continue, he stretched out on the cot in one of the cells and fell asleep listening to "Reservations", Shannon's first hit.

❧

Shannon stayed close to her father after John and Donna left. Mama Lou and Savannah were the last ones to leave.

"You married a lady," Mama Lou said to her son. "She lived an upright life, raised her children to be kind, respectful adults, and she made you happy. I can't say more than that."

Shannon went to check on Leila and found her sitting on the floor holding Brown Bear, her favorite nighttime toy. Shannon joined her.

"Hey, Brown Bear." She leaned over and made a face. "Can I please have a kiss?"

"I have a boyfriend," Leila confided as she held the toy to Shannon's face. "He gives me cookies from his lunch. Granny won't let me have cookies."

Shannon smiled. "I had a boyfriend when I was your age. His name was Alva. Does Granny prepare your lunch when you stay over there?"

Leila nodded. "She gives me tuna sandwiches. I don't like tuna. I like apples, but she always gives me bananas. And you know what else? Blue is my favorite color. Grandmommy said it was your favorite color, too." She became sad. "I miss Grandmommy. She was teaching me to read. She said she would teach me numbers when I'm older."

"I'll teach you numbers, sweetheart. I'll be here to help you read in English and French, and I'll teach you numbers. I love you with all my heart."

# Chapter 6

Unable to sleep, Shannon tossed and turned until she knew Thierry had started his day and then called him. His voice gave her comfort.

"*Mon agneau*, I am so sorry I could not be with you today. How is your father?"

"Stone-faced most of the time, but he has broken down twice. John and I were both emotional today."

"*Bien-aimé* Leila?"

"She's so precious, Thierry, and so grown up. You wouldn't believe the conversation we had tonight. She makes my heart stand still."

"Bring her back here to live. I'll bring Madame Duprat to stay with her. When will you come home?"

"I'm trying to sort things out. I can't leave Daddy just yet, and I can't take Leila away from him at this time. He's lost so much already."

"Take your time, *Mon agneau*. I understand."

She knew he would understand, even if she decided to stay in Shepherd, but not if she missed the scheduled engagements he had contracted. "Is it possible to cancel whatever engagements you have scheduled until after New Year's? I just can't think of performing now."

"I shall try. Are you planning to stay that long?"

"I can't say right now."

She knew she would probably leave Shepherd, but she would never leave Leila.

~

Edison stopped in to see the mayor early the next morning. "I'm trying to get a lead from Bobby Joe. I think he knows something, but every time I try to hem him in, he disappears. I went by his house early this morning, but he wasn't there. I'll find him. When I do, I'm not letting him out of my sight until he gives me something."

"I thought we would have had more leads by now. Is there anyone else you think might know something?"

"There is. It's just that I know Bobby Joe better than I know my own brothers. I'll find a way to make him talk."

The mayor turned around in his chair. "On a personal note, I'm going to venture into the none-of-my-business category. Are you sleeping in your jail these days?"

Edison pursed his lips. "Mayor, that's a whole 'nother story altogether. My ex-wife is home. My mother and the woman I thought I was going to marry have both gone crazy. My little girl understandably wants to be with her mother. I have to stay focused on my job. The only way I know to do that is to stay away from my mother and Jeannie, so yes, I am."

"I see." Mayor Townsend leaned on his desk, his face filled with concern. "I'm sure it will all work out. In the meantime, you can use our guestroom anytime you need it."

"Thanks." Edison smiled and nodded.

He went back to his office. Shannon dominated his thoughts. He could not give her the things she and Leila had enjoyed in Paris, but he wanted more evenings like the one he'd just had with her family. Leila's face had lit up when she spoke of Paris. He had been surprised that both she and Shannon spoke so casually of Thierry. Even that had hurt his heart.

He wanted to see Shannon, maybe drive over to Crowley and have dinner, just the two them. Before he did that, he knew he would have to settle things with Jeannie.

Shannon took Leila shopping in Jackson and spent the afternoon at Family Supermarket, helping Donna with inventory. While Leila played in the back with her cousins, Shannon learned more than she wanted to about Edison's relationship with Jeannie.

"I had not planned to talk about this, especially now, but I feel you need to know," Donna said. "Tori was in town a couple of weeks ago and went to Velma's to have her hair done. She's the baby of the family, so she's much younger than the rest of us, and certainly too young for Jeannie to recognize. Tori started listening to the conversation when someone teased Jeannie about getting married. She said she was already Mrs. Edison Page, and didn't plan to change a thing. She went on to say that under no circumstances would she raise Shannon Travers's daughter."

"I suspected that was the reason they hadn't married."

"This happened on a Saturday. Tori had been here with the kids most of that morning. She had just said how bright and beautiful Leila is. She left here, went to Velma's and heard Jeannie running off at the mouth. She jumped all over Jeannie. Your parents knew about it. Someone called my mother. She called me. My sister specializes in child behavior. She told Jeannie if Edison heard those remarks made in front of his child, he'd go off, and so would she. Miss Etta thinks Jeannie is sweetness and light, but she's a first-class bitch."

"I'm glad you told me. Rest assured, Jeannie will never have to raise my child."

"Hey, you two." Edison walked toward them. "If that look on your faces is directed at me, I think I'd better run."

"It's not directed at you, Sheriff," Donna said, hugging his waist. "Just venting."

He gave Shannon a quick hug. "I was about to ask if the kids were back there, but I hear them."

"They're back there. I'm taking the boys back to day school tomorrow. I drove out there the other day, but I couldn't leave them." She looked at Shannon. "Your mother had an assigned parking spot right across the street. My boys looked over there and cried so much I didn't have the heart to leave them. It's very hard to explain death to children. When we got to my mother's, the boys ran to her like they were afraid she wouldn't be there."

She looked from Shannon to Edison and back. "Are you planning to take Leila back to day school?"

"Yes, I guess…" He stopped and turned to Shannon. "What do you think?"

"Let's wait until next week. I'm enjoying being with her so much. Even with her visits to Paris, I've missed so much of her life. I was planning to come back here tomorrow after I run a couple of errands. I'll help with the kids."

"Fine with me," Donna answered. "And I'm sure it's fine with them."

"I know it's your time with her, but I think she needs me a lot right now."

Edison nodded. "Walk back there with me, or I might not ever get out."

Shannon followed him through the aisles and stood back when the boys and Leila ran to greet him.

"Are you taking us fishing?" Trey asked, and the others echoed the question.

"Not today, but I'll take you very soon." He saw Shannon's smile, and added, "But Shannon can't go. Last time I took her fishing, she caught all the fish. Didn't leave a single one for me."

"I want my mommy to go!" Leila yelled.

Shannon left Edison tussling with the boys and walked back to where Donna was checking items off her inventory list.

Donna commented without looking up, "It just seems natural, doesn't it?"

"How did you know what I was thinking?"

"I saw the look on both of your faces." She straightened up and faced Shannon. "You two belong together. He's good with kids. My boys love him. He needs a woman who shares his feelings."

"For a few minutes back there, I almost forgot we were no longer married. I can't tell you how much I've missed him."

"Tell him how you feel."

"I can't. He's engaged to Jeannie."

"I've given you more advice since you've been home than I've given my sisters in all their adult lives. I've got one more thing to say, and then I'll keep my comments to myself. If you let that man marry Jeannie, I'll be damn disappointed." She smirked. "More importantly, so will he."

"I'll keep that in mind."

"In case you haven't noticed, the sexual tension between the two of you is strong enough to blow the windows out of this place. Did you see him about to kiss you when he first came in?"

"Old habit, nothing more."

"You don't believe that, and neither do I."

She was not sure if Donna was right about Edison's feelings, but she was very sure of her own. She had wanted to kiss him, and more. The same thing had happened when he started to leave. She wondered if they could ever stop bickering long enough to just let it happen. After all, he and Jeannie were not married yet.

She and Donna worked side by side until J.P. came to close the store as he usually did each night. Shannon enjoyed the short drive home with Leila. She prepared dinner while Leila went to wash up. Answering a knock on the back door, she looked at Edison in surprise.

"Hey. I didn't expect to see you tonight. Is something wrong?"

He sheepishly entered the kitchen. "No, nothing's wrong. I just wanted to see my little girl before she went to bed. Did she tell you that I never miss a day of seeing her, no matter how busy I am? Did she tell you that?" A look of sheer joy spread across his face as Leila ran into his arms.

"Yes, she told me. We've had some very interesting conversations –"

"Don't tell, Mommy!" Leila giggled and tugged her mother's arm. "Don't tell him about you-know-who."

"Trust me, I would never do that." Shannon shook her head and winked.

"What's this? Secrets from the old man? I thought you were my girl?"

"I am, Daddy, but I had girl talk with Mommy." She hugged his neck. "I love you!"

Shannon watched the two of them, and thought of Donna's parting advice. "Stay for dinner? We have enough food to rid the world of hunger."

"Please stay, Daddy! Mom made a French dessert. She's a good cook, and you know what else?"

"What, honey?"

"Mom sang me a song last night—in French!" Her large dark eyes danced with delight.

"Your mommy can really sing, can't she? Okay, I'll stay for dinner." He turned to Shannon. "You're sure it's all right?"

"Sure." She knew he wanted to stay. She also knew there was no way she could sit with her daughter and ex-husband for dinner and not regret allowing her family to fall apart.

They ate amid a lot of chatter. Leila told her father everything that she and her mother had done since they last talked. Shannon was glad for the company, especially for her father's sake. Edison stayed long after dinner was over, talking to J.P. while Shannon and

Leila did the dishes. After Leila's bath, he helped tuck her in.

"That was a great dinner," he said when they went back downstairs. "Thanks for inviting me. Our little girl seems so happy. I'm glad you're home, Shannon. Really glad."

She frowned in surprise. "Thank you for saying that. The circumstances are regrettable, but spending time with Leila makes me happier than you could know. I hope you agree that she's approaching the age where she really needs a woman—a mother—in her life."

"She always has."

This time his tone was dry, and she stiffened in anticipation of an argument.

"Then I hope you'll agree that Leila needs to be with me." She slumped down in the chair, waiting for the sparks to fly.

"I know she needs you. Only you. I just can't imagine not seeing her, and I know that will happen when… if you take her to Paris. I'm not wealthy like you. I can't afford to fly halfway around the world to see her, and I can't let her grow up without a father. That Thierry guy of yours sure as hell wouldn't make a good father. We've got to work this out for her sake."

She stood and poured herself a glass of wine. "Suppose I tell you that I'm not taking Leila to Paris? That I'm staying here. Do you think you could live with that?"

"If you really mean it, I can live with it just fine." He shook his head when she offered a glass to him. "You wouldn't say that and then take her away, would you?"

"We both need to do what's right for her. She's not happy when she's with you because you leave her with your mother. She's a very perceptive child. Talk to her. More precisely, listen to her. Let her tell you herself. I didn't make this up."

"I know how Mama feels about you, but she would never hurt Leila. Even if you stay here, I'll still want her with me as much as possible. Just give me time to work everything out. Stay here or go back to Paris. Your career is there, and so is Thierry."

She walked him to the door. "I know you love her. She loves you, too. I don't want to take her away, so change what you just said. Make it 'we'll work this out.' "

The phone rang as he was driving away.

There was no hello, only a stern demand. "I'm callin' to let you know I'm on my way over there to pick up Leila. Edison asked me to bring her home. Tell her to get ready."

"Hello, Miss Etta. Edison just drove away. He knows Leila is staying here for the time being."

"Well, he musta changed his mind. He just told me to come get her, and that's what I plan to do."

She hung up before Shannon could answer. "Guess who that was?" she said to her father while dialing Edison's number. "She said she's coming to get Leila. Says Edison told her to."

"Edison just kissed you on the cheek and walked out of here. She's lying."

"Well, he's not answering his phone."

"He's probably checking his messages or talking to one of the deputies."

Shannon dialed the number again, left a message and was about to start her bath when she heard her father's greeting.

"Well hello, Etta. I was just thinking that you're the only neighbor who hadn't been by to pay their respects. Come on in."

"I am sorry 'bout your wife, but I'm here for Leila. Is she ready?"

"Leila is in bed." Shannon walked into the room. "Edison helped tuck her in. As I told you on the phone, she's staying here for the time being."

"Then like I said, he must of changed his mind. It's his time with Leila. He's got 'nother month with her, so get her ready. I ain't got all night."

"I don't want to go with you," Leila screamed from the hallway. "I want to stay with my mommy. I want to stay here!"

"It's okay, Leila. Go to your room and get the book we read last night so you can show it to Granddaddy. We'll be up there very shortly." She waited until she heard the bedroom door close. "As you can see, she doesn't want to go with you, Miss Etta. I left Edison a message to call and discuss this, though I hardly think that's necessary."

"Ask Edison who he put in charge of Leila when he ain't around. I'm her legal guardian."

"And I'm her mother."

"You didn't think 'bout that when you went away from here with that—"

"Hold it right there," J.P. interrupted. "I just buried my wife two days ago. For God's sake, have some respect. You've always hated my daughter, and we all know it. I never said anything before because I didn't want to be a mettlesome old bag of wind like you, but this has gone too damn far. You get the hell out of my house, Etta."

The patrol car came to a screeching halt in the driveway and Edison ran up the steps.

J.P. was still fuming. "Edison, if you're half the man you should be you'll put an end to this. If not, go ahead and use that gun on your hip. Forget how shamefully your mother treated my daughter. Look at what this is doing to yours."

"Go home, Mama. I told Shannon that Leila could stay with her for the time being."

"You just let her—"

"Stop it! Stop it!" The scream came from the hallway before Leila ran to Shannon's arms. "I don't want to go with you, and if you make me I'll run away and never come back!"

Shannon lifted Leila in her arms and held her tight against her chest. "Shhh, honey. It's okay. Everything is okay."

"Look at your grandchild, Mama," Edison said, taking Miss Etta's elbow and ushering her around to face Leila. "Look what you've done. Even if I had planned to take her, I wouldn't do it now. I don't know when all of this started, but it's obvious she's been unhappy. Everyone knew about it but me, so I guess that makes me a bad father. We'll sit down and work this out like reasonable adults—Shannon and me."

"Just like I thought. Ya still can't control her."

"I never attempted to control Shannon or anyone else, but I see that I should have kept you out of my personal life. Just leave. Right now, please!"

Edison reached out for Leila as his mother backed from the room. "No one is going to take you anywhere, honey. I didn't realize you were so unhappy at Granny's. Why didn't you tell me? I don't ever want anything or anyone to hurt you. Don't you understand that?"

She nodded and he leaned in and kissed her salty cheeks. "Your mother is a wonderful person, and you're the best daughter in the whole world."

Shannon looked at him and tried to pry Leila from her shoulder. "Honey, let Granddaddy take you upstairs. Your father and I have to talk."

"Please don't yell anymore," Leila said, her voice full of pain.

"No one is going to yell, baby. I promise," Edison said softly.

"Leila, your father and I created you because we loved each other, and we wanted a little princess to share that love. I know things have gotten out of hand, but we will work this out. I promise."

Edison placed his arm around both of them. "Your mother is right, honey. Go on with your grandfather and we'll talk before I leave. Okay?"

Shannon passed Leila to J.P.'s arms, reached for the remote control, and turned up the volume on the television. Taking Edison's hand, she led him into the kitchen. "I don't want to upset that child anymore, and I don't want to upset my father. I can't believe your mother is so insensitive that she would come in here and carry on like that. I can see why Leila doesn't want to be there, and you should have seen it a long time ago."

"I won't even try and defend my mother. She was wrong."

"I made a mistake. I left my husband. I left my child. No matter what the reason or the intention, I was wrong." Shannon's voice overflowed with pain and anger. "I'll say that to the people who matter. Everyone else can go to hell, and that goes double for your mother."

133

"You have every right to be angry. I'm sorry. I wish none of this had happened. I wish I'd never…" He moved away. "It's getting late. I've got police business that I have to take care of. That's where I was heading when you called. I'll see you tomorrow."

"Say goodnight to Leila before you go."

He went upstairs, and J.P. joined her in the living room.

"Are you okay?" he asked.

"I'm okay. It's Leila I'm worried about."

"She's okay now," Edison said as he returned, looking tired and ashamed. "I'm so sorry about all this. I tried to stop her after I got Shannon's call. I didn't ask her to come here, and didn't know she planned to do it."

"I've known your mother longer than you have," J.P. said. "I understand. I just hope you won't let it happen again."

Shannon walked him to the door. "I know this is hard on you, but I can't deal with your mother anymore, and Leila wants nothing to do with her. That's not my fault, Edison."

"Mama has a giant blind spot when it comes to you. It's nothing you've done, just who you are." His eyebrows lifted when he turned to go to the car. "I just remembered. I have a jar of honey for Leila. It's in the cone, just the way she likes it. Just don't let her have too much."

She walked with him and took the jar. "Nice. You love honey, too."

"You remembered." He half smiled.

"I remember everything, but I only hold onto the good memories."

"It was good, wasn't it? I was so happy with you."

They were standing so close together she felt his breath on her neck. Just as she lifted her face to his, she caught sight of a small face in the window. "Someone is watching us."

He smiled and waved. "Well, we're not yelling, if that's what she's afraid of. I don't want to do that anymore." He kissed her forehead and waved at Leila before driving away.

"Daddy's not mad anymore, is he?" Leila asked when Shannon went upstairs.

She shook her head. "Your daddy isn't mad. I'm not mad, and everything is okay."

"So now can I stay with you and Daddy?"

When Shannon didn't answer, Leila prodded. "Why can't we stay together? You and Daddy both want to, don't you, Mommy?"

"It's not that simple, sweetheart. You'll understand when you're older."

Leila rolled her eyes. "That's what Daddy says, but I don't understand anything. I'll ask Daddy if he wants to do it. If he says yes, will you say yes, too?"

It was a request Shannon wished she could fulfill.

# *Chapter* 7

Edison drove back to his office, which was located in the basement of the courthouse. Emmett Paul, his chief deputy and longtime friend, was still there.

"Sorry," Edison said as he rushed through the door. "Where is he?"

Emmett nodded. "Back there. I told him he couldn't leave until you got here."

Edison went into the cell, walked over and kicked the side of the cot. "Bobby Joe. Wake up, man."

"Edison, man, why ya'll wanna lock me up like a criminal? I didn't do a damn thing."

"The door wasn't locked. Emmett just wanted you to stay here until I got back. I've been looking all over town for you. Where have you been?"

"I've been home. Didn't Carmen tell you?"

"Carmen said she hadn't seen you in two days. That's the second time you promised to get information for me and then disappeared. In case you don't realize it, I was concerned."

"I don't know a thing. If I had heard something, I would have come back and told you."

"It's me, man. I know you know something. The only reason for not telling me is that you're mixed up in it. I don't want to believe that."

Bobby Joe stood and brushed his hands down his shirt. "Hey man, remember when we took those girls to the creek for that picnic? We were fifteen. That was our first time. I'll never forget that. What ever happened to Joyce and Gloria Jean? Those girls were hotter than fire." He giggled. "Remember you couldn't decide which one you wanted?"

"Yeah, I remember. Now I'll tell you something about that evening. Nothing happened with Gloria Jean and me, and I know nothing happened with you and Joyce. See, I know when you're lying. Now, let's get back to the subject at hand. Man, this stuff is hurting our kids. People are getting robbed. We've got to stop it, Bobby Joe."

"I'll try and find out something by tomorrow."

Edison placed his arm across the doorway. "That's what you said last time."

"Okay, but you can't say I told you. I don't want those guys gunning for me."

"Would I do that?"

"I don't know as much as you think I do, but I know Boise Park is their drop. They meet on the campground at night."

"What night?"

"Most nights, actually. That's the drop for the whole area." Seeing Edison's skeptical grimace, he added, "I'm not lying. Go see for yourself."

Edison moved his arm and Bobby Joe hurried to the door, but stopped. "Hey, man."

"Yeah? What is it?"

Bobby Joe looked across the room at Emmett.

"What, man? You got something else to say?"

"Just be careful. Okay?"

"Did he give you anything?" Emmett asked.

"I'm not sure. He said they use Boise Park for the drop, and they're there most nights. He's holding out on me, but maybe it's a start."

"I'll go with you." Emmett reached for his hat.

"I'm not going out there tonight." He rubbed his neck. "We need to ask… no, make that beg for some new cots. I've slept better on camping trips. I'm either sleeping in a bed tonight or finding myself a place to live tomorrow. Go on home. Melvin is out on patrol. I'm going home–wherever that is."

Edison saw Jeannie's expression change when he walked in the door.

"I was about to go to bed. I didn't think you were coming." Her eyes were misty as she reached out for him. "I'm sorry about the other night. It's just that I liked the way things were between us," she cooed. "I thought you did, too."

"I liked the way things were, except for having to leave Leila with my parents instead of having her with me. Shannon isn't planning to leave any time soon. We can marry and the two of us can spend more time with Leila together. By the time Shannon leaves, you two will be comfortable with each other. Sound okay?"

She grimaced and then smiled. "I love the two of us being together. Why can't we keep it the way it was, or let Shannon take Leila with her? I'm sure she'll agree to bring her back to spend time with you. After all, her family is still here, and I know she wants to help her father adjust to the loss of his wife, so she'll be home a lot."

"Cut the crap, okay? We've been practically living together. We have bank accounts together, we've bought property together, and we share expenses. If your only reason for not getting married is Leila, let's just call the whole thing off right now."

"I don't beg, Edison."

"Neither do I." He went to the closet and took out racks of clothes. "I'll get the things I need for now and come back tomorrow for the rest. I'll do it while you're at the diner and drop the keys off afterwards."

"I don't want it to end this way."

"But you don't want to help me raise Leila."

She looked down at the floor. "No."

"Enough said. Do we need attorneys or do you think we can separate our assets without a hassle?"

"I'm not trying to take anything from you, and I've given you all I have to give. I want to be your woman, your lover. I want to be your wife. I just don't want to raise Shannon Travers's child. I'm sorry."

He smiled broadly and sincerely. "Don't be."

He filled the squad car with his belongings and left without saying another word. Instead of driving to his parents' house, he went back into town and transferred everything to his truck. Surprised that he felt no anger and not much pain, his thoughts went directly to finding a house to rent and buying furnishings.

He saw four cars parked in front of his parents' home, and knew his mother had sent out her usual distress call to his sisters and brothers. He started to turn around, but did not. He opened the front gate just as his father and his brother Ray came into the yard.

"Hey, man." Ray raised his fist in greeting. "How's life treating you these days?"

"Hey, Ray. Daddy. Man, I think you already know the answer to that. I've got my hands full."

"Just don't let your mama interfere anymore," Tito said. "We just told her she ought to be 'shamed for causing trouble over there tonight. I can't blame that child for not wantin' to come over here. Your mother is getting crazier every day. I can't talk no sense into her. Ray tried and she just about took his head off. I'd just leave her 'lone right now. Let her simmer down. I get out in that shed, turn on my TV, put my feet up, and just let her fuss by herself."

"I've tried very hard to keep everyone happy. Consequently, no one is." Edison walked past them and opened the front door. "Evening. Everybody doing okay?"

His youngest sister, Nancy, hurried over and hugged his neck. "Hey, big brother. I heard about that meeting the other day. Come on in the kitchen. I brought that casserole you like. You've probably eaten, but you'll have it for tomorrow."

"Thanks." He looked at his mother's frowning face. "What you did was wrong, Mama. There's no nice way to put it. How would you feel if you just lost Daddy and somebody came in here yelling and carrying on like a madwoman? It was disrespectful and wrong. Your granddaughter was already afraid of you. Now I doubt if she'll ever want to set foot in here again. You and Jeannie both have behaved poorly toward the Travis family, and toward my baby. In case you don't know, that little girl means more to me than anything in this world."

"It's late. Let's just forget about this for now," Nancy insisted. "You've got to be tired and frustrated right now. Everything will be okay."

Etta stood and faced him. "Shannon poisoned that child again' me. She's the one to blame. You the one actin' disrespectful, toward Jeannie and towards me. I'm your mama. That oughta mean somethin'."

"It means a hell of a lot, Mama, but you had no right to do what you did."

Ray came in the front door and took Edison's arm. "Just do what you have to do, man. You don't owe anybody an explanation."

"Is Shannon taking Leila back to Paris with her?" his sister, Brenda, asked. "You'd let her do that?"

"He'll let her do whatever it is she wants to do, and that's the gospel truf," his mother said. "That's the pro'lem."

Edison looked around the room. He loved his family. "Stay out of my life, Mama. Your personal feelings have clouded all sense of reason. Don't go near Shannon, and don't ever say another word about her to me or in front of my daughter. I came here tonight because I was tired and needed some peace." He looked around the room. "I don't need this."

Ray and Nancy followed him from the room.

"Come stay with me until you get everything together," Nancy offered.

"I think that's a good idea," Ray added. "You'll never keep Mama out of your business as long as you're staying here. Did you and Jeannie split up?"

"Yes. Jeannie and Mama get along so well because they're so much alike. Thanks for your offer, sis. I need to drive around and clear my head. I'll see you guys later."

He would drive around. Maybe he could check out Bobby Joe's story, but there was no need to clear his head. For the first time in a long time, his head, his whole life, was crystal clear. He loved his child and he loved Shannon. He drove by the house they had shared and thought about everything she had said since she returned home. Her feelings were not as clear as his, but he felt almost certain that she loved him, too.

❧

Shannon was up early the next morning. She made scrambled eggs, bacon, and pancakes, but did not take time to eat.

J.P. focused on Leila's continuous stream of questions about their plans for the rest of the day. "You'll stay with me until your mother completes her errands. We'll go to the store."

"And I'll meet you there later," Shannon added.

She kissed them and went to the bedroom for her purse, dreading the tasks before her, but knowing they had to be done. Carmen and Jackie had been her backup singers and best friends for many years. Jackie was happily married, a mother and a nurse. Carmen's life had been in shambles, practically since high school. Her mother had provided dramatic updates on the many personal setbacks she had suffered, including the loss of her mother, her troubled relationship with Bobby Joe and raising two children alone.

Shannon had tried to talk with her several times, even offered her money. Jackie had never blamed Shannon for accepting Thierry's invitation to Paris, but Carmen had. Feeling the need for closure on many things in her past, Shannon felt she owed them an explanation and an apology.

When the door cracked at the dilapidated house where Carmen's parents had lived, Shannon tried hard not to cry. Carmen's face was pocked with dark spots and scars. The wig she wore looked ratty, as did the bathrobe she clutched to her chest.

"Hi, Carmen. I hope you don't mind me stopping by like this. I would have called, but I didn't want to give you a chance to say no."

Carmen moved into the doorway. "I'm sorry about your mother."

"Thank you." Looking at her bloodshot eyes, everything Shannon had planned to say seemed inadequate. "I have something to get off my chest, so I'll just say it and go. I'm very sorry I couldn't persuade Thierry to take us as a group. I did try. I hated leaving you and Jackie. It would have been so much better if you had been there."

Carmen shrugged. "Don't sweat it. You were looking out for number one. I ain't hatin' on you for that. I probably would have done the same thing."

A man's voice asked who was at the door.

"Just someone I thought was my friend. I'll be there in a minute."

"Take care of yourself." She looked at the troubled, angry face. "If there is ever anything I can do...you know...I love you."

"You can't do crap for me. I know you tried to ease your conscience with them little trinkets you sent Jackie and me. Don't bother. I ain't no charity case. Besides, why would you think more of us than you did your husband and child?"

"I'm sorry," Shannon muttered. "My offer still stands." She hurried away. Accusations from Etta Page only made her angry. Carmen's words hurt. The trinkets she had sent Jackie and Carmen were designer handbags filled with French cologne and diamond earrings at Christmas. There was guilt, but her feelings and the gifts had been genuine.

She drove through town, noting that Edison's squad car was parked in the usual place near the courthouse entrance. She parked her father's car in a shaded area and walked inside the cool building that was a new edition to Shepherd General Hospital. Jackie had married just after high school, completed a nursing course, and started her career at the hospital.

Signs directed Shannon past admissions and the gift shop to the large cafeteria. With few restaurants in town, many of the older citizens ate there on a regular basis, mostly for the price and the portions. Her mother had volunteered to drive senior citizens there twice a week. She had said it was probably the only nutritious meal most of them ate.

She spotted Jackie's broad smile as she turned the corner, and hurried into her arms.

"I didn't get much of a chance to talk to you at the funeral. I'm so sorry. I loved your mother. I think everyone did." She stood back. "And you look hotter in person than you do in the magazines."

"Thank you. You're looking pretty good yourself. How's that handsome husband of yours and those beautiful girls?" Shannon was godmother to Jackie's oldest daughter.

"They're all well. Driving me crazy. I plan to take that trip you offered and get away from them for a while. I can't wait to see Paris." She gave Shannon a serious nod. "How are you holding up?"

"I never thought anything could hurt so much, Jackie."

"I know. Come on over here. I've got us a table. The food isn't Paris good, but it's okay."

Jackie left her at the table and returned with two plates. "I don't know if you'll like the meal, but I know you'll like dessert. It's Miss Dee Dee's peach cobbler."

"You're kidding! That was the best part of school. Peach cobbler on Tuesdays. Daddy told me Miss Dee

Dee had left the school, but I didn't know she was working here. I assumed she retired."

"She did. She's well past seventy now, but she's here every day. God don't make women with her strength anymore." She placed her hand on Shannon's arm. "I hope you know I'm here for you. I saw your dad at the store yesterday. His brave face didn't fool me. I've never known a man to love a woman more than he loved your mother."

"They were happy together." Shannon gathered her thoughts. "There's something I need to say to you, so let me get it out before I lose the rest of my resolve. You and Carmen were the sisters I never had. I love both of you, and I shouldn't have left you. We made a pact to stick together and I should have kept it. I shouldn't have gone to Paris. I hurt my family, destroyed my marriage, and hurt the two of you. I hope you can forgive me."

Jackie had stopped eating. "Is that it? Girl, I thought you were about to say something awful. Now you listen to what I have to say. I can sing. Carmen can sing. You're the one with real talent, stage presence, and incredible beauty. I heard Thierry tell you he didn't need a group act. He needed a hot, sexy female with a great voice, and that was you. I'm not a crab trying to hold everyone in the barrel because I didn't make it out. I'm proud of you. There's no need to feel guilty, and I'm sick and tired of hearing how you deserted your husband and child. You left Leila with her father and your parents. I told Edison the same thing."

"I appreciate that, but I had responsibilities here that should have come first. By the time Edison filed for divorce, I had made commitments in Paris. Thierry didn't hesitate to remind me about the lawsuits that would follow if I didn't keep them. I told Edison I wouldn't sign any more contracts and would return home as soon as those ended, but he didn't believe me. How could he? I had broken a few promises already. I just wanted you to know that I regret the whole thing, especially hurting the people I love."

"Everything happens for a reason. Don't look back, honey. I admire you so much. Hell, I live my life vicariously through you." She took a sip of tea. "Please don't say any of this to Carmen. That girl is really messed up."

"I already did." She told Jackie about her visit. "She hates me."

"She hates herself. You just gave her a convenient whipping post. I don't know who is worse, her or Bobby Joe. Carmen's sisters don't talk to her anymore. Of course, Jeannie and Bobby Joe have been at odds since their father died. He talks bad about her and she tells people she's sorry they're related. I don't know—"

A woman in scrubs came over to the table. "I hate to interrupt your lunch, but we've got a gunshot wound in the ER. It's Sheriff Page."

Shannon heard but the words did not register until Jackie grabbed her arm.

"Oh, God. Is it serious?" Jackie asked.

Shannon tried to stand, but the only movement was the frantic pounding in her chest. As the woman nodded, darkness closed in around her.

≈

"This is unreal. It can't be happening." Shannon leaned against her father's shoulder, still trying to clear her head. "First Mom and now Edison. I don't know what to do. Should I tell Leila now? And how do I tell her? If Edison—"

"We can't think that way," J.P. said. He held her head to his chest. "Wait until we know more about his condition before telling Leila. Donna said she knows something is going on. You promised to meet us at the store, so she's been asking why you're not there. She's young, but still too bright to be kept in the dark for very long."

"What kind of person would do something like this?" She left her father's arms and started pacing the confines of the room where Jackie had taken them after the waiting room filled with Page family members.

"That part I don't have to wonder about. We've had more crime here in the last five years than I'd seen here my entire life. I don't have any firsthand knowledge of addiction, except maybe to coffee, but from what I hear it takes away the very soul and conscience of a man. They'll do anything to anyone, with about as much forethought or guilt as you would feel for swatting a fly."

John joined them, his face covered in perspiration. "I just went over to the station and talked to Emmett. He's as broken up as I am, and frantic to find out who's behind this."

"Who was the last person to see Edison?" J.P. asked. "Do they have anything to go on?"

"He left to go home, Emmett told me. Seems Edison has been sleeping at the station for the past two nights. Emmett said he was dog-tired. He went to Jeannie's and his parents', but for some reason, he came back. He left in the squad car but it's now parked at the courthouse. His pickup was found at the scene, filled with his clothes." John looked at Shannon.

"Emmett said he had been looking for Bobby Joe. When he left you last night, he was going to the station, but had to come back to deal with his mother. Emmett held Bobby Joe until he got there. He was trying to get information, but Emmett said he didn't seem pumped up about what Billie Joe said. It was something about drug drops being made in Boise Park. Edison was found in that area."

"And what does Bobby Joe have to say?" J.P. asked.

"Nobody can find him. Emmett's been down there questioning the boy who brought Edison in. That Lincoln boy. The crazy one, Bo."

"Did he shoot Edison?" Shannon asked.

"Emmett seems to think so. He roughed the boy up pretty good, but Bo keeps saying he found Edison lying close to his truck and brought him in. Seems unlikely he would have done that if he had shot Edison, but Emmett is still skeptical."

John stepped away to answer his cell.

"I just don't know how I'm going to deal with this," Shannon said to her father. "How am I going to tell Leila?"

"Well, you'd better think of something quick." John shook his head as he rejoined them. "That was Donna. Leila's been asking for you, and she's pretty upset. She thinks you've gone back to Paris."

"I'll drive you over there." J.P. took her arm.

"I can't leave until we hear something. Jackie said she would come for us when the doctor had a clear assessment of Edison's condition. I have to be able to tell Leila how her father is doing. At least prepare her for…"

"I'll stay here and wait for the doctor. You go to Leila, if only to assure her that you didn't leave her." John walked them to the door. "I'll call when there's word. I'm glad Jackie was on duty. She said it might be awhile before they're able to determine the severity of his injury. He was shot twice. One bullet made a clear exit. The other one is still in him."

≈

J.P. drove and Shannon sat next to him, lost in thought. When they reached the store, Donna met them at the door.

"I think she cried herself to sleep. The boys were upset, too. They've never seen Leila this way. I think they all passed out back there." She hugged Shannon and J.P. "John just called. The doctors will have something to tell us pretty soon. I've prayed harder today than I have in my entire life, and I know you have, too. I don't know how you're going to break it to her, but at least she'll know you're here for her."

"Thanks." Shannon gently touched her already sore eyes with the edge of a tissue, took a deep breath and tiptoed through the double door that separated the offices and storage from the shopping area. She stood in the doorway, feeling her heart leap at the sight of her little girl, lying between her cousins on the sofa with Trey's arm wrapped protectively around her waist.

*God please give me strength to handle this.*

She reached down with shaky hands and lifted the sleeping child into her arms.

Rubbing her eyes, Leila clutched her mother's arm with one hand and twisted the other in her hair.

Shannon had noticed her doing it before when she was upset.

"Mommy?"

"Yes, baby. Mommy's here."

She rubbed her eyes. "I thought you'd left again."

"I'll never leave you again, Leila. I promise. I'm not going to leave you."

"Then why are you crying?"

Shannon walked to the office and sat in her father's chair. "Honey, I've been crying because something happened that made me very sad, and now I have to tell you about it. I know you're very bright for your age, but do you fully understand what your father does for a living?"

She nodded. "He catches bad guys so they won't hurt the good people in Shepherd."

"That's right." Hesitating, she kissed Leila and held her close. "Leila, I love you very much. No matter what happens, I'll be here for you. If I have to leave and go to Paris, I'll take you with me. I will always be here for you."

"Is my daddy all right?"

Shannon choked, but managed to get the words out. "Your father was out last night, and one of the bad guys shot him. He's in the hospital. Now I know you've learned to pray. I want you to pray to God that your daddy recovers. I came to tell you that, and to let you know that I'm here for you, and, until God decides otherwise, I always will be."

"Is my daddy going to die?" she asked between sobs.

Swallowing back a flood of tears, Shannon answered slowly. "Honey, we are going to pray very hard that your daddy will be all right. God hears the prayers of sweet little girls like you, so pray as hard as you can."

Silent tears rolled down Leila's face. "I don't understand why people die. Daddy is good, isn't he?"

"Your father is one of the best people I know. He's good and kind and he loves you very much. I can't explain why bad things happen to good people because, quite frankly, I don't understand it myself. But God can help us through this. If it's God's will that your father doesn't make it then we'll have to be strong, you and me. Sometimes God has plans that we can't understand. Your grandmommy used to say that God wants good people, too."

J.P. had come in during her explanation. His eyes filled with tears before he turned quickly and left the room.

Leila stopped crying and struggled from Shannon's arms. "Can I see him?"

"No, honey. None of us can go into the emergency room until the doctors have finished examining him."

"He's dead, isn't he?"

"No." Shannon shook her head. "He's not dead, but he is hurt very badly."

"Then why can't I see him?" Her eyes became hard and cold. "I don't believe you. If he's not dead, I want to see him."

"I wouldn't lie to you, honey. Your father isn't dead. You can see him, just not right now."

A sob broke from her throat. "I want to see my daddy!" She looked into her mother's eyes and said in a tone Shannon found heartbreaking, "Please."

The boys ran to the doorway and looked on in wonder. J.P. and Donna rushed in.

"Granddaddy, is my daddy dead? Is he dead?" She ran to J.P.'s arms.

"No, baby. Your father is not dead. He's wounded. Someone shot him, but he's not dead. He's at the hospital."

"Then why can't I go there and see him? Why can't I see my daddy?"

"You can go to the hospital," Shannon said. "I'm not sure if the doctors will allow us to see him just yet, but I'll take you there."

Without another word, Leila took her mother's hand.

Emmett was standing inside the doors of the emergency wing when they arrived.

She hurried inside while J.P. was getting Leila from the car. "Emmett. What happened? Is he going to be all right?"

"We don't know, Shannon. He's got a bullet lodged near the base of his brain that has to come out. The doctor says it will kill him if it's not removed, but may paralyze him if they take it out. He's lost a lot of blood. No one knows how long he was out there on the side of the road. If that boy hadn't brought him in when he did, he would have bled to death."

"Where were you? Why was he out there alone?" She knew Edison never took unnecessary risks with his life or the lives of his deputies. One of their first rules was to patrol in pairs. She knew Edison sometimes rode alone on routine patrols, but not if foul play was suspected.

"Bobby Joe told him a wild story about a drug drop out there, but Edison said he wasn't going there tonight. He said he was going home. If I had known he was going, I would have either gone with him or followed him there. I know he went to Jeannie's when he left the station. I followed him out of town and saw him turn into her driveway."

"Do you think Bobby Joe set him up?"

Emmett shrugged. "He trusted Bobby Joe. That could have been a mistake."

Shannon scanned the crowd and found Jeannie's plump, dark face immersed in a throng of Page family members. She noted that Jeannie had gained quite a bit of weight, and wondered, as she had initially, why Edison had chosen her. Shepherd was a small town, but there were other women available.

Shannon walked to the center of the crowd and held out her hand. "I'm so very sorry, Jeannie. I don't see how something like this could happen. Did he come home after he left Emmett? Do you know why he was out there alone?"

Jeannie took her hand but quickly pulled away. "He came home, to my house, that is, but he only stayed a few minutes. He didn't say where he was going."

She looked at the floor and Shannon immediately knew there was more to the story.

"Who was the last to see him?" She looked from one to the other and determined by the guilty look on their faces that each of them knew more than she did about Edison's situation. "Someone must know why he was out there."

Miss Etta took Jeannie's hand and pulled her aside. "We were prob'ly the last to see him, but he didn't say where he was goin'. My guess is that he was driving 'round tryin' to calm down from all the ruckus around here."

Ray stepped forward. "Tell the truth, for God's sake. Don't let him die with a lie hanging over his head." He turned to Shannon. "He came by to talk to the folks around nine-thirty. I was there. He said he and

Jeannie broke up, and then he talked to Mama about what happened earlier at your parents' place. Edison was more upset than I've ever seen him."

"Ain't no need to tell his business!" Miss Etta yelled. "Ain't nobody here got no business knowin' about it."

"The hell they don't," Ray replied. "He was mad when he got to the house and even madder when he left. Jeannie told him she didn't want Leila living with them, and Mama said things that made it worse. He left the house about ten. That Lincoln boy didn't find him until this morning. He's very lucky to be alive."

She turned to Emmett. "Do you have any idea who could have done this? Did you question Bo Lincoln?"

"He's half crazy, Shannon," Emmett answered. "Just poor white trash. That whole family is crazy, and they're all racists. He's still down at the jail, but we'll have to let him go. There's no proof he's ever owned a handgun."

"Why do you say he's a racist? Why would he bring Edison to the hospital if he was the one who shot him?"

"I can't swear that he did. I was just surprised when he brought Edison in. Back in school that boy used to say that just because his name was Lincoln he sure didn't free no slaves, and if he had his way they never would have been freed. The boy ain't got much education and even less sense. They come from way up in the woods outside of Shepherd. There's a whole bunch of them, and they're all worthless."

The crowd stared, open-mouthed, when J.P. walked in with Leila.

"What's this child doing here?" Miss Etta asked, looking at Shannon rather than J.P.

Before she could answer, Jackie came out with the doctor in tow.

"Everyone, this is Doctor Welch." She made the introductions. "This is Shannon Travers, Edison's ex-wife and…" She looked at Leila.

"I should explain," Shannon said. "Normally, I would not have brought my daughter here, but my mother's death has left her quite shaken. Seeing her father was the only way to confirm he was alive. Doctor?" She sought affirmation.

"Under the circumstances, it's probably not a bad idea to have her here. I'll explain that later, but let me start with the sheriff's condition. I've conferred with Emmett, and as near as we can pinpoint, Edison lay out there in the woods for hours before Bo Lincoln found him. A bullet pierced his left shoulder, well above his heart. Flesh only, no bone damage. The danger is the piece of lead close to his brain. There's a lot of swelling. The lead is sort of floating around in the fluid and tissue. I feel, and Emmett, who knows weapons better than anyone, concurs, that it was a ricochet. Even a small caliber bullet would have done more damage if it were a direct hit. This was a high-powered weapon. His condition is grave. The bullet needs to be removed."

Shannon lifted Leila into her arms.

"Nothing can be done until the swelling goes down, but once that happens we'll have to move quickly. Now, all of you know this is a small hospital with minimal services. We have a great staff of physicians, but we don't have surgeons who can perform this operation. I've called hospitals all over the area, asking for a neurosurgeon with the kind of expertise to remove that bullet without damaging the brain. We've located several surgeons noted for performing delicate operations such as this. I'm waiting for word on their availability."

Shannon looked at her father and nodded to Leila.

"Come on, honey." J.P. took Leila from Shannon's arms. "Walk with Granddaddy to the water fountain."

Shannon waited until they had crossed the corridor before turning to Doctor Welch. "I appreciate everything you're doing and I know there are no guarantees, but what are his chances for survival? What is the likelihood of a successful surgery with a noted neurosurgeon?"

"That's hard to say. A lot depends on the location of the bullet once the swelling subsides. With any luck, it will drain downward. An experienced surgeon would have a pretty good chance of removing it, but it's still a risky procedure. The other side of the coin is that without the surgery, that bullet will penetrate vital areas of the brain."

"How long can he…make it without the surgery?" Ray asked.

"Every minute is crucial. We have to monitor the swelling closely and take our cues from that. He's lost a lot of blood and needs to stabilize before we attempt to remove the slug. The surgery is lengthy."

Doctor Welch looked from one to the other. "His strength, both emotional and physical, will play a key role on his recovery, especially before the surgery. No upsets, no irritations. Does everyone understand this?"

J.P. returned with Leila, who quickly observed the look on everyone's face and asked, "Is my daddy going to die?"

"We'll do everything we can to see that he doesn't, and for that, we're going to need a lot of help from everyone. I want you to pay attention to this part, Leila. Your Aunt Jackie says you're very intelligent, but you're hearing a lot of information right now, and you're understandably upset. I want you to ask questions if you don't understand what I'm about to tell you. Okay?"

"But you didn't answer my other question. Is my daddy going to die and go to Heaven like Grandmommy?"

Shannon choked back sobs.

"Your daddy has a good chance of living through this, Leila. I wish I could give you a yes or no answer, but I can't. Doctors are trained to make people well. Sometimes we can't. In your daddy's case, we're going to try extra hard, and you can help. We're going to tell you how."

He turned to Jackie. "I think you'd better explain this part."

Jackie looked at Shannon first, and then Edison's parents. "One of the reasons it's taken the doctor so long to give you an update is that we were trying to get a full understanding of Edison's state of mind. He opened his eyes about an hour ago. He seems to be totally aware of what happened and where he is. He knows he's been shot. He didn't see who did it." She looked from Jeannie to Shannon. "When he first opened his eyes, he asked for his wife. Since Doctor Welch knows he's divorced, he asked me to find out why he said what he did. I asked him a lot of questions and he immediately knew the answers."

She frowned and held out her hands. "There is only one area that's unclear. He doesn't know that he and Shannon are divorced."

"What?" Miss Etta asked. "How'd he know everythin' else and not know that?"

"That's a good question, Mrs. Page," Doctor Welch answered. "Memory lapses are very common with trauma patients, but Edison seems current on all but one thing."

"Since Edison keeps up with everyone from high school, I asked a lot of questions that I already knew the answers to, and he didn't miss a beat," Jackie continued. "He remembers Leila's age, her birth date, and that Miss Doris just died. He also knows that Shannon was given a chance to record in Paris, but in his mind, she still hasn't gone."

"Are you sure, Jackie?" Shannon asked.

She nodded. "He asked me to make sure you don't leave."

"He's just afraid I'll return to Paris. He must remember…" She stopped as Jackie shook her head vigorously.

"No. That's what I thought at first, but he's still back in the past, honey. He said he knows how badly you want a career and he knows you have talent, but he doesn't want you to leave him and Leila, especially since your mother is gone."

"I might as well go home." Jeannie stood with her hands on her hips. "She's the wife and I'm nobody."

"Listen to me, all of you." Doctor Welch's authoritative voice hushed the murmurs. "After what he's been through, I'm thankful he can open his eyes. It's not uncommon for a patient who has undergone this kind of trauma to wake up in an altered state."

"How long this here state 'sposed to last?" Miss Etta asked.

"That's not something I can predict. It's seldom permanent, but I must advise you that a shock to his system could send him to a much more painful place in his head."

"I don't understand," Leila said.

"Honey, Doctor Welch and Aunt Jackie are saying your father is having trouble remembering certain things. He thinks he and I are still married and that we still live in the house down the road from Granddaddy. He'll remember everything when his head gets better, but for now, we have to make believe so we don't upset him."

"Is it like that game you bought me where I pretend I'm a singer like you? We have to pretend you and Daddy are still married together?"

"That's exactly what you have to do," Doctor Welch said. "Your Aunt Jackie was right. You really are an intelligent little girl. Of course, your grandmother was the best teacher I've ever seen." He looked at Shannon. "Do you think you can do it?"

"I can do it. Thank you, Doctor. Please keep us updated."

"Absolutely. We'll do everything we can to get the sheriff back into that uniform. You can go in when you're ready."

"Is it okay for Leila to see him? I promise it will be brief."

"Jackie can escort both of you in for a brief visit, and then bring Leila back to her grandfather. The rest of the family can take turns." He started to leave, but turned with a final warning. "Under no circumstances should you tell him he's divorced, or anything else that would upset him. That's crucial."

"Don't you worry none, Jeannie. Edison will come to his senses." Miss Etta rolled her eyes in Shannon's direction.

"We're not having any of that, Mama," Ray said.

"He's right," Nancy agreed. "Would you rather have him married to Shannon or dead?"

Shannon walked away with Jackie, still holding Leila.

Miss Etta retreated, but continued muttering. "I just knowed somethin' bad would hap'en. My son ain't in his right mind. We can't say nothin', but we can pray for him to see the light."

John had been standing next to the wall, listening silently. Large in stature, he was quiet and seldom volunteered an opinion.

"Tell me something, Miss Etta. How many of your children have to die before you learn to stay out of their business?"

Everyone gasped.

J.P. touched his son's shoulder. "Calm down."

"Not this time, Dad. This is something I've wanted to say. I didn't think it would take the possibility of losing somebody I love like a brother to bring out the words, but since it did, I might as well say them now. I loved Carol. Did you know that, Miss Etta? I loved your daughter. All the things you said, that I was just trying to use her, that it was all about sex, you were so wrong. You were the one who never saw your daughter's true worth. Carol was beautiful and bright. She could be funny and carefree, but your nagging usually took care of that."

Everyone gathered closer.

"I would have married her, Miss Etta, loved her, and tried my best to make her happy, but you drove her from my life and into the arms of the man who killed her. Now you're treating Edison the same way."

J.P.'s jaw dropped.

"My sister went to Paris to do what most of us never have the talent, opportunity, or the nerve to do. She's good at it. Whether she should or shouldn't have gone was between her and Edison. Now it's between her, her conscience, and God."

He looked back at Emmett. "Keep those handcuffs handy, because the next person who uses the word 'abandoned' in connection with my sister is going to find my foot up his or her ass."

"You ought to be 'shamed to talk that way to your elders. God will—"

"Save it for church, Miss Etta. You came into my father's home two days after he buried my mother and stirred up a pile of crap. That's why Edison is lying in there with his life in the balance. He left work to go home. He was tired, not just from working, but from sleeping on that little cot at the jail. He did go home. I guess he found more stress than he could handle and went out in those woods alone. We all know Edison doesn't usually take chances."

No one stepped forward to defend Miss Etta, not even her husband. J.P. finally moved next to John and tugged at his sleeve.

"Everything you say is right, John, but let's not stoop to that. We should all be in prayer for Edison's life right now. He's a good man." He looked into Miss Etta's face. "When Leila heard you talking about taking her with you, that child raised a cry that was heartbreaking. I can't help but wonder why. There's more at stake here than what we think of one another."

Ray and Nancy stood together, holding onto each other.

"He's right," Ray muttered. "Nothing we say can change what happened. Let's just pray for Edison." He reached for J.P.'s hand.

The mayor walked in and joined them, as did Emmett. Heads bowed. A communal 'amen' followed J.P.'s passionate prayer.

# Chapter 8

Jackie took Leila from Shannon's arms. "A lot is riding on your ability to calm him down. I know you can do it."

Shannon stared at the bandaged body. She loved him more than she could say.

"Come on, honey," Jackie whispered. "He needs you. Edison has lost a lot of blood, which makes having surgery more dangerous. You go over there and reassure him. Tell him whatever you have to so he'll relax and get stronger."

Shannon moved to Edison's side and touched the fingers of his right hand. She felt encouraged by the warmth of his skin and leaned forward, placing her mouth close to his ear.

"Hi, honey."

His eyes opened slightly.

Jackie nudged her closer. "Hold your face over his so he doesn't have to struggle to see you."

Shannon bent down and gripped the sheets to hide her trembling. "Don't try to move. I'm right here."

"I want …I want you to promise me something." His voice was weak and raspy.

"You're going to make it. We need you. We love you. Please don't lose sight of that, but I'll promise anything."

"Don't leave…Leila. Don't go to Paris. If I…don't make it, she'll need you more…"

She touched his lips with her fingertips. "I'm not going to Paris, or anywhere else. I'm going to be right here for Leila and for you. I'll be by your side forever, just like we promised when we married." She kissed his damp forehead. "Now I need you to make me a promise. You have a bullet in the back of her head. The doctors can't remove it until you're stronger. You have to promise that you'll lie very still and get as much rest as possible, okay?"

He lowered his eyelids and nodded slightly. She kissed him again.

Jackie went to the other side of the bed and bent over with Leila in her arms. "Hey, dude. This beautiful young lady wants to give you a kiss before I take her out for some fresh air."

Leila stared, unsmiling, and reached out and touched his cheek. "I love you, Daddy."

"Leila." Tears crept into his voice. "I…I love…you m…more than anything."

"We have to go now, so tell your daddy he'd better stay calm and get better."

"I prayed for you, Daddy. Just like Mommy told me to do."

Shannon's knees buckled.

"Then…I'll get better. Bye. Bye, baby. Love…you."

Shannon saw tears in Jackie's eyes as she left the room. Determined to face Edison calmly, she took a deep breath and placed her face close to his. "I love you with all my heart. I'm not going anywhere."

He tried to smile. "Don't forget…" His voice faded. "…how much you mean to me."

"I won't forget, but I want you to tell me every day, so you've got to get better." For a moment, she felt they were in the same place. He was her husband, and she wanted him back in her life.

He closed his eyes, and Doctor Welch, who had entered the room in the middle of Leila's goodbye, took Shannon's arm and guided her to the hallway.

"That was wonderful, Mrs. Page. Perfect. Now we just have to wait, hopefully no more than twenty-four hours, and pray that he's strong enough to stand the surgery. We're transfusing him, but he's very weak."

"From your experience, what are the best- and worst-case scenarios once the bullet is removed? Is there any possibility that he will fully recover?"

He slowly shook his head. "I wish I could be more positive. I'm shocked that he's speaking so clearly, which just goes to show how little we know about these things. All I can promise is that his chance of survival is about seventy percent with the surgery and zero without it. We'll just have to take it one step at a time."

Leaning against the wall she let the tears wash over her burning face.

Jackie hugged her shoulders. "Your baby just pushed Miss Etta's hand away when she tried to take her. John is driving her back to the store. I don't know what was said out there, but according to Emmett, John just told Miss Etta she was responsible for Carol's death and Edison's condition. I'm glad he told her. She's dabbing at her eyes now, trying to act pitiful. Jeannie left when Emmett started asking about Bobby Joe."

"Oh, God."

"Doctor Welch called all the way to Johns Hopkins and to Walter Reed, searching for a good surgeon. Two doctors have responded and he's waiting to hear back from the others. I know he'll do his best to help Edison. We all will."

"I know. Thank you for being here for me, Jackie, and for Edison and Leila. When I arrived here after Mom's death, I didn't think I could feel worse."

They hugged and Shannon walked down the hall and into her father's outstretched arms. "Oh, Daddy, I'm so scared."

"It's going to be all right, honey. We have to believe that."

"He's asleep now," she said, looking at Ray and Nancy. "He's lost a lot of blood. His voice is weak, but the doctor said just the fact that he is so alert is a positive sign."

～

Shannon and J.P. drank coffee and talked about many things. Tito, Ray, and Nancy visited back and forth. Shannon stretched and started toward the water fountain, but stopped when she saw a face peeping around the wall at the end of the corridor. He quickly moved into the shadows, but not before she had seen his eyes. She had noticed him there for the last hour, darting behind the wall that led to the entryway. The same inquisitive blue eyes.

She walked back to her father and Tito. "A man down that hallway keeps looking over here and then hiding every time I turn around. Don't look now, but turn quickly after I walk away."

J.P. moved to the side of the room and came back. "If I'm not mistaken, that's Bo Lincoln." He walked down to the drinking fountain and back. "That's him, all right. I guess they had to let him go. I'll find out what he wants."

"Let me." Shannon walked slowly down the hallway and past the water fountain until she was face to face with the man behind the wall. His eyes were half hidden by a hank of scraggly hair. The shoulders of his plaid shirt drooped down his arms.

"Mr. Lincoln? My name is Shannon Travers." She held out her hand.

He looked at her quickly before dropping his head. "I know about you. You're famous."

"Thank you for remembering me, Mr. Lincoln, and thank you for what you did for Edison. You saved his life."

"So he's gonna be all right?"

"We don't know yet, but whatever chance he has, we owe to you. Thank you. Thank you very much." Undaunted by his glazed stare and the crude tattoo on the side of his face, she leaned forward and hugged him.

"Mr. Lincoln, did you see anything out there when you found him?" she asked. "Anything that might help them figure out who could have done this?"

"Oh, I know who done it," he said in a matter-of-fact tone.

"You know who shot Edison?" Shannon moved so close that he had to face her. "Did you tell the deputies? Did you tell Emmett Paul?"

He shrugged his shoulders. "They won't believe me. They think I'm stupid."

J.P. joined her, and so did Ray and Tito.

"Where's Emmett?" Shannon asked. "He needs to hear this. Mr. Lincoln says he knows who shot Edison."

"Emmett just left," Ray answered. "I'll call the station and have them send him back." Ray took out his cell phone and Shannon got a cup of coffee for herself and one for Bo. There was nothing offensive about the man whom everyone seemed to dislike and distrust. He did appear very ill at ease, so she kept talking, hoping to win his confidence.

"I don't want to go back to that police station. They don't like me down there. I don't mind telling what I know, but I don't want to go down there. They just let me go 'cause I was over to The Junction when the sheriff was shot. I fell asleep in my car waiting for my brother and then went back to the house. I was out looking for my dog when I found the sheriff. I just come here to see if he was okay. They wouldn't tell nothing down at the courthouse."

"Do you know Emmett? He's very anxious to get whatever information he can on this crime, Mr. Lincoln. I'm sure he can take your statement here. Right here."

"You promise to stay here when I talk to him? I don't like them lawmen."

"I'll sit right here with you. I can't tell you how grateful I am that you came along when you did."

She continued expressing her gratitude until Emmett rushed through the door.

"What's going on, Shannon? I was just outside in the patrol car. Foley said you have some information." He turned toward Bo Lincoln. "His alibi checked out. We had to let him go."

"He didn't shoot Edison, but he knows who did. He doesn't want to go to the station. I promised you would question him right here."

"You know who shot Edison? Why didn't you say so?"

Bo turned away.

"He's not comfortable talking to you," Shannon whispered. "He saw enough to help you. Just listen to him." She smiled. "Go ahead, Mr. Lincoln."

"I didn't see it happen but I saw a big oil spot over there where I found the sheriff. Oil had been leaking something fierce. That was Junior Vinning's truck. You know Junior?"

"Yes, I know Junior, but how can you say he shot Edison just based on an oil spot? I'm sure there are dozens of cars around here that leak oil. Is this all you have to tell us?"

He looked at Shannon. "See? I told you they wouldn't believe me. That's why I didn't say nothing before. They all think I'm simple, that I don't know nothing. I know a lot of things, and I know Junior shot Sheriff Page. He also robbed a gas station over in Moss Point."

"You're not simple, Mr. Lincoln, and you're a very nice man. Thank you for helping the deputies catch the person responsible for this."

"You're welcome." He grinned. "I like you."

"I like you, too. Just tell me everything you know about this man, Junior Vinning."

"He's all right, I guess. He likes my little sister, but they ain't married or nothing. Every time he comes over that old truck of his leaks oil all over the ground. He asked me to fix it for him—I'm a good mechanic—but he didn't have no money to buy the parts yesterday. He woke me up at daylight. He had money this morning, and I know he was over in Moss Point yesterday. He did some other things, but I don't have tell you 'bout that, 'cause it ain't revel...rev...shucks, I don't know the word."

"Relevant." Emmett was now paying attention. "Tell us what you saw when you found the sheriff."

"Like I said, I saw a lot o' oil. Oh yeah, I saw bullet holes in Junior's truck this morning."

"Had Edison's gun been fired?" Ray asked.

"Yeah. Looks like he got two rounds off before he went down. I just don't know why Junior would shoot him. Bo, was Junior involved in drugs?"

"Junior likes whiskey." Bo giggled. "Me, too."

"Why do you think he shot Edison?" Emmett asked.

Bo shrugged. "I don't know that."

"Do you know Bobby Joe Stanberry?" Shannon asked.

"I know who he is, that's all."

"Is he involved with Junior?" Emmett asked.

Bo shook his head. "Shoot no. Ain't no coloreds come over to The Junction where Junior hangs out."

Emmett shook his head and Bo looked at Shannon. "I don't mean no harm by that."

"No harm taken, Mr. Lincoln. Did you know the sheriff before this happened?"

"I knowed him some. He saved my sister."

Emmett nodded and Shannon looked to him for clarification.

"I had almost forgotten about that. Bo's sister went into labor one night and their daddy's car broke down on the way to the hospital. Edison was out patrolling and saw them. They didn't have a cell phone or nothing so he called it in. The baby started coming and she was having problems."

"My daddy didn't want the sheriff to help, him bein' colored and all, but my mama said Jean Mae was dying. The sheriff took my shirt. That's what he put the baby in."

Shannon smiled as Emmett finished the story.

"Edison helped the baby through the birth canal. He's real attentive to stuff like that during our training sessions. The girl had lost a lot of blood. The medic said she probably wouldn't have made it if Edison hadn't happened by."

"That's why I wanted to help him, just like he helped Jean Mae. I know y'all think I'm just poor white trash, but I'm honest. My daddy told me to always be honest, and I am. I drink whiskey and I swear sometimes, but I ain't no heathen."

"If we thought that about you then we were wrong." Emmett reached out for a handshake. "I apologize to you, Bo."

"She called me Mr. Lincoln." He looked at Shannon.

"Mr. Lincoln it is." Emmett smiled. "Thank you, Mr. Lincoln, for bringing the sheriff to the hospital, and thank you for giving us this information. If anybody calls you names again you tell them Deputy Emmett will kick their butts." Emmett patted Bo on the back, winked at Shannon, and told her he would let her know how things turned out.

Most of the family had left the waiting room when they returned. Ray told his parents what had transpired. Jackie sat next to Shannon in the gray chairs against the back wall.

"I can't tell you how proud I am of you. Those people are just jealous, especially that thing Edison is talking about marrying. She knows he still cares for you and that's eating her heart out. I'm surprised he would even consider marrying her."

"He was hurt," Shannon said. "I understand."

"We talked a few months ago—back when your parents went to visit you. I told him you and I still talked all the time, and he asked if you and Thierry were getting married. You should have seen his face when I told him you weren't even interested in Thierry when you first went to Paris, and that nothing happened between the two of you until much later."

"Edison was suspicious of Thierry from the beginning. You know he kept saying Thierry was a con artist, that he had no plans to record my music, just get me in bed. I wasn't surprised that he didn't trust Thierry, but I was both surprised and hurt that he didn't trust me. Maybe Thierry did engineer keeping me beyond the date he knew I had planned to leave, but it wasn't because we were sleeping together at that time."

"How are things with the two of you now?"

"Nothing like Edison or Daddy suspects. We've never discussed marriage. He was married before— three times, actually—and I don't think he wants to do it again. He probably thinks I don't, either. He's very set in his ways now, which is mainly answering to no one."

"You never told me about him. You know I'm dying to hear." Jackie looked around. "Hopefully Edison will sleep for awhile. Let's go over there in the nurses' lounge and talk." She led the way to a door at the end of the hallway. "I'll get us some coffee from the nurse's station. It's damn near lethal, but if it doesn't kill you, it'll put hair on your chest, so to speak."

They sat in the orange and gray chairs holding Styrofoam cups and talked the way they had talked in high school. Shannon shared her disappointments and the fears of leaving home.

"Thierry was there for me all the way."

"Tell me the story. You know how boring my life has been here in Shepherd. Every time I heard or read something about your career, I tried to imagine what it must be like. So come on." She rubbed her thumb and forefinger together. "Give."

"I don't know that it's all that exciting. Being a second-generation nightclub owner, Thierry had connections. By the time he became a producer, he already had a stable of talent lined up. He wasn't looking when he heard us, but he thought I was sultry. I guess that would be the right term. He never developed a love for hip-hop."

"So when did the two of you go past your business relationship?"

She told Jackie about her episode of claustrophobia. "I was shaking like a loose hubcap that day. Thierry almost had to carry me inside to see the stage layout. When we got back to the hotel, he plied me with champagne and kept telling me how much everyone loved me. Said he thought I was the most desirable woman ever."

"Edison said you were living with Thierry."

"I stayed in a hotel at first, but Thierry insisted I stay in his guest quarters, simply for practically. He managed my career the same way he managed all of his businesses. To him, paying rent in a luxury hotel was stupid, and I wasn't about to live in a fleabag. I was frightened enough as it was."

"So you started living with him then?"

"I lived in his house, in the west wing. It's a large house in the city with servants and everything. He also has a chateau outside of Paris with gardens to die for. Thierry had a parade of women coming and going in both houses. Honestly, I never dreamed he and I would be together at all. Looking past the cultural and racial difference, and the fact that he's almost fifteen years older, I was still very much in love with Edison." She stopped and rolled her head back to relieve the tension. "Thierry also had a masseuse. I sure could use Ian right now."

"See, that's what I'm talking about. How many of us will ever visit a masseuse, let alone have one at our disposal? I'm glad you lived out your dreams. Damn glad."

"It really was a dream come true. We traveled so much. Thierry had other acts, and when I started accompanying him, we were seldom home. I had just finished a tour of Brussels, England, and Spain when Daddy called. Thierry and I had been home two days. Just being in Paris was living a dream. Jackie, strolling in the gardens on Sunday evenings, where even the homeless people wear furs, was heaven."

"Tell me about Thierry. He's cute in that French sort of way. I never thought the two of you were having a thing. I know the kind of men you like, and they all resemble the one lying in that bed down the hall."

"Thierry is handsome and worldly, but he's also sweet and very passionate. He started taking care of me from the moment I arrived in Paris, but in a detached sort of way. Everything was more businesslike. At least, that's the ways I saw it. Things changed after I had that claustrophobia attack."

She thought for a second before continuing. "I was upset and ashamed. I guess he knew it. He was always tender and nurturing, but the way he comforted me was so touching, I started looking at him differently. As a man. I started missing him when he was away, and looking forward to his calls. After one of his weeklong trips to England, he called and said he was coming back early because he missed me. I went shopping for the perfect peignoir set. It was pale peach, silk, very clingy. I guess I could have worn an old nightshirt, but Thierry is older, refined, sophisticated. I wanted to look special."

A woman from an adjourning table recognized her and came over to ask if she was performing in town. After exchanging pleasantries and signing three autographs, she continued her story.

"Usually he would come in from a trip, toss his bags down for the maid to unpack, and fix himself a drink. I didn't give him a chance to get comfortable. I pushed my chest out, and waited for his response. It had been so long."

"I'm sure you didn't have to try too hard. I won't even tell you the things men would say about you when we were performing, even my cousin Evan. Edison would have punched his lights out if he had heard."

"I don't know how Thierry viewed me that night, but he put his coat over the chair, took a box from the pocket, and told me to close my eyes. I felt his hands on my shoulders and something cold on my neck. He guided me to the corner mirror to see the diamond necklace I had admired in a showcase when we were together one day. I was shocked. That necklace cost over three hundred thousand dollars."

Jackie shook her head. "He must have really wanted to make a point."

"Well, he certainly did. I had admired it while trying to calculate the exchange rate. When I realized how much it cost I walked away."

"Do you still have it?"

"Oh, yes. It's in a safety deposit box back in Paris."

"Don't stop now," Jackie clamored. "Tell me what happened next."

"He kissed my neck and told me how much he had missed me and we fell into each other's arms," she concluded. "It was a wonderful night."

"Oh, no, honey, you don't get off that easy. I want details. I keep hearing about how romantic the French are, but not whether they're good lovers. I want a first-hand narrative. Give it up."

Shannon looked embarrassed. "Jackie."

"Don't *Jackie* me. I've been stuck here with one-position Fred for all these years. Give me something to swoon over, and you know I won't tell anybody. Did he do anything outrageous, like cover your body with whipped cream?"

They laughed together.

"Thierry is awed by the female physique. He likes to make love to the entire body, not just the breasts and usual places."

"So he spends a lot of time in foreplay? I wish I could make Fred do that."

"Most of our lovemaking was foreplay." She looked at the table as Jackie let out a yell.

"Girl-l-l no! You mean he . . .oh-h-h!"

Shannon struggled for words. "Okay, think about this. Big brass bed, silk sheets, me in that slinky nightie, Thierry naked. He starts kissing my face, my eyelids, my ears, my neck. His hands are everywhere, and just when I'm flaming hot, he quits."

"What? Quits and does what?"

"He just lies next to me and tells me how desirable I am. He kisses me, soft kisses that become intense. Then he starts all over again. When Thierry said make love all night, he wasn't exaggerating."

Jackie moved closer. "Did he suck your toes? I hear that turns them on."

"Toes and everything."

"Is he well-endowed?"

"Very much so." She looked around. "I can't believe I'm telling you this. I feel like we're back in high school. I told you the first time Edison kissed me—I should say I kissed him. Remember?"

" 'Course I remember. That's what best friends are for. Thierry sounds yummy."

Shannon looked forlorn. "None of those things made up for losing Edison. Thierry knew it. He never asked for my love."

"Honey, if Edison was better than that, I don't know how you stood it. Hell, I'd give anything to find a romantic like Thierry. All I get is 'You got something for me, baby?' followed by 'That was great' and a good night kiss."

"I was deeply in love with Edison. There was no need for special effects. Thierry is a wonderful man, probably not a faithful one, but wonderful just the same. He's kind and loving, attentive to a fault, all of those things. I love him, but I'm not in love. There was nothing missing with Edison. I would rather be in his arms than anywhere else in the world."

"You will be. He's going to make it and the two of you—the three of you, and maybe a few more will be together."

Shannon squeezed her eyes shut. "Let's pray on that."

⮞

Jackie left Shannon alone with her thoughts, which were mostly about Edison. Things were all wrong. She closed her eyes and spoke with her heart.

*Edison shouldn't be lying in that bed fighting for his life. He shouldn't be planning to marry a woman who doesn't like his child. Oh, God, please let him live.*

She left the hospital only long enough to take a change of clothes to John and Donna's for Leila the next morning. Edison was awake when she returned. Rushing to his side, she hesitated before speaking, not certain of how focused he was.

"Have you been here all night? You look tired, baby." His words were barely audible.

She nodded. "I left for a while, but I'm back now." Relieved, she brushed her lips over his.

"I can't feel my feet. Did the doctor say I was paralyzed? I know he was here earlier, but I was too drowsy to remember anything."

"The doctor didn't say you're paralyzed. Once you're stronger and the swelling in your head subsides, they'll remove the bullet. You have to rest and stay calm. I'm staying close by to make sure you do." She tried to smile but couldn't hold back the tears.

"Don't cry. I'm tough." His words slurred more than before.

"These are happy tears. I'm glad I still have you to love."

She stayed by his side all night. The doctors came by several times and said his breathing was better and his vital signs were closer to normal.

"He's a very strong man," Doctor Welch said the following morning after they had taken Edison for more tests. "The swelling is beginning to recede and the bullet is moving in a good direction. It's not lodged in the brain, and that's wonderful news. Keep talking to him. It seems that you're able to calm him better than the medication."

"Has one of the neurosurgeons you contacted agreed to do the operation?"

"Two of them have agreed, but we're having scheduling conflicts. A neurosurgeon in Houston is exceptionally skilled in this type of procedure and is anxious to help, but he's also quite busy. Now that Edison's condition is more stable, I'm hoping we'll be able to move him to Houston. We'll know more in a day or two."

Shannon left, but instead of going to her parents' house she went to the house she had shared with Edison. She had planned to put her things in storage after Edison left, but changed her mind. Instead, she'd sent rent to her parents, who insisted on depositing the money in Leila's savings account.

She sat on the edge of the bed, surrounded by joyous memories. The beginning of their marriage. The promises they had made to each other.

"And I broke the most important one."

Leila's baby things were there as well. The stuffed lamb wind-up toy that she had slept with, the bassinet Edison had loved, and her mother's pillow made from rhyme-time print. She held the ruffled edges to her face. The baby smell was still present. Leila's favorite rattle was next to the tiny satin-covered Bible that John and Donna had given Leila when she was christened.

Overcome with pain, she ran from the house, locked the door, and drove to John and Donna's. Rushing inside, she held Leila as close as she could. Leila misread the outpouring of affection.

"Did my daddy die?" she wailed.

"No, sweetheart. I'm sorry I frightened you." She hugged her close. "Your daddy was asleep when I left. He's getting stronger every second. I just needed to hold my little girl. To feel you in my arms."

"I love you, Mommy."

Not wanting Leila to see her desperation, Shannon placed her back in the midst of her cousins and prepared to leave. Donna walked her to the car.

"I know something happened. Is Edison okay?"

"As far as we know." Tears ran down her face. "Oh, Donna, I'm so torn. Being with him this way is like we never parted. I went over to our house. We were a family there. The memories were just too much. I should have stayed there with Edison and Leila. I would have missed out on the thrills, but I would have my family. Leila would be sure of her position in my life, and Edison wouldn't be near death."

Donna put out her hand in a halt position. "You were both young, and let's face it; you're a beautiful, talented woman. Things could have gone differently if you had stayed—positive or negative. You're certainly not to blame for Edison's condition. Other than hearing sour remarks from Etta, your baby has been loved. No one could be more of a mother than the one you had. Until God called her home, she was the same with Leila."

"You're right. I just walked around in that house and remembered. The birthdays, the day we brought Leila home from the hospital. The first time we made love in our home, our new bed. Donna, I have missed all of that more than I can say."

"You're still connected to that life. We all have to live with the decisions we've made, both the good and the bad ones, and most of us have made our share of bad ones."

"When I walked out on that stage and heard the applause, when I walked down the street and people stopped and ran after me, I felt so good. Fame was exhilarating, but it didn't take the place of the people I love."

"Leila is getting closer to you every day. Things will work out."

"I just hope Edison makes it, Donna, even if he goes back to Jeannie and forgets what we're doing now. I just want him to get well."

"That's the prayer we all have. I'm no expert, but I've heard that in times of unbearable stress the mind goes back to the last time there was true happiness. Edison is acting out the past because it was where he felt most comfortable, just like the memories you bumped into in the home you shared. Don't forget, Edison drives by that house every day. You got a reprieve, but he's been right here with those memories."

❧

"He's doing well," Jackie informed her later that afternoon. "Doctor Welch is excited about this neurosurgeon in Houston, but apparently he's having trouble scheduling time away from the hospital. Right now, they're afraid to move him. Since he is stable, it gives him a chance to get stronger. That's very important for his survival during that long procedure."

Shannon arranged the many vases of blooms and assorted potted plants that were already piling up. She wanted to wait outside with the rest of the family, but settled for a hug from Ray and Nancy while avoiding Miss Etta's scowls. She was drained, but too concerned to rest.

"Now you look like my little homemaker." Edison spoke very clearly.

Knowing she had to face him and lie was heartbreaking. But was it really a lie? She hurried to the bed. "How do you feel, sleepyhead?"

"Like I did on the football field when three big linemen hit me from different directions. I must look awful, too."

"Oh, we can fix that. Be right back." She said a prayer while wiping his face, but moved away when she saw that his eyes were resting on the open folds of her blouse.

"The doctors have located a surgeon to get that bullet out. You have to cooperate by getting stronger. Jackie said Mr. Snow has found one of those medical transport planes to take you to Houston if Doctor Welch feels you're strong enough to make the trip."

"I know where I'd like to be right now." His eyes glazed with lust. "Lying somewhere with you next to me."

"Give me a second and I'll try and lie down next to you."

"Don't play coy with me. You know what I mean. I remember those little messages you used to put in my lunch bags telling me what to expect when I got home. I still keep them in my wallet."

"Listen to you. Doctor Welch wants you to relax, not get excited."

"If Doctor Welch was looking at a wife as luscious as mine, he'd be salivating, too. Talk about pain. This one is as bad as the one in my head and shoulder. At least we know something still works."

He reached out and she nuzzled his chest.

"It feels like years since we made love. If that's part of my injury, tell Doctor Welch I want to hold onto to it. If you think I'm kidding, put your hand under this blanket."

She felt blood rush through her body. "I don't have to put my hand under the blanket. Anyone who walks in here can see your problem."

"Ah, come on. Don't you feel a little of what I'm feeling?"

She stroked his chest and looked deep into his eyes. "I feel a lot of what you're feeling. So much so that I'm tempted to crawl on top of you. That's why I don't want to talk about it."

It was not hard for her to say because every word was true. She wanted to be a wife in every way. "We'll make up for this lost time. We'll make up for everything. I promise, baby." She kissed his arm.

"Hi, Mama. I didn't hear you come in."

Shannon kept her face buried in the crook of his arm and prayed his mother had not heard the conversation. "I think I'll walk down to the cafeteria and let your mother spend a little time with you. Can I bring you anything back?"

He gave her a wicked smile. "Something cold would be nice."

Shannon hurried past Miss Etta without looking up. She wished Jackie was still on duty, but found an obliging cafeteria worker who duplicated the snow cones that Edison loved by filling a cup with crushed ice and pouring cherry juice on top. Holding the cup in one hand and an iced tea in the other, she rounded the corner and literally bumped into Miss Etta.

"I'm so sorry, Miss Etta. I was taking Edison—"

"I know what you was doin' in there. You oughta to be 'shamed of yourself."

Feeling her face blanch, first from embarrassment and then from anger, she managed to keep her voice at an even pitch. "Miss Etta, every word I've said to Edison about my feelings for him are true. I'm not enjoying lying to him about the two us still being married. I'm simply trying to help. When I came in, Jackie said he'd been asking for me. His blood pressure was elevated and they had to give him medication. Why can't you just accept all of this as part of Edison's recovery? When he walks out of here, you can go right back to hating me."

"Mama?" Nancy took hold of her mother's arm. "I know you've not giving Shannon a hard time for doing what the doctor asked her to do."

Miss Etta left in a huff.

"Are you okay?" Nancy asked. "Don't let Mama get to you. Like Daddy always says, she's miserable unless she has someone to put down. I'm sorry it's you, especially now. Edison needs you."

"I won't leave him. This is getting harder, even without your mother's nagging. I'm just trying not to fall apart."

"I know it's difficult. You just lost your mother. You can talk to me if you need to unload. I've never blamed you for anything that happened, and neither has Ray. I'm getting married on Valentine's Day. I haven't even told Mama and Daddy yet. They just don't understand."

Shannon remembered Nancy's teenage rebellion, and Miss Etta's deprecatory response. "I do try and let her comments roll off my back. Some of it is age difference. Their world was so simple. Find a way to share your good news with them."

"I'm trying, but every time I mention Enrique's name, Mama goes into another spasm. I'm glad you're with Edison, even if it is pretend."

She wanted to say it was very real. The only difficult part was knowing he would probably forget everything but the pain she caused him.

# Chapter 9

She spent most of the day with Edison, listening, talking, and wishing.

Pretending to be his wife was easy because she had never stopped feeling like Mrs. Edison Page. She had never stopped loving or wanting him. The pain she felt was in knowing he no longer belonged to her. Did she even have the right to hope that one day he would?

When J.P. arrived with Leila, Shannon took a break. Miss Etta was waiting in the hallway.

"I want you to know, I wasn't tryin' to start nothing with you. I want my son to get well, and if you can help him, I'm grateful. It don't bother me none 'cause you're here. It bothers me that Jeannie don't want to be here no more. She loves Edison. She's being put aside by all this, and that's jes a shame."

"So what do you want me to do? Tell me, and I'll do it. I love Edison, too, but if you want me to stay away just say so. Then you go in and explain it to Edison. Maybe he'll just laugh it off. But if he doesn't, if his blood pressure rises and his heart rate doubles, his death will be on your head. Just tell me, Miss Etta, because I'm tired of this."

"How you plan to 'splain this to him later on? The doctors don't know everythin', but I can't be the one to say no. They want you to lie to him, so go ahead and do it. I just don't like any uh this."

"And you think I do? I know it hurts Jeannie for him to ask for me, and believe me I wish he didn't. I wish he was well and could go on with his life." She started to walk away then turned back. "I still love Edison very much, Miss Etta. I'm not proud of myself for doing something that helped end my marriage. I loved my husband. I also remember your husband going off every fall to work on some kind of harvesting job in Louisiana. He was gone from early fall to just before Christmas."

"He went where the work was. You didn't have to leave here. It ain't the same thing."

"There are always choices, Miss Etta. Your husband left because he couldn't stay here and give you the things you needed, just as I felt I couldn't stay here and miss the chance to do something spectacular. I wish I hadn't gone away, but I did. I didn't marry Edison with the intention of leaving for any reason. When someone offered me something I really wanted, I felt compelled to go. I didn't leave Shepherd because I didn't love my husband and baby. I also didn't leave, as you've claimed, to be with Thierry. I made a choice. I now feel it was the wrong one, but I didn't at the time. If we were all content living under minimal conditions, this world would be one sorry place, don't you agree?"

She left the question dangling and sped off down the hall, wanting to get far away, but knowing she could never leave again. Edison slept most of the evening, but opened his eyes just as she was about to go home.

"Leaving me, beautiful?"

She went back to the bed. "I'll stay longer if you're going to keep me company."

"Where's Emmett? I don't know what's going on at the station. Did they find out who shot me, and why?"

"Emmett was here earlier, but you were asleep. Just about everyone in town has been here. Emmett arrested Junior Vinning. They're still trying to piece this all together. There's still no sign of Bobby Joe."

"I barely know Junior Vinning. I saw a truck back onto Boise Creek Road so fast it spun around twice. I pulled him over. I just wanted to find out what he was doing back there. Bobby Joe said these dope dealers were meeting back there. I've got to stop them." He tried to raise his right hand. "I can't do anything. I can't even hold a gun."

"But you will, baby." She spoke quickly. "Don't worry about that. Emmett and the others will get them. Do you remember Bo Lincoln? He's the one who brought you in." She felt he was blocking out certain things, after having been told about Bo several times. "I don't know the whole story, but apparently you helped deliver his sister's baby. Saved her life and the child's. I'm giving him…" She stopped abruptly. "I've been giving thanks to God for Bo."

When he settled down, she hurried to the car, and let out a big gasp. She had almost told him about giving Bo autographed copies of her CDs. She sat in the car and thanked God for helping her to get through another day, wiped her eyes, and drove home.

J.P. had brought dinner from the diner. "Don't worry," he told her. "I sent someone else in to get it."

Shannon smiled, and so did Leila, leaving Shannon to wonder if her baby was even more perceptive than she recognized. Worn down from the grief and tension, she gave Leila a bath and was about to tuck her in when Leila voiced her observation.

"Is it just make believe with you and Daddy?"

"Why do you ask, honey?"

"I want it to stay this way. I want you and Daddy to live together like Uncle John and Aunt Donna. I don't want you to fight."

"Don't let the arguing fool you, kitten. Your father and I will always love each other. I'm not sure about the two of us getting back together." She remembered Miss Etta's comments about Jeannie. Ray had said Jeannie and Edison broke up, but she knew if Miss Etta had her way, she'd get them back together. "Your father was planning to marry Jeannie before this happened. He still may do so."

Leila closed her eyes. "She hates me."

Stunned that Leila would use such a strong word, Shannon tucked her in and went back to the kitchen. When she told J.P. what Leila had said, he placed his coffee mug on the table and shook his head.

"I'm sure you're going through yet another rough situation trying to deal with Edison's memory loss, his mother, Jeannie, your child, and the loss that has to be tearing you apart, as it is me. You're strong and you're morally superior to the ones who criticize you. Don't let them get you down. Let's first hope Edison pulls through. After that, my only advice is to follow your heart. If you want him back in your life, fight for him."

Outside, rain beat heavily against the windowpane. Shannon rested her arms on the counter and held her head in her hands. Her father was counting on her strength, Edison needed her, at least for the moment, and her daughter would need her always. She couldn't give up or give in to the pressure.

She took Leila with her the next morning, but found Edison restless enough to summon Doctor Welch. After a brief examination, he offered reassurance.

"He does seem anxious, but his blood pressure and heart rate are amazingly normal. Swelling around the head wound has continued to decrease. That bullet keeps dropping further from critical areas. We'll still have to operate, but the longer he remains stable and gains strength, the better his chance will be. Did something happen to unnerve him?"

"Not that I'm aware of. One of the deputies was here when I arrived. I didn't hear the entire conversation, only that they can't find a connection to the attack on Edison and drug trafficking."

"Did they locate the Stanberry boy?"

She shook her head. "Bobby Joe has not been seen."

"You hang in there, Mrs. Page. Have the nurses find me if there's any change."

She started to remind him that she was no longer Mrs. Page. His name and his child were all Edison had requested in the divorce.

❧

Shannon waited until he had calmed down enough to fall asleep before taking Leila to the store to join her cousins. She stayed there, helping Donna for most the evening.

"I called Carmen this morning," Donna told her. "Bobby Joe is a fool, but he is the father of her children."

"I know. I've thought of her since this whole thing began, but I'm sure she wouldn't appreciate a call from me."

"Don't even think about it," Donna advised. "You've got your hands full and then some. Has Etta been giving you a hard time?"

"She did yesterday. Nancy intervened."

"Nancy is okay. I think she got a dose of reality when she went away to school."

Shannon felt an extra measure of guilt for Carmen's suffering, but knew there was nothing she could say or do that would help. Edison was asleep when she returned later in the evening. After a long conversation with Jackie, she sat next to the bed with a book. Exhausted, she fell asleep with her head on the bed, and awakened to the warmth of Edison's hand on her back.

"Hi, angel. You must have been really tired."

Still groggy, she realized darkness had set in and became alert. "How long did I sleep? I've got to get Leila."

"She's with your dad. Donna came in and told me. She prepared dinner at her house and your father took Leila home afterwards."

"How are you feeling?"

"I could feel much better." He started fumbling with the buttons on her blouse. "All I need is you."

"All in due time, my horny husband. Now lie back and relax." She sang until his eyelids started to flutter.

"I'm not asleep," he said when she started to leave. "I need you. Please, baby. You said you'd do anything to help me get better. Please do this."

She looked around to the door.

"Don't worry, I've been keeping track of the nurses' schedules. No one is coming in for another hour. That's how long we have to enjoy being close."

"I'm just not sure, Edison. You have to rest and stay calm."

"Then help me do it. I can't rest when I feel this way. It's all I can think about. I could never be near you and not want you, but I've never hurt this way before. You gotta help me. Please."

⤸

Overcome with concern, Shannon did not leave until after the nurse had checked Edison's vital signs and he was sleeping soundly. She replayed every second of the evening during her drive home. He had needed her. She remembered nights during their marriage when she had been tired from caring for Leila, and still unable to resist Edison's pleas.

She parked in the driveway and called the nurses' station. "I just left, but I'm worried—"

"He's still asleep," the nurse interrupted. "I promised I would call you if his condition changes, and I will. Try and get some rest."

Shannon did try. After updating her father on Edison's conditions, and watching Leila sleep, she hugged her pillow as a parade of scenarios sifted through her mind. Maybe Edison was madly in love with Jeannie, and she had disrupted their relationship, or more importantly, maybe she had just harmed rather than helped him heal. Thierry's face appeared before her and she felt an extra measure of guilt.

She tossed and turned for most of the night, and hurried to the hospital the next morning. Jackie was a welcome sight.

"He's fine. I checked his chart when I first arrived."

Breathing a sigh of relief, Shannon watched Edison sleep for hours. She thought of all the ways she had missed him, and prayed for a chance to prove his importance in her life. His condition improved rapidly over the next two days, prompting Doctor Welch to schedule a flight to Houston for the following Monday.

Leila was back with her cousins and friends at day school. J.P. returned to his job, but the first day seemed to tire him considerably. Shannon reminded herself that her father was aging. Losing his wife was taking a toll on his strength.

A long day at the hospital and another confrontation with Miss Etta had left her frazzled. Pressing her palm against the throbbing pain in her head, she filled the tub with very warm water. Just as she sank onto the warmth, her cell phone rang.

"Shannon, it's Jackie. The doctor asked me to tell you they're going to have to do the surgery now. Edison was fine earlier. Really fine. One of the nurses said he was talking and joking before he fell asleep. We're thinking he had a bad dream. I was called back here to help and they want you back, too."

The load suddenly became too much. "I don't know, Jackie. Miss Etta told me that while I'm not the cause of Edison's injury, I'm still responsible for the turmoil in his life. Maybe she's right. I don't know if I can take anymore."

"I can only imagine how painful this must be for you, but he needs you, honey. He's counting on you, and so is Doctor Welch. He keeps saying Edison is most calm when you're at his side. Do this for him, and if she gets in the way, I'll kick her ass myself."

"I'll be there in twenty minutes."

The temperature had dropped. Gusts of wind pushed the jagged clouds around the sky and chilled the earth. Shannon felt the weight of all that had happened and could not stop the tears.

"I don't know if I can be of any comfort, Jackie. Look at me." She held out her trembling left hand. "He'll know I'm falling apart."

Doctor Welch joined them. "I know this is tough, Mrs. Page. I thought we had more time, but just as that piece of lead shifted through the tissue and away from his brain, it's now moving the other way. We don't know what happened, so I asked his father to limit visits by family and friends. You've been the major player in keeping him calm. You have to endure the stress until the neurosurgeon arrives."

"You mean he's coming here."

"They're coming here," he said, smiling. "Two of the country's best. They've both shifted patients around to make the trip."

Miss Etta joined them and Doctor Welch continued his explanation. Shannon watched Miss Etta's frowns of concern.

"He's in pain and that's causing restlessness. We need him to calm down before the surgeons arrive if that's possible."

"Do you think the pain makin' this hap'en?" Miss Etta asked. "Did he get his mem'ry back?"

"We're not sure what's happening, only that he was sleeping peacefully, awakened in a panic and hasn't calmed down since then. There's a chance he relived his encounter with the shooter."

Hearing him groan from the hallway, Shannon brushed past his mother and tiptoed to the bed.

"Hi, baby." His voice was no more than a whisper.

"Hi, handsome. I hear you have a pressing date with two of the finest neurosurgeons in the country. Aren't you special?"

She kissed him and stroked his arm. "The doctors are going to remove that bullet. They don't want to give you too much pain medication, so I'm sure you're hurting." She kissed his face. "Do the best you can to relax. I'm here with you."

"Everything hurts, except my legs." He nodded to the tubes in his arms. "These things bind my arms and I can't even move my head. I feel so helpless. I want this to be over."

"It will be over very soon. Just concentrate on walking out of here with me on one side and our baby on the other. That should calm you down."

"Why can't I think of what we're going to do when our baby goes to sleep?"

"I doubt that would calm you down, so do as I ask. Right now, I'm just thinking of how much I love you. How much I need you in my life." She sat next to the bed, stroked his arm, and crooned softly.

Doctor Welch stood at the foot of the bed and was soon joined by two other men in white. He introduced them as Doctor Marcus Spivey and Doctor David Thom from Methodist Hospital in Houston. They spoke in hushed tones while watching the monitor as a nurse administered a sedative.

"Remember our first date? The homecoming dance? You came to pick me up, so handsome in your new blue suit." Brushing away the embarrassment of speaking so privately in front of an audience, she continued her journey back to happier times.

"Everyone watched when we danced. It's still the most magical time of my life."

"I was the luckiest man in the room."

"You parked and I kissed you." She leaned closer and kissed him repeatedly.

The sedative was taking effect, but he smiled broadly. "I…I kissed you back."

"That you did."

"And you two were the best looking bride and groom I've ever seen," Jackie said. "You know I'm partial to little girls, but I think you should have a little boy now. You both have height, so maybe this one will play basketball or some other sport."

"I'd like that." His eyelids fluttered rapidly. "I'd like that a lot."

Shannon kissed him again and hummed softly. After he was wheeled away, she sank to her knees in tears.

"Here, honey. Drink this. It's freshly brewed." Jackie placed the cup in Shannon's hand. "I have to get back to my duties, but if you need me, just go to the nurses' station and have me paged."

Shannon walked to the opposite end of the hall. She had seen the Page family, minus Jeannie, and wanted to avoid another confrontation. Ray and Nancy came and sat next to her.

"Shannon, I'm very sorry for everything that's happened." Ray took her hand. "I love my mother, but she can be so far off the track it's pitiful. To this day she can't admit that Edison loved you and that the two of you were good together; she can't stand to be wrong."

The tears had stopped and numbness had taken over. "I can't blame it all on her. Right now, I just want him to live."

"I want my brother to live and, when he's better, I want to see the two of you married again, no matter what anyone else says." Nancy pushed the hair from Shannon's face.

"That goes for me, too," Ray said. "I'm glad you're here for him now. They don't understand, but Edison is living out the feelings he has deep inside. Maybe that's what kept him alive out on that highway. Don't let them get to you."

"I feel bad for Jeannie," Shannon said. "I know this hurts her, but your mother wants to believe that I'm enjoying causing her pain, and that's not true. I almost didn't come when Jackie called me earlier. I just lost my mother, I'm not sure how much more I can take."

"Well, don't worry." Ray frowned. "When I stopped by the diner today Jeannie said Edison never really cared for her. I don't know about Edison, but I never cared for her. I don't even like the way she treats her brother."

"You came home to your mother's funeral," Nancy said. "Sometimes we forget just how precious, and possibly brief, our lives can be. We'll have to help him through this."

J.P. joined them, and so did Emmett.

"Old Bo was telling the truth," Emmett said. "We finally caught Junior Vinning just as he was about to leave town. He had some of the money he took from that gas station and the back of his pickup was filled with cases of motor oil. A bullet from Edison's gun was found embedded in his truck and we recovered the gun he used. How stupid can you be?"

"We owe Bo Lincoln," Ray said. "Big time."

"Bo Lincoln has been unfairly judged, just like so many others," J.P. said. "After all we've seen in our lives, some of us can't get past the ignorance and intolerance long enough to see people for what they are. What do you know about this Junior Vinning, Emmett?"

"There's not much to him, but he had never been in trouble with the law before this. His daddy, William Sr., is a roughneck. Folks used to say he beat the crap out of his wife and his kids. I'm glad you talked to Bo," he told Shannon. "Catching this bastard means a lot to me for many reasons. I've worked with Edison since we both joined the department and I could never want a better sheriff or a fairer man to work with. It would just about kill me to know the man who shot him was out there free."

Emmett then added another perspective. "I'm glad it was someone other than Bo. Right after Edison was shot there were two reporters here in the hospital trying to work the angle of racial violence. I told them that was absurd. When Edison ran for sheriff he got seventy-six percent of the votes. Shepherd is only sixty-two percent black, and I can assure you, they all didn't vote. Quite a few whites thought he was the best man for the job, and I think just about everybody likes him. There's been some grumbling lately because it's an election year and we're overrun with crime right now. Too many idle hands. I've never heard anyone say anything bad about Edison or the way he runs the department."

"I remember the first day he wore his deputy's uniform," Shannon said. "I was apprehensive about everything, including the reason old man Buford had chosen him for that job. I saw a ghost around every corner back then. I guess I just wanted to protect him. Keep him safe. I never got used to the idea of him wearing a gun, but back then, life was a lot simpler."

"And that's when he had a lot of open prejudice in this town," J.P. said. "Your feelings were natural, honey. We always want to protect the ones we love."

"I remember what he said that first morning when I kissed him goodbye and told him to be careful.

'Thanks, baby. I'll be careful. I want all of Shepherd to be proud to have me.' Emmett, I'm glad he accomplished that."

"Come on now, honey. He's going to be okay." Doubt peered through J.P.'s reassuring words, but he smiled and hugged Shannon. "I still believe in good over evil."

When no one was around Shannon confided to Donna, "I know this is selfish, but I'm afraid of how Edison will feel about our relationship when he awakens. I can't tell you how great it was to have him in my life again without the animosity."

"He'll experience many emotions before this is over. I think he asked for you the first time he awakened because he has never stopped thinking of you as his wife." Donna placed her hand over Shannon's. "Don't lose sight of that. Make him forget the anger. I know he wants to."

❧

The wait seemed never-ending. Shannon squirmed in her chair, then stood and paced, always keeping her distance from Edison's family. Ray often paced with her. John's arrival made her feel much better. She needed his support.

"Donna said he's in surgery." John hugged her. "Have you heard anything?"

"Not yet. I'm scared, John. I keep thinking I'll never see him alive again. That's the worse thing imaginable. The next is that he won't remember the closeness we're shared this last week."

"We'll pray for number one. When he's out of danger, I'm sure he'll remember many things. Maybe not the recent ones, but the ones where you two were happy together."

Jackie made several trips to inform them of the doctor's progress. The last bulletin was that the surgery was taking longer than anticipated, but Edison was holding his own. Shannon asked Ray if Edison had ever been ill. She could only remember the one time he had kidney stones.

"No. He takes good care of himself. Works out. Eats well. I'm praying that helps him now."

When the three doctors walked through the double doors at the end of the hallway, Shannon was too frightened to move. Emmett and J.P. held her between them.

"We have some very good news, and some not so good news," Doctor Welch said. "Doctor Spivey will explain."

Shannon braced, praying the good news outweighed the bad.

"Edison came through the surgery like a champ," Doctor Spivey said. "He's doing quite well. We won't know for sure until he's awake and we can examine him better, but there was likely some damage to the motor nerves. Given time and therapy, he could be as good as new, but some paralysis could remain."

"When will he awaken, Doctor?" Shannon asked.

"Give him a few hours, and even then he'll still be groggy," Doctor Thom answered.

"I have to tell you a little story, Mrs. Page," Doctor Welch said, with a smile. "We played your CD while we performed the operation. Jackie brought it in. Everyone in the OR found it amazing that he responded to your voice even when anesthetized."

Shannon was puzzled. "How did he respond?"

Doctor Welch cocked his head to one side. "He smiled."

Knowing she could make him smile made her warm all over. She left to tell Leila that her father was going to be all right. The explanation was more difficult than she imagined.

"Remember when Granddaddy had his tooth pulled last summer and his face was a little stiff? Well, your daddy might have some stiffness in his face and he may sound a little different."

Leila nodded. "Can he walk and everything?"

"The doctors aren't sure just yet. The main thing is that your daddy is going to get better. He'll be here to love you, just as he's always done."

When she returned to the hospital, Edison had awakened and his mother was with him. Shannon waited until everyone had taken a turn in the small recovery room before she poked her head in the door. Just to see him lying there, eyes open and alert, made her happy. She stared at the smooth texture of his skin, from which a four-day stubble had grown. There was no doubt in her mind that she loved him and that she always would. He opened his eyes and saw her.

"Hi. Come in."

She smiled as she had instructed Leila to do in spite of his slurred speech. "Hey. You look wonderful." She bent to kiss his forehead.

"Did they tell you I could have all kinds of impairments?" He closed his eyes as he spoke.

"The doctor said there was some nerve damage. Of course it will take a lot of hard work to regain your strength, but right now I'm just glad to see your eyes open and hear you speak. The other we'll deal with day by day."

He soon erased her uncertainty about his recent memory.

"Is Jeannie out there?"

Her heart sank. "I'm not sure. I didn't see her. I went home to tell Leila that you were going to be okay. She's so happy. I was going to bring her with me, but decided that maybe we shouldn't tire you out too much just yet."

"Maybe it's best not to bring her here."

"She's already asking to see you. She loves you so much, you know. She'll be happy to see her daddy's face and hear you talk to her."

"Is that what I'm doing? Sounds like I'm babbling like a retard. I'm surprised you're still standing there listening to me."

"I'm not that superficial. I prayed harder than I've ever prayed in my life for God to let you stay with us. For Leila to still have her father. I'll be here for as long as you'll let me, and I'm not the least bit repulsed. It isn't nearly as bad as it seems to you. You're still as handsome as ever. There's still swelling and the bandages, of course." She smiled and stroked his brow.

"I had a dream. A long dream. In it we were still married and you were here with me, telling me how much you loved me. You said you would be waiting for me to come home. I could feel your face close to mine as we talked about what would happen after we put Leila to bed." He became embarrassed. "I must have dreamed it for a long time."

It occurred to her to tell him the truth, but she was afraid to upset him. It was a good memory for her in spite of the awkwardness it caused. She decided to steer him in another direction.

"Sounds like good memories to me. We did have a nice life together. Leila has been so worried about you. When I told her you were going to be okay she jumped up and down and yelled. You know she won't be convinced that you're better until she sees with her own eyes. Do you think you'll be up to a brief visit maybe tomorrow?"

"I don't think so. I can't move my left arm because of the wound. Now I can't move my right one very much either."

"She's a mature little girl. She'll be happy to see her father. Your condition isn't severe enough to upset anyone who cares about you. If she doesn't see you soon she'll begin to think I'm lying about your condition."

"Let's just wait a few days. Give me a chance to adjust to this. Jeannie and I had a big fight. I told her it was over between us, so I guess she's still angry. I thought she would have been here, if only—"

"She was here. She was here when you were first brought in." She changed the subject. "I don't know how much you remember, but a man named Bo Lincoln found you and brought you to the hospital. He also told Emmett who shot you and Emmett arrested him. I think Emmett beat the crap out of him, because he gave a full confession. Do you remember any of that?"

His face became dark. "Yes. I remember all of it. I stopped a pickup for speeding, and to see if he was one of the drug dealers Bobby Joe told me about. Green pickup. The man got out and began firing before I could say a word. Did Emmett find out why?"

"Yes. The man's name is Junior Vinning, some low life who had just committed a robbery. Bo Lincoln knew this man's truck was leaking oil, and he saw a big stain when he found you. "

"I'll have to thank him for what he did. I admit, I thought Bo was a few bricks shy of a full load and flaky as a fresh biscuit."

"I thanked him for bringing you in. He's not all there, but in a nice way."

"That's amazing. I remember a man getting out of the truck and firing. He must have dived into the bushes afterwards. I went down, pulled my gun and fired back. That's all I remember except for that dream." He looked wistful. "It was a nice dream."

The nurse came in and said Edison needed to rest. Shannon left for home but decided to stop at the diner. Jeannie met her at the door.

"I've never seen you here before. Did you come to tell me something about Edison?"

"Yes. He's awake and he's asking for you. He thinks this is the first time he's been awake since he was shot. I know it was tough for you before. That's all over now. He needs you."

"There's no reason for me to go down there now. It's over between us, so you can just get your little marriage back together and then break his heart like you did before. It's no longer my problem. *He's* no longer my problem."

"I don't consider Edison a problem for anyone. He's asking for you and I thought you'd like to be there with him regardless of where your relationship goes from here."

"Well, you thought wrong. You can play nurse. I don't want the job."

"I don't know you, but people have told me you're a real bitch. I'll make sure they add cold-hearted to that. Whether he recovers or not, he's too good for you."

John was there when she got home. "I went to the hospital and Edison said you'd just left. He's going to be all right. I know it's going to be a hard adjustment, but it's not nearly as bad as I thought it would be."

"I went to see Jeannie." After telling John about their conversation, she added her conjecture. "No wonder she gets along so well with Miss Etta. They're both witches. He's asking for her and she's refusing to see him."

"And that tore you up, didn't it?"

She nodded. "I feel like I'm living in a nightmare, John. First being swept into the fantasy of the whole Paris thing, then Edison filing for divorce, and then losing Mom. It seems surreal. Then Edison was shot, we were bonding, and now this. I'm not much of a drinker, I'm afraid of drugs—even prescription ones—but I'm not sleeping well. I keep feeling that if I could just fall into a deep slumber, I would awaken and my life would be whole again. "

# *Chapter 10*

The room seemed bright when he opened his eyes but Edison felt engulfed in darkness. Pieces of awareness fluttered in his head. He knew he was alone and in a hospital bed. There seemed to be holes in his life, little pockets filled with question marks.

While the dark spots did not go away, some things were painfully memorable. In his line of work, he had been shot at more than once. His luck had finally run out. Just thinking of the piercing metal tearing into his shoulder was excruciating. The second shot obviously didn't give him a chance to feel the pain.

"Hey there, old buddy."

He heard Jackie's voice and saw her walk into the room, but could not focus on anything but the agony and uncertainty he felt inside.

"You're looking great. Can I get you anything?"

"Just my strength." He couldn't pretend to be chipper.

"I think you're pretty strong, all things considered. The doctors have been amazed at your strength. You lost a lot of blood. That alone is enough to make you weak."

"Tell me the truth, Jackie. What are my chances of beating this? I can't hold a gun in this hand. I can't hold my child. I'd rather be dead."

"Don't you dare say that. Do you know how hard we all prayed for you to live? I've been at this hospital long enough to see a lot of things, and believe me, your condition could be a hell of a lot worse, so don't you dare say something like that. That waiting room was packed with people praying for you, and I was one of them. You have a lot to be thankful for and a lot to live for. You have a family and a beautiful little girl who loves her daddy."

"I see you carefully omitted Jeannie."

She moved about the room, rearranging the flowers on the table, and everything on his nightstand. "I don't know what's going on with you and Jeannie. I do know Shannon was here day and night."

"Shannon just felt sorry for me, or guilty, or she did it to win her daughter's trust. She'll leave like she did before and that will be the end of that. She wants to bring Leila here. I'm not sure that would be a good idea."

"I don't see why not. Leila is mature for her age. She'll understand and she'll be happy to see her daddy. As far as Shannon is concerned, I know she loves you."

"I doubt that. Can you dial the number to the diner for me, please? It hurts like hell to move any part of my body."

"Sure. You had a bullet in your shoulder so that arm's going to be useless for a while. The good thing is that there's no permanent damage. You'll regain full use."

She leaned over to get the phone, then turned to face him. "I'm not supposed to discuss a patient's condition, but I love you like a brother so I'm going to open my yap and tell you everything I know. There is almost no movement in your legs, but there is feeling. Your reflexes aren't sharp, but there is a reflex. What that means is that you'll have to work like hell to get the use of your limbs back. You may not be able to dance like you used to, but there's more than a good chance you'll walk again." She dialed the number and put the receiver in his hand.

When he asked why she hadn't been there, Jeannie's voice was loud and distinct. "You broke up with me, Edison. I guess that slipped your mind. When you first woke up, you asked for Shannon, not me. You've made your choice. I'm just abiding by it."

"There are lots of things…Jackie, don't leave yet. There are lots of things I don't remember, but I do know we have joint accounts at the bank, we own property together, and I thought we cared enough about each other to be there if one was in trouble. I don't remember asking for Shannon, so obviously I wasn't clear-headed at the time."

He did remember. It wasn't a dream. He had to talk to Jackie. "I'll let you go. Do whatever makes you comfortable." He passed the receiver back to Jackie. The room began to spin. His head throbbed, but in a different way. So did his heart.

"Tell me what happened between the time I was brought here and yesterday, and please don't lie."

∽

Shannon kept Leila as busy as she could, hoping she would not insist on seeing her father until he was ready. When the phone rang and she realized it was Jackie, she sent Leila to the kitchen. "Honey, go in the pantry and see if you can find some potatoes. Mommy needs to start dinner soon."

She waited until the door closed. "What's wrong?"

"He's depressed as hell and raging mad. Jeannie just reminded him that he asked for you when he woke up. He wants to see you. Probably so he can vent. It's up to you. I can say you're busy, but I know he'll keep asking."

"Thanks for telling me. I'll be down there as soon as I drop Leila off at day school."

The waiting room was empty as she hoped it would be. She wanted to spend time with him before the crowd, particularly his mother, arrived. He lay motionless, with his face turned away to the wall. Shannon watched, thinking he was asleep until she saw his shoulder shake violently and realized he was crying.

She closed the door softly and walked back down the hall. In their years together she had never known Edison to cry. She checked with the desk and found that Jackie was not available. Not knowing what to do, she waited in the hallway until she saw a nurse go into the room. She followed her inside, walked quietly to the bed, and touched his arm to let him know she was there. When he lifted his head, her heart found new places to break.

"Good morning. Before Leila left for school I promised I would come and see you this morning. She really wants to visit, and she made you this." She held the happy face drawing up to his face. "Pretty good, don't you think?"

His silence was frightening. When he finally spoke, she fought to keep her composure.

"Why didn't you tell me, Shannon? When I told you about the dream I had, why didn't you tell me it wasn't a dream? You people let me make a fool of myself while you stood around laughing. Was that your revenge for my filing for divorce?"

"No one was laughing at you. We were praying that you gained enough strength for the doctors to remove that bullet before it caused more damage. The doctor asked me to try and console you. He said that time was of the essence in removing that bullet, but you were too weak to undergo surgery. I was trying to help."

"Why didn't someone just tell me the truth? Was that so hard to do?"

"I can answer that question for you, Sheriff." Doctor Welch walked to the foot of the bed. "I advised them not to do or say anything that would upset you. I needed every second of tranquility to allow you to regain enough strength to get that bullet out. Don't blame anyone but me. They followed my orders."

Shannon moved to the window and tried to calm down. He was too angry to realize he needed her, but she did. Turning back to Doctor Welch, she tried to sound cheery. "How's our patient progressing, Doctor?"

"Quite well, actually. His blood pressure is elevated and he'd better learn to relax. Sheriff, sometimes our minds take over when our bodies are too weak to function, and that's what happened when you first awakened. It's quite normal following drastic shock and loss of blood. Your mind chose another entry into consciousness, maybe to a time and place that had great significance in your life.

"At the time it happened, telling you would have worsened your condition and afterwards, well, it didn't seem to matter. Everyone was focusing on your recovery. Your ex-wife understood. She tried to calm you and obviously told you what you wanted to hear because you responded better than we had hoped. We were able to operate, and that was crucial to saving your life. Looking at where you were and where you are now, that's an awful lot."

When he concluded his exam, Shannon thanked him and went back to Edison's side. "I'm sorry."

"Like the doctor said, you told me what I wanted to hear and I bought it. I guess you're good at role-playing. If your voice fails you can always take up acting."

Tears sprang to her eyes. She waited until Doctor Welch left the room. "When Doctor Welch and Jackie came out to tell us about your memory lapse, I was holding our daughter. She didn't believe you were alive, so I had to bring her here to see for herself. Daddy took her walking while Doctor Welch gave his prognosis, but she was there when he started explaining what had to be done. Doctor Welch advised Leila to listen carefully and ask questions if she didn't understand. She asked if all he wanted us to do was make believe you and I were still married."

She felt a tear fall on her cheek. "I didn't think I could do it, but Jackie and Doctor Welch said any kind of shock might cause your death. He called me Mrs. Page. I started to correct him, but didn't. The next time he said it, I didn't correct him because I felt like Mrs. Page. I pretended we were still married, but everything I said to you was true. I'm still very much in love with you. I never stopped, Edison."

"So you lied to Thierry? You must have told him you loved him at some point."

"I do love Thierry. I always will. He gave me something special, not just the opportunity to sing, but to adjust. I love him, but I couldn't fall in love with him. I still loved you."

"So why were you with him? Just to pass the time?"

"I guess I could ask you the same thing about Jeannie. Let's just say in all of my heartache, in the stress of walking onto a stage and hoping to be well-received, in my loneliness, Thierry was there."

"I suppose I should thank you for keeping me calm, as the doctor said."

She swallowed her anguish. "You don't have to thank me. You were in fierce pain. You're back to normal now and aware of anger. I'm sure Jeannie will understand now that you're able to communicate your feelings to her. You love her, not me. She must understand that."

"Oh yes, she understands. She wants nothing more to do with me."

At a loss for words, she patted his arm. "I'm sorry, Edison. I'm really sorry this happened, but I have to say that your memory failure couldn't have triggered enough hurt to send her away. There's more to it. Ray said you broke up with her before you were shot. He said it was because she didn't want Leila to live with the two of you. I know you love Leila, so I'm sure that must have hurt, but it doesn't have to end this way. I'm here for Leila. You and Jeannie can have a life together if that's what you want. If you would like, I'll try talking to her again. Maybe I can make her understand that you love and need her."

"No. You're right. It wasn't just the memory thing. We did have a big fight before this happened. Matter of fact, that's why I was out driving around. She said that she never wanted Leila to live with us. I was so angry I just walked away and started driving. I went to the house and got into it again with Mama. I wanted to come over and talk to you but I couldn't bring myself to do it. I was also worried sick about Leila. You don't know how it made me feel to see her crying and pulling away from my mother—even from me."

He lifted his hand and waited until she took it. "I'm still worried about Leila. I don't know what to do." He hung his head. "In my condition there's nothing I can do."

"There is absolutely no need for you to worry about Leila. I'm taking care of her and loving it. What's more, she's very happy with me. Her only concern now is you."

"But what happens when you go back to Paris? Your French friend will probably feel the same way Jeannie feels about having her around, and Leila made it quite clear she doesn't want to stay with my parents."

"I've told you I'm not leaving my baby. My heart isn't in Paris right now. My father just lost the only woman he ever loved. He's devastated. Even if I could take Leila with me, I can't take Daddy. I want to be here with my baby and my family. If I decide to return to Paris later, I can get a place for Leila and me." She looked into his eyes. "I don't want to leave you."

"I wish I could believe that. What about your relationship? Are you just going to drop Thierry?"

"My personal relationship with Thierry is something I'll have to deal with, but he and I have a business arrangement. He knows I'm planning to stay here and he's trying to get releases for my upcoming performances. If he can't, I'll have to fulfill them. I owe him and the fans that much."

"Are you going to hang around so you can pity the poor cripple?"

She laughed mirthlessly. "I'm trying so hard, and you're doing everything you can to make it impossible. I think it's time for me to leave. Can I bring Leila here, or would you rather wait longer? You're the man. Just tell me what you want me to do."

"Bring her here if she wants to come. You can bring her this evening after school. She'll have to see me this way sooner or later."

"Take this any way you want, but I am concerned about you and I do care, so please try and relax." This time she didn't kiss or embrace him. She just walked through the door. As she headed down the hallway she saw his mother and father walking toward her.

"Good morning." She tried to smile.

They both spoke and Shannon decided to throw caution to the wind and let them know how poorly Edison was reacting to everything around him. "I'm sure you don't want to hear this from me, but I'm going to say it anyway. In spite of what you might think, I care very deeply for Edison, but right now I'm not the one who can help him. He's distraught over his condition and the fact that Jeannie wants nothing to do with him. You seem to be close to her, Miss Etta. Can you talk her into not doing anything to further upset him? He needs reasons to fight right now, not reasons to quit."

"I tried talkin' to her but she says she can't marry him after the way he treated her. I don't know nothin else to say."

"Now, Miss Etta, you've never been at a loss for things to say, certainly not to me. Your son's life has been severely altered by this shooting. He needs everything, and I do mean everything, he can get to make him want to fight to regain the use of his limbs. Having the woman he loved turn her back on him is not going to help. You and I both know that what happened when he first awakened was a fluke. He was worried about Leila at the time of the shooting. Subconsciously he flicked back to the past and his concern for me leaving and going to Paris. It meant nothing. If Jeannie cares for him at all she'll get her butt up here and go about the business of trying to help him get better. Even if she doesn't love him she can't just walk away now. She must feel something for him."

"I guess her pride is pushin' her to do it," Miss Etta answered. "I can't talk her out of it. I tried. She says that everybody in town knows Edison wishes he was still married to you, and she's just can't deal with that. It's her pride."

"If I hadn't encountered it firsthand, I wouldn't believe there could be so many cases of misplaced pride here in Shepherd."

"I'll try talkin to Jeannie," Tito said. "I've been thinkin' on Edison's illness, and I figured he'd have a hard time acceptin' it. You're right, he sure don't need somethin' like this piled on top of everythin' else."

"I don't think Jeannie wants to leave Edison. She just jealous of you. It might he'p if you stay away from Edison." His mother spoke calmly but with conviction.

"I'm bringing Leila back here this evening. I promised. I'll let Edison choose. If he wants me to stay away, I will."

She drove home in tears. She wanted to tell her father but he was preoccupied with his mother's problem. "She's getting worse. She left the teakettle on the stove this morning and almost set the house on fire. Savannah is a good girl at heart, but she's not focused. She can't hold a job and seems to attract nothing but worthless men. Talk about dysfunctional. My mother had thirteen children, and there are still seven of us left, but no one wants to accept responsibility for her care. This whole thing sure came at a bad time. I don't know what to do."

"I promised to take Leila to the hospital this evening. I'll go out and get Mama Lou in the morning. I'll look after her. I'm a lot bigger and stronger than she is, and I don't mind taking care of her at all."

"Don't trouble yourself, honey. You have to spend time with Edison. He needs you right now."

Not wanting Leila to hear the conversation, she assured her father that she would have the time to care for her grandmother. "I've been told that I need to back off. Jeannie is not comfortable with this arrangement and she's been avoiding him. He needs her now more than he needs me."

J.P. quit eating and stared at her. "Okay. If you're sure, I'll go get Mama tonight. I have to go to the store and lock up. Donna is going to an open house at the school and that worthless manager we hired is sick, again. I'll stop by and get Mama on the way back. I'll tell her that you want to spend some time with her. I think she'll like that. That is, if she remembers who you are."

Shannon thought she might live to regret her offer, but she did want to help. Having told Leila they were going to the hospital, she proceeded to get her dressed. "I want you to look especially pretty tonight for your daddy. Now remember what I told you, don't look surprised that his face is a little different, or that he can't move too well. The blessing is that he's alive and he's going to get better. He needs to know that we love him regardless of his condition."

"But I do love him, Mommy."

Leila wiggled about impatiently as Shannon combed her hair. "Hurry up, Mommy. Daddy might go to sleep if we don't get there soon."

*So grown up.* She recognized so many of her own traits in her daughter, especially impatience. "Then you have to kiss him and wake him up. Let's go and practice your brightest smile."

Leila ran to Edison before Shannon could restrain her and jumped on the bed. "Daddy! I was worried about you. Mommy said you were going to be all right, but I wanted to see for myself." She stood back. "You look just like my old daddy."

Edison smiled broadly. "I'm so glad to see you, honey. Give your old daddy a kiss. I can't move very well. There's a nasty old needle in one arm and the other arm's in a sling."

"That's okay. You just have to get well, that's all. Just like I did when I had the measles. Remember? I was a mess."

They all laughed and Shannon told Leila they could not stay too long. "Your father needs his rest, honey, and I need to talk to him alone, so why don't you go into the waiting room with your grandparents? I'll come and get you to say goodbye before we leave." She escorted Leila to the waiting area and returned.

"What do we need to talk about?" Edison was alert and anxious.

"Your mother told me earlier that maybe my presence here is keeping Jeannie away. I don't want to do anything to hurt you or your chance to marry the woman you love. Also, as upset as you've been with me, it may be best if I don't come back."

"What are you saying? You're not going to bring Leila back here again?"

"That's not what I'm saying at all. Whenever Leila wants to come here or whenever you want to see her, my father or John can bring her by. If they're not available, I'll come myself. I don't know if your mother is right about this, but I don't want another crime hanging over my head."

"And what if I want you here? Don't I have a say in this?"

"Of course you do. I'm not throwing you away." She smiled. "If you need me, just call, or have Jackie call. You might not believe this, Edison, but there's not much that I wouldn't do for you, including staying away and allowing you and Jeannie to patch up your relationship. I'll come if you need me—anytime."

After hearing her father's car pull into the driveway Shannon pushed past her apprehension and went to greet her grandmother. She watched them walk down the driveway, got a good look at the silver-haired matriarch, and was amazed that someone deemed incompetent could appear so fit.

"Mama, look there on the porch," J.P. said.

Shannon smiled as her grandmother squinted against the porch light.

"That's my baby. That's Shannon. I'm not incompetent, J.P. I know Shannon is home. She brought me here last week, remember?"

"Hello, Mama Lou. I'm so glad you came to spend some time with us. You look great."

"Oh, shoot. You're only saying that because they've told you I'm on my last leg, but you look like the beautiful woman I knew you'd would grow up to be. Help me inside and show me to my room. I'm usually asleep by now, or at least in bed. That crazy Savannah treats me like a little child. Time to go to bed, Mama Lou. Time to get up, Mama Lou. Eat your food. Take your medicine. Makes me mad as hell."

Shannon laughed. "You're a pistol, Mama Lou. Just like always. I remember spending weekends with you and making popcorn in that big black pot. That's one of the fondest memories from my childhood. You would tell ghost stories and Savannah and I would pretend to be scared."

"You pretended. Your cousin was scared. She still is. Well, look at this little woman." She opened her arms when Leila came into the room. "She looks just like you did when we used to make that popcorn."

When Leila had gone back to finish her last half hour of television, Mama Lou looked at Shannon. "I know this is so hard for you. Losing Doris and now Edison. Doris was the sweetest person in this town. She was good to me."

She was silent for a moment before sending Shannon and J.P. into gales of laughter with her next remark.

"If I didn't say this before, I'll say it now. I'm glad you're home to take care of your baby. I heard she was over there with old Etta Page. That woman is the devil's handmaiden. Crazy as a road lizard. Keep that baby away from her and her family. Edison's the only one that's got a lick of sense in that bunch. Makes you wonder if maybe there was some inbreeding going on there."

Shannon looked at her father and they both laughed. "You've got that one pegged right, Mama Lou. I'm not letting my daughter out of my sight from now on."

After getting her grandmother settled in the guestroom, Shannon sat down for a last cup of coffee. "Daddy, she is totally alert. I can't imagine her behaving the way you described. Are you sure there isn't some kind of mistake? Maybe taking the wrong medicine?"

"I wish it were a mistake. One minute she's talking like she did when I was a boy, and the next she doesn't even know who or where she is. Be careful with her. She'll trick you. Are you certain you're up to this?"

"I promised Savannah I would help with Mama Lou. I've agreed to abide by Etta's wishes and stay away from Edison. From the way Jeannie talked when I stopped by the diner, I doubt that my absence will help, but I'm willing to try. Other than helping Donna at the store, I have nothing to do all day, so I'll be glad to keep Mama Lou company. How much trouble could it be?"

She made a quick breakfast for Leila the next morning and coffee for her father before going in to help her grandmother. "Mama Lou! You're up and dressed."

"Yes, I am. Pretty good for an old lady, don't you think?"

"You're amazing. Come on in the kitchen and keep me company. We didn't have much of a chance to talk the last time you were here. What would you like for breakfast?"

"Can you cook?" She looked doubtfully at her granddaughter.

"I sure can. You tell me what you want and I'll fix it for you. If you like things prepared a certain way just let me know."

"Thank you, Lord. Finally someone in this family who's worth the salt in their bread. Can you make potato pancakes? I don't mean the kind from that damn package Savannah makes. I want real potatoes in my pancakes."

"You got it. I'll get us some coffee while breakfast is cooking." Thinking Mama Lou was a little too eager for potato pancakes, she decided to pry. "Mama Lou? Is there some reason you're not suppose to have potato pancakes? Are you trying to pull the wool over my eyes?"

She laughed. "I always said you were the smartest one in the family. They keep saying I don't need foods with a lot of salt. You don't have to put much salt in the pancakes. I just want to taste that crusty brown potato, that's all."

"Okay. I'll make them extra crusty." Overcome with sadness, she imagined what it was like to be her grandmother, once again a child. When they settled down in the kitchen, Mama Lou started asking questions about Shannon's life abroad.

"I'm so glad you saw some of the world. It's a damn shame to live your entire life in this briar patch. Tell me about Paris. Did you go to the Louvre?"

"Oh yeah. It took three visits to see all of the paintings. Paris is loaded with museums of all kinds. I stood forever in front of the Mona Lisa trying to figure out what all the fuss was about. Then there's Venus de Milo. Today she would be known as a big old transvestite."

They laughed and Shannon continued. "I became fascinated with art over there, Mama Lou. Art and history. America is too new to have that kind of history. I was alone for much of the time when I wasn't rehearsing, and spent a great deal of it learning about art. I love the great impressionists. I had been living there a year before I finished my tour of the museums. Once I did, I studied art and the artists. Did you know the Louvre was built as a fortress in 1190?"

"That's interesting."

"You would love it there. Nothing brings you closer to the history of Paris and of France than Notre Dame. It's located in an area called Ile de la Cite, which means cradle of the city. Mom loved the stained glass best of all. Leila hates the gargoyles. Dad liked the art. He remembered so much of it from his tour of duty and enjoyed visiting the city again."

"Did you buy any of those paintings?"

"Only prints. They're far too expensive for me. Thierry had three, but of course Thierry is filthy rich."

"Thierry's just plain pretty. Can I have him now that you and Edison are getting back together?"

"Mama Lou. Why do you say that?"

Shannon listened to her grandmother's logic until the telephone interrupted their conversation. It was J.P.

"Hello, honey. How's it going with your grandmother?"

"We're having a good time, Daddy. I made breakfast and we're about to eat. I'm really enjoying Mama Lou's company."

"I suppose you know she's going to try and talk you into letting her have foods that she knows she's not supposed to have?"

"Been there, done that. We were just discussing Paris."

"Good. Just watch her, Shannon. She could fade out at any time."

"Thanks, Dad. I'll see you and Leila when you get home."

Mama Lou was smiling when she got off the phone. "I'll bet he told you to keep a close watch on me." She rubbed her knuckles against the palm of her hand. "I try to fight this aging thing. My right hand and elbow hurt a lot so I learned to write with my left."

"I know it's hard getting old, but I'm so glad you're still with us. Mom didn't have a chance to grow old."

"I don't mind getting old. That's part of life. It's being less than myself that's so demeaning. That Savannah and the rest of them never sit down and talk to me like you're doing. They're always talking to me like I'm two years old, and that hurts me so bad."

"It's okay, Mama Lou. As long as you're with me we'll have fun talking about the things we've done in our lives. I want to hear about your youth. I can only imagine how difficult life must have been back then."

"And I'm glad you have to imagine it, because it was pure hell."

She followed Shannon through the house, talking about the past, her family, her husband, and her youth. Shannon was fascinated that her mind was so clear and her memory so sharp.

"I have a great idea, Mama Lou. Thierry bought me a tape recorder that I keep in my purse. Do you mind if I record the stories you're telling me? I'm sure Leila will remember you when she grows up, and we have photographs, but I want her to hear you tell about your life. She can pass it on through generations."

"I don't mind, but are you sure you want to record the ramblings of an old woman? Your grandkids probably won't care."

"I want to do it very much, first for me, and then for the next generations. I'm sure they'll be fascinated."

Each day they had breakfast and talked for hours. Shannon used three tapes to cover tales of post-slavery, Jim Crow, and the hardships of farming in rural Mississippi. Mama Lou also covered the very romantic story of her courtship, and the pairing of two families and two small pieces of farmland.

Shannon played a sample for her father, Mama Lou's description of the day he was born, and watched tears gather in his eyes.

After almost a week Shannon was beaming with pride. Everyone loved the meals she prepared. She tried to make her father's adjustment less painful by keeping him engaged when he was home. It also helped keep her mind off Edison. Leila glowed and Mama Lou enjoyed the attention. She found that by giving her some of the things she liked to eat, it was easy to persuade her to follow the rest of the prescribed diet. A small potato pancake would get her a dish of fruit. A small pork chop made the bowl of vegetables more appealing.

John had taken Leila to see Edison twice, but it was Jackie who kept Shannon updated. "The doctors keep asking why you're not visiting. The only smiles I've seen on his face were the stingy ones he gave Leila. He was in a lot of pain when I checked on him early this morning."

"I told him I would come if he needed me. I'm just waiting for his call." She finished making the beds and was about to load the dishwasher when she heard the front door close. Thinking her father had forgotten something, she ran out and found her grandmother gone. Her sweater was still draped across the kitchen chair, and the temperature had dropped overnight. Grabbing a coat from the closet she dashed out the door and spotted Mama Lou walking toward the street that led to the highway.

"Mama Lou! Wait!"

Mama Lou shot her a quick glance and began walking faster. Shannon broke into a full run and finally caught up with her on the corner.

"Mama Lou, where in the world are you going? Hold still and let me put this over your shoulders. It's chilly out here, you'll catch pneumonia."

Mama Lou's stare was blank and unknowing.

"Come on, Mama Lou, let's go back to the house. Where are you trying to go?"

"I'm going home. Leave me alone, I'm going home."

"You need to come back to the house with me. If you want to go somewhere, I'll take you there in the car."

"I'm not going anywhere with you! I don't know you! Get away from me! Help! Help! Get this woman away from me! Help!"

Shannon shrank in embarrassment from the passing stares. The more she tried to talk to her grandmother, the more Mama Lou yelled and screamed.

"We've got to go back to the house right now. Granddaddy is waiting for us. I just heard him calling you. Didn't you hear him? He said 'Come on home, Puddin' Pie.' Didn't you hear him?"

A hint of remembrance crossed the wrinkled brown face and the struggle ceased. Shannon helped her into the coat, buttoned it, and led her back to the house. Once they were inside, she coaxed Mama Lou into taking a mild sedative the doctors had prescribed.

Overcome by the sadness of the past few weeks, she collapsed in tears. She wanted to call her father, but waited until he was home to fall into his arms.

"Oh, Daddy, it was awful! I just couldn't believe how much she changed—in just a few minutes. She was like a different person. I thought I was doing so well. I failed."

"Oh, no, you didn't. You did more than her children were willing to do, and you did it gladly. You've never failed at anything."

"It was a good week. I enjoyed being with her. It helped take my mind off everything else."

"Same here. I suppose that's one of the ways for us to survive the bad times. It's just like the man with the terrible headache. He moaned to his friend to do something to help him forget the pain. His friend walked up to him and stomped on his foot—as hard as he could. The man screamed, 'You damn fool! You just broke my toe.' The friend said, 'Well at least for the time being you forgot about your headache.' That's part of it, honey. We'll get through this."

Mama Lou remained in a state of confusion for three days, only acknowledging Leila with a faint smile. The family had a meeting and decided the only place she would receive constant care was a nursing home. Shannon cried when they left her there with the white coats and antiseptic smells. When she said goodbye, Mama Lou thanked her for caring, which made her cry harder.

Shannon called the hospital and talked to Jackie for updates on Edison's condition, and was not surprised to learn he had fallen deeper into depression. Jackie also said Jeannie had not visited. Shannon applied for a teaching position and tried to find ways to keep busy while Leila was in day school. Donna gladly accepted her help at the store. Thierry called several times, each time becoming more insistent that she return home.

"I'm not asking you to leave your daughter. Bring her with you. If this place isn't big enough we'll get another one. I know your family needs you, but I need you, too. How can I run this business without my major attraction?"

She cried after the last conversation, missing him, but knowing her loyalty and her heart were there in Shepherd. Even if she considered taking Leila to Paris, she could never do it with her father still grieving and Edison feeling the way he did. She busied herself with reading and going to the surrounding towns to shop for nothing in particular. The phone rang as she was about to leave for the store on Friday morning.

"Shannon? Can you come down here today?" Edison's voice was steady but sad. "I need to see you, to talk to you."

"I'm on my way."

She spent the fifteen-minute drive in wonder, but his smile eased her worries.

"Thanks for coming. I missed you. I wanted to wait until Leila came home before asking you to come, but I needed to see you now."

The touch of her hand on his face was magic. She held his face to her own and kissed his forehead. "You look swell. I'm glad you're better."

Using the back of her hand, she stroked his cheek and watched him smile. "Leila has been asking about you since her last visit. Of course I talk to Jackie every day. I've been keeping Mama Lou, but we had to take her to that facility on the highway." She immediately regretted uttering those words.

"I'm sure that's where I'm heading. I can't care for myself."

"Don't be ridiculous. We didn't put Mama Lou there because she's physically disabled. She's strong as a horse. I should know." She told him about her frightful experience, and to her surprise he began laughing.

"I'm sorry. I'm not laughing at your grandmother, but I just got a mental picture of the two of you. I know it was traumatic, but you have to admit it was kind of humorous."

"Yes, I guess it was. I was standing there tugging on her and she was screaming for help and pulling away. If the grandpa trick hadn't worked I would have had to pick her up, throw her over my shoulder, and physically restrain her. Now that would have been something."

"What's going on here?"

Their laughter stopped as Miss Etta entered the room. "I thought we 'greed that you'd stay outta Edison's life and let him and Jeannie work out their problems?"

Anger quickly replaced the smile on Edison's face. "Shannon did as you asked. She stayed away. And guess what? Jeannie still didn't come to see me. Instead I got these."

The all too familiar envelope from one of the town's two attorneys made Shannon tremble. She began stroking Edison's brow. "I'm sorry."

"Don't be. It's not your fault, and I had better not hear anyone say that it is. We had problems before I was shot. I doubted we would get back together, but I never thought she would act this way. She had an attorney write to let me know the things I left in her house were being placed in storage, and detailed what she kept for herself. I don't know why she felt the need to go to all of this trouble. A simple 'goodbye, cripple' would have sufficed. I called and asked Shannon to come here, Mama. I want her here. Do you understand?"

Miss Etta shook her head. "If you'd tried to talk to Jeannie, I know she'd a' been here. She's just hurt that—"

"Don't say it, Mama. Don't ever say it again. That woman doesn't love me. She never did. You look at her and see what isn't there, just as you look at Shannon and see so much less than she is. I don't want you or anyone else stopping people from coming to see me." He took Shannon's hand. "Can you bring Leila up this evening? I've missed her more than you can imagine. Or maybe you know exactly how it feels to miss a part of you."

She smiled down at him. "Of course I will. She's missed you, too. She loves her father, and that isn't dependent on whether or not he can walk." She tilted her head, gloating silently, and took Edison's hand.

On her way out, Jackie stopped her and asked if she had a minute to talk. They went down to the lounge and found an empty table.

"I hope you don't mind, but I suppose I've become Edison's confidant. We've been talking a lot, mostly about you. I know how the two of you got together. How frightened he was when he first asked you out and how much he still loves you. He was never in love with Jeannie, and he's sorry as hell he filed for divorce. I'm only telling you this because I know he won't."

"I believe you. I just don't know if I can do daily battles with Miss Etta. Edison has been through so much, I hoped it would make him emotionally strong. It may have. He did tell his mother that he wanted me to visit and that she had better not try to stop me from coming here." She took a deep breath and smiled. "Do you have any experience with Alzheimer's patients?"

"In the nine years that I've been in this place I've seen everything there is. Are you talking about your grandmother?"

"Yeah. I thought I could handle her. I tried to keep her with me during the day so they wouldn't have to put her away in that place on the interstate. It was going quite well until she spaced out on me. It was shocking, Jackie. She's not ill, not physically. We talked every day and her mind was clear as a whistle. All of a sudden she was walking down the street, going away from the house. I ran and caught up with her and she didn't know who I was. Fifteen minutes earlier we were having a nice conversation. She remembered things I had forgotten, and then suddenly she didn't know who I was."

"It's an awful disease. They say two glasses of red wine a day will prevent it. I've been telling Fred to drink it. I sure would hate having to deal with that."

"It's no fun, believe me, but it made me think. A few months ago my mother was healthy and vibrant, now she's gone. Mama Lou is physically healthy, but unable to care for herself. I love Edison, Jackie. I've always loved him, and I know I always will. If he doesn't get better I can take care of him. I can earn money, I can take care of the house and him and Leila. I may have to strangle Miss Etta, but I'm not letting anyone put him away."

"You have no idea how glad I am to hear you say that. I was wondering what would happen when he goes home. Take him home with you. Tell Miss Etta to shove her attitude up her ass. He's your husband, divorce or not."

For the next week she made daily visits to his room, and came back again most evenings with Leila. His condition improved and he began physical therapy, starting with trying to bend his legs. It was excruciating to watch, but whenever he felt a sensation, he laughed and Shannon laughed with him. The fact that there was some feeling gave them hope. She and Leila would slip into the room when he was asleep and leave little notes on his pillow, or sneak in his favorite French fries.

The holidays loomed before them, bringing a certain amount of sadness for Shannon and John, but especially for J.P.

Shannon tried to replicate the thing that she knew would bring remembrances to her father and to Leila, beginning with the wooden pilgrim set her mother had used for a centerpiece. The brown and gold wreath was placed on the front door and the Thanksgiving dishes were taken from the top shelf of the cabinet, washed, and placed on display in the baker's rack. Things were going well at the store, but the week before Thanksgiving the wholesale supplier failed to make a delivery and some of the shelves were almost empty. Shannon remembered what J.P. had said about the man with the headache.

There was also the matter of her grandmother. She had visited at least once a week since leaving her at the nursing home. Mama Lou was seldom coherent, and severely depressed when she was. Shannon told her father that she was bringing her home for Thanksgiving regardless of her mental state. She asked Savannah to drive out and get their grandmother, and then called her Aunt Rose when Savannah said she'd made other plans. When no one else would go, she made the drive to the facility, packed a small bag with necessities, and headed back into Shepherd.

"You're a good child, Shannon. The others were glad to drop me off with strangers and go on about their lives. J.P. and Doris did a good job of raising you — both of you. You and John are the only grandchildren I can count on to visit me in that old folks' prison."

"I hope you realize why we put you in that facility. We love you so much, but you need constant care and none of us are knowledgeable enough to give you that. Please don't think you've been abandoned. I love you, and I will always visit you and bring you home to be with us whenever I can."

"I understand, my dear. I really do. Sometimes my mind just goes blank. I know it does because there are long periods of time that I can't account for, days even. I try to fight it. I try so hard. Now don't you cry, honey. I know you didn't want to put me away in that place, and neither did your father. See, I hear a lot of things that are spoken in my presence, especially when people think I've gone off into space. I know your mother was planning to stay home and take care of me. I heard Savannah say so. Some of the people at that home are dropped off and forgotten. They're the ones that are not treated well."

"Do they treat you well?"

"Let's just say they'll never win congeniality awards. I trick the old birds, and that keeps them on their toes. Some of the patients are always lost in space, but they know I'm myself quite a bit. What they don't know is when. One day I pretended to go blank. I asked for my mother. When one of them made a wisecrack I told her that she should be ashamed of herself. I said I hoped when she was old, which won't be long, she'll have to wear diapers and eat baby food. She was horrified that I caught her with her drawers down."

Shannon laughed. "You're a hoot. I love you so much."

"I love you, too, baby, and I don't want you to worry about me. Just come to visit when you can. How is Edison? Is he making progress?"

"He's much better now. We're still not sure how much motion he will regain, but he is making progress. I spent time with him before I came to get you."

"Can we go by and see him before we go home?"

Shannon hesitated. "Are you sure you feel up to it? We don't want to tire you out."

"I feel fine, but if you're afraid to chance it, I understand."

"I'm not afraid at all," Shannon lied. Turning the car north, she drove back to the hospital and helped her grandmother inside. Miss Etta and Ray were in with Edison when she peeped her head in the door.

"Hi. I have a surprise for you." Taking Mama Lou's hand she led her to the bed.

"Hello, son. I wanted to come by and see you, and your wife was kind enough to bring me. How are you feeling, Edison?"

"I'm feeling better every day, Mama Lou, and I'm so happy to see you. Come and give me a hug. This is a wonderful surprise."

"Guess you don't 'member that Edison and Shannon got a divorce," Miss Etta said.

"Yes, Etta, I remember that quite well. I know they're not married anymore and *I* know why. That doesn't much matter. They still love each other. God makes one person for each of us. Sometimes it takes us a while to realize it, but when we do, our lives become complete. We don't see other men or other women, just the love we have for each other." She smiled sweetly as everyone looked on in amazement.

"Mama Lou, that was brilliant." Shannon hugged her. "I hope one day I'm half as wise as you are."

"I hope you're never stricken with this damn disease I have. Live your life to the fullest. Don't let your condition get you down, Edison. Keep your head held high and your heart wide open. Hold onto each other, and don't ever let go. Don't waste a precious second of life or love."

"Mama Lou, you truly are the wisest person I've ever known," Edison said. "I wish I had you around every day to give me the wisdom of your years."

"And I wish I could do that, too, but you wouldn't want me around every day. Most of the time I'm okay, but I've been told I'm a mean old hag when my mind starts to wander." She looked at Miss Etta. "At least I know my shortcomings."

She kissed Edison. "I want you to come up to that old folks' prison and see me, and I want you to walk in the door. You just keep fighting and praying. God will do the rest."

Shannon kissed Edison and wished his family a good evening. Inside, she was overcome. The sadness she had felt earlier was drifting away, leaving her soul more at peace than she had known since coming home.

Mama Lou waited until they were in the car to express her thoughts. "That Etta Page is a bitch if I ever saw one. I don't know how she managed to raise a fine son like Edison. That other boy of hers is nice as well. Guess they took after Tito, except they can talk."

Shannon laughed. "Your visit made Edison feel better. I try and dodge Miss Etta's crap because Edison is worth it. I'm making Thanksgiving dinner tomorrow. I have all of the ingredients for a traditional turkey and ham dinner. Is there anything I can get for you? Maybe a special favorite of yours?"

"As a matter of fact there is something I've been craving. I want a glass of good brandy to settle that fine meal I know you're going to cook. Does J.P. have any at the house?"

Shannon laughed. "Should you have alcohol?"

"Now don't you do me like the rest of them. If you ask a person what they want, have the decency to give it to them. Look at me. What the hell can it hurt?"

"I love you so much. I can't think of anyone I'd rather spend time with. Yes, we have brandy. Daddy replenished the bar yesterday."

With Donna working late on Wednesday, Shannon did most of the cooking and everything was a success. It was customary for the oldest and youngest persons in the family to say grace. Mama Lou was still alert and filled with humor.

"Thank you, Lord, for this fine meal, and thank you for my wonderful granddaughter who prepared it. I can't complain about the burdens I'm saddled with because you have given me so much. I pray that on this family holiday you will lift our hearts and fill them with only kind remembrances."

Shannon tightened her grip on her father's hand.

"Bless us all, Lord, and if it's your will, give me the power to turn those crabby nurses at the home into toads. Amen."

Everyone laughed except John, who had griped about having his grandmother institutionalized.

"Okay, Leila, it's your turn now." Shannon stroked her daughter's hair and smiled.

"Dear Lord, I'm thankful for everyone here, especially my mommy. She's the best cook in the world and the prettiest mommy, too. Thank you for our food, and please give my grandmommy a hug from me. They said she's in heaven, so I know you'll see her. Amen."

All eyes filled with tears, even those of John's two boys. Everyone raved over the dinner and the special desserts. John and J.P. went off to watch the ball game, the kids retreated to Leila's room, and Mama Lou stayed in the kitchen, helping Donna and Shannon wash the dishes.

The conversation was light, but Shannon's heart was heavy. She carefully washed and dried her mother's holiday china. Most of the holiday napkins and tablecloths were handmade.

After dinner she dished up generous helpings of everything for Edison, pried Leila away from her cousins, and went to the hospital. They said a prayer of Thanksgiving with Edison and he attempted to eat.

"No appetite today?" Shannon asked.

"I'm sorry. The food is delicious, but this is my third Thanksgiving dinner. I'm going to burst if I finish all of this."

"I knew your mother would bring you a plate. Who brought the other one?" Shannon asked.

"Jeannie. I guess she felt guilty for the bomb she dropped on me. My mother can instill guilt in almost anyone if she sets her mind to it. We finally had a talk, and I think we both agree that there's nothing left for us."

"I'm sorry, Edison."

"Don't be. After all, this is what I did to you, isn't it? I'm sure that in the grand scheme of things we all reap what we sow. I'm happy the two of you came. My day is now complete."

Shannon was glad as well. Her mother's absence had made it impossible to be really happy, but it had been a good day. She went home and spent the rest of the evening talking with her grandmother and Leila. Before going to bed, she called Edison's room and held the phone for Leila to say goodnight.

"You're special," he told her. "I don't deserve your thoughtfulness."

She thanked him and said goodnight. There was more she wanted to say, but she wasn't sure if there would ever be a good time to say it.

# Chapter 11

The wholesale truck arrived at the store on Friday morning. That ended one panic and started another. Donna had been frantic that the shelves were empty but now she had to wonder who she could get to help stock the goods.

Shannon had planned to spend the day with Mama Lou, but it was clear that her grandmother was trying very hard to hang onto her lucidity. She did not want Mama Lou to leave, and knew there would be tears and recrimination.

"Shannon, would you come help me get my things together?" Mama Lou asked. "I feel pretty good right now, but I probably won't stay that way, so let's say goodbye while I still know what it means."

Their goodbye wasn't as heart-wrenching as the last time. Shannon promised to visit on Sunday and bring something good to eat. "If you need me before then, just pick up the phone and call me. I'll make those nurses wish they'd never messed with my Grandma Lou."

"She does mean that, Mama." J.P. helped carry Mama Lou's things to the car.

Shannon kissed her cheek. "I'm very glad you're physically strong. That makes me worry a little less. I also know you're too sharp to let those nurses get past you."

John had also volunteered to help at the store. The adults took turns looking in on the kids, who played in the part of the storeroom that had been equipped with toys and a television. Shannon found work quite therapeutic. Soon they were laughing about Mama Lou or something they remembered from their childhood.

"You know guys, I don't mean to sound sappy or anything, but it's good to be here with the two of you. You have no idea how much I've missed my family."

Her father joined them and made it a real family project. John offered words of caution.

"Sis, I hope you're still happy at the end of the day when your back and legs begin to ache and your nerves are worn to a frazzle, but I do know what you mean about family. It's good to have you home."

"What about Thierry's family?" J.P. asked. "You said they weren't opposed to you, but was there any closeness for you there?"

"When I first went back to Paris, Thierry made it clear that after three unsuccessful marriages and three children he did not seek family togetherness. His youngest child lives in Versailles with his second wife. His parents live there as well. The little girl spent more time with Thierry's mother than with Thierry, which didn't seem to bother him. His oldest kids, the ones from his first marriage, are in boarding school in Switzerland, and only visit during the summer and holidays.

"He comes from a large family, and of course he's wealthier than the rest, so he provides for his parents. They welcomed me, but I had a feeling they were concerned about the continuation of their support if Thierry married again, especially if he married an American."

"Did the two of you ever discuss marriage?" Donna asked.

"No, not really. He kept me entertained with trips to Versailles or Milan. We did visit his family often. I spent enough time with his daughter to form a tight bond. She loved Leila, but she's getting more into being a teenager now. I think he spent more time with his daughter while I was there than he had done with her or the other kids. They became closer and I developed a fondness for his mother."

"I know my opinions are old fashioned, but I don't get these relationships," her father said. "You explained your situation with Thierry, but I know he calls often. Is he aware of your current plans? Has he asked you to come back?"

"He does each time we talk. I know he loves me and I love him. As I told you, I was never in a position to give Thierry a commitment, and I doubt he wanted one. When there's love without commitment, the doors are left wide open. We had a monogamous relationship—at least I know I did—but Thierry always knew I was still in love with Edison, and now I've got Leila's welfare to consider." She gave her father a pleading look. "Can we change the subject?"

"I'm sorry. I didn't mean to embarrass you. It's just that I saw a different side of Thierry when we came to visit. He appeared devoted to you, and quite at ease with Leila. I heard him reading to her in French when the two of you tucked her in. Your mother and I were touched. I don't speak the language very well, but I know the word love when I hear it. We always thought you would take Leila to live with you and Thierry when she was older. Your mother commented that it would be a great experience for her to live and study in Paris. I don't want to see you give up your life there, and later realize you and Edison aren't getting together."

"Edison is Leila 's father. I don't feel right taking her away, especially now. I also toured quite often, and that would mean leaving her with someone else or dragging her around with me. I just think it's best for all concerned if I stay here. As for Edison, I'm not sure where that stands. After all, there's still that chubby little woman over at the diner."

They all chuckled and went on to discuss other things, but Shannon saw Edison's face before her, the face she very much wanted close to her own. After leaving the store for the evening, she took Leila to the hospital and they sat with Edison until they were all yawning.

"I'll be working at the store all day tomorrow. Saturdays are busy and I don't think Donna will have time to do the office duties, so I'm going in to help. I'll try and come by for lunch."

She kissed him goodnight and headed home with Leila, singing and enjoying her daughter's company. When she arrived home, a blue Chrysler was parked in front of the gate. She noticed the rental company name on the front fender and someone sitting in the driver's seat. She recognized the mane of salt and pepper hair.

"Thierry! I can't believe you're here! Why didn't you call? I've been trying to reach you at home, and in Versailles." She failed to mention that she'd assumed he was with another woman and simply didn't wish to take her calls.

"Since you didn't come home for the holidays, I thought I'd come to you." He reached for her, but drew back when he caught Leila's angry stare.

"Hello, Leila, darling! Come and give Thierry a big hug."

Instead of going to Thierry's open arms, Leila clung to Shannon's leg. "Mommy is not going back to Paris."

"Darling, I'm not going to take your mom back to Paris unless she wants to go, and I've already told her

261

she can't return unless she brings you with her. Actually, I was thinking of taking you back with me. Wouldn't you like to live in Paris? Attend French schools? Go to Switzerland for ski trips once a month?"

Her face briefly lit up, and then filled with frowns. "I would, but we can't leave my daddy. He was shot. We have to stay here with Granddaddy, too. Now that Grandmommy is in Heaven, he needs us a lot." Then she relented enough to allow a hug and a kiss.

When they were alone Thierry offered sympathy. "I can see what you're up against. I wanted to cry when she made that statement about your dad needing the two of you. As far as I'm concerned, the three of you can come to Paris. I like your family, and I love you. I've missed you so much. I've wanted to fly over since you left."

"Leila is afraid right now because of all that's happened. Edison's mother has alienated her with the same gripe about my leaving, and, with her father lying in that bed and my mother gone, she has no one other than her grandfather and me. The woman that Edison planned to marry didn't want her to live with them. I have to stay here, Thierry. I can't let them down."

"Are you speaking of your family or your ex-husband?"

"I'm speaking of my daughter, primarily. She's my responsibility. I've shifted that responsibility to others long enough. I love you and I miss our life together, but I can't leave my daughter right now, and I can't take her away from her father until he's better."

"How long do you think this will continue? I love you, but life does go on."

She didn't consider his statement an ultimatum, just a simple declaration of facts. "I know that, and I'm not asking you to alter your life or your plans. We all have choices to make, and in this case I have a responsibility to make one that is in the best interest of my daughter. You've been wonderful to me. You've built my career to heights I never imagined, and you were there for me when I needed you. I will always love you for that. I know this isn't fair to you. I wish it could be different."

"My life has never been as good as it is with you. I don't want to lose you. I knew you would have to accept responsibility for your daughter at some point, and I'm prepared to live with that. I love your little girl. Leila can live with us in Paris."

"I know you're not comfortable with children. You don't spend time with your own kids. I couldn't do this to you or to her."

"There's something you don't understand. You're speaking of my feelings back when you first came to live with me. Things changed over time, Shannon. I've changed. I would not just accept your daughter into my life, I would welcome her, love and care for her as my own. Give it some thought. I'm going to Chicago tomorrow, then on to New York. I was hoping to spend the night in your arms, but I can see that's not possible, so can you just sit with me for a while. Let's not say goodbye just yet."

They talked for a long time and Thierry kept reminding her of what she stood to lose if she didn't return to pursue her career. She accepted his goodnight kiss, but her face was immediately shadowed in guilt.

"I've missed you so much. I've missed being loved." Shannon could admit her feelings, but did not offer a final resolution to their relationship. There were no easy answers. The next morning she told him she would keep in touch and watched him drive away.

❦

After Leila and J.P. went to the store, Shannon dressed in the red outfit Edison had admired and went to the hospital. He was sitting on the side of the bed with his feet propped on a chair.

"Hey. This is a new position for you. What gives?" She bent to kiss his forehead and was gently pushed away.

"I thought you would be halfway across the ocean by now."

She stood back and stared at his angry face. "Thierry had business in the States and stopped here to discuss my plans."

"I wasn't asking for an explanation. You preferred him to me when I was healthy, so I'm sure you wouldn't trade a romantic Frenchman for a cripple. I don't need your pity, and you can resolve your guilt on your own time. Go on to Thierry. I've heard that Frenchmen are excellent lovers. Is that true?"

"Is Jeannie a good lover?"

"You're right. I shouldn't question you about your private life. It's none of my business. You have a right to live as you choose. I'm glad you came by. I wanted to tell you that I've changed my mind about you taking Leila to Paris. There's nothing I can do for her now, so go ahead, take her with you. Just make sure she's treated well, and let her write to me sometimes."

"You don't know what you're saying. If you're upset that Thierry was here, just say so. There's no need to take this to the table. I'm not going with Thierry."

"Why not? That's where you belong. You're urbane and sophisticated. There's no place in Shepherd for a woman like you. I want Leila to grow up with her mother's sense of style and grace, so she should be with you. Jeannie and I are getting back together. She'll take care of me, so there's no need for you to feel guilty about leaving. I don't need you, and I don't want you here."

She stared in disbelief. His controlled anger was worse than the times he yelled. She began walking toward the bed but was stopped by a verbal attack she would never have believed Edison capable of launching.

"Give it up already! I'm marrying Jeannie and that's all there is to it. You should leave before she gets here. Just bring Leila to see me before you take her away."

She stood still, too shaken to move.

"It's okay, Shannon. You can go now. I'm fine. I don't need all these complications in my life. I have enough already."

She still did not move.

"Would you just get the hell out of here?"

"What's going on?" Jackie hurried into the room "Is Edison okay?" She looked at Shannon's face. "Come on outside with me. You're shaking."

"He found out that Thierry was in town," Shannon said after they walked into the hallway. "He and Jeannie are getting back together. He wants me to take Leila and go to Paris."

"And you believed that? You told me you were going to stand your ground and let Edison know how you felt about him. Now you're running away?"

"He said—"

"He's full of shit!" Jackie interrupted. "Jeannie hasn't been here and they aren't getting back together. He lied to keep you from feeling sorry for him."

Miss Etta walked past Edison's room, peeped in the door, and headed over to Shannon. "Lord, what you done now?"

Jackie spoke quickly. "Shannon, I'm not trying to defend Edison, and he would probably kill me if he knew I was telling you this, but he's had a terrible morning. He had some tingling in his legs and thought he could walk. The therapist left a walker close enough for him to reach, so he tried to go to the bathroom." She looked from one woman to the other. "Needless to say, he didn't make it. Not only that, but he failed to tell the nurse who found him that he needed a bedpan. Now you know a man like Edison is going to find that hard to deal with. He's hurt, angry, and ashamed, and he's taking it out on you. Don't leave him now. He needs you desperately. He and Jeannie are not getting back together and you know it. That was his pride talking. Foolish pride, if you ask me. Now go on back in there and stand up to him."

Jackie held her arm out as Miss Etta turned to go into the room. "Let her help your son deal with his frustrations. When they've had a chance to talk, you go in and show him how much you love him. That's what he needs, Mrs. Page. He needs the love and support of those who matter."

Shannon took a deep breath and charged back into the room.

"Don't worry, I'm not going to hang around until Jeannie gets here. I just need to ask you a question. It's a very important question, but you should be able to answer it fairly quickly. I've been labeled the selfish, manipulative bitch who deserted her husband and child. Now, I want you to think back to when we were first dating. I passed on opportunities to attend prestigious universities to be at Grambling with you. What did you give up before, during, or after our marriage?"

"I wondered if you blamed me for that. It was your choice. I didn't ask you do it."

"You had your say, now it's my turn, so just shut up until I finish. And yes, I decided to go to Grambling because I loved you and wanted to be with you. You didn't ask me to and I don't blame you. I also agreed to get a teaching certificate, though I had no intention of teaching. I returned here because this was where you wanted to come and join the police force, which you did against my strong objections. Stop me if I say something that isn't true. You didn't sacrifice a damn thing you wanted, Edison. Nothing."

The beaten expression on his face tempted her to quit, but she kept going. "Everything we did was at your behest. It was what you wanted. My feelings didn't count. When I wanted to do something for myself, you filed for divorce. You preached about having time with Leila, but went on to Jeannie and left her with your mother. We both know how that turned out."

His expression made her profoundly sorry for him, but that was the one thing she could not admit. "I've been here with you because I wanted to be. That's the only reason. Not because I pity you, and certainly not because I feel guilty. I'm not the one who drove you into the night to meet up with a bullet."

His head fell to his shoulder.

"I don't need to feel sorry for you. You're doing a great job of that all by yourself. That bullet took away your manhood, and I don't mean your legs. It took away the determination in your heart. It drained your will to fight."

Her eyes were filled with tears but she continued. "I went to Paris to fulfill a dream. Nothing more. I should have returned when I promised, or never gone at all, and that I'll always regret. I guess I never believed you'd divorce me. When you did, my heart shattered in a million pieces. In time, when the pain and loneliness became unbearable, Thierry was there. He was kind and sweet. I love him a lot."

She did not allow the frown on his face to impede her release. Everything that was kept pent up inside suddenly came tumbling forward in pain, anger, and determination. "I love him…but I was never in love with him. You see, Edison, there wasn't enough left for him. My love was still here with you."

Sobbing, she pulled a tissue from the box on his table. "Now I'm leaving. You go on back to Jeannie. I wish the two of you nothing but happiness. I did not go back with Thierry, and I have no plans to return to Paris to live, but don't worry, I won't interfere with your life. Daddy can bring Leila here to see you. That is, if you still want to see her."

"Don't leave. I'm sorry." He held out his limp hand. "I took my frustrations out on you."

She waved. "Don't sweat it. I'll live. I hope you can walk out of here soon and I hope you have a happy life. Whenever you want to see Leila just give me a call. There are no restrictions on your time with her."

"Come over here. Please. I'm not getting back with Jeannie and I don't want to. Don't you know how much you mean to me? I don't want you to go. I don't ever want you to go. I…I just don't know if I'm going to be able to cope with this, and I don't want you or Leila to see me fall apart. I'm not brave like you are. Right now I'm scared to death. I'm afraid of not being able to walk, of spending my life as an invalid…" He paused. "I'm afraid of looking at you and seeing pity on your face. I don't want to live that way. I'd rather be dead—"

She covered his lips with her fingers, put her arms around him, and they cried together. "You're wrong about me. I'm not that brave. I'm scared of everything, but I have tried to brave the storm because I didn't know what else to do. The day I got those divorce papers in the mail I was so frightened and so devastated I forgot to breathe. I stood there with no one to hold onto. Strange place, different people, and no one to love."

She accepted the warmth of his body against hers. "I'm still scared, for myself and for you. I'm scared of what life in a wheelchair will do to you. I can deal with it and so can Leila. We're not feeling sorry for you. We love you. We need you. I need you, in whatever form God gives you to me."

They held onto each other fiercely, kissing the tears away. "I promised to be with you through sickness and health. I've always loved you."

"I love you, too, and I've been such a fool. I suppose I should thank Jeannie. I would have been miserable without you. I'm sorry I hurt you, and if you'll let me, if you can love me this way, I'll spend the rest of my life trying to make it up to you. If you can accept me the way I am, then please marry me. Marry me again and stay with me forever."

Etta cleared her throat behind them. "I hate to in'erupt, but I need to talk to you 'fore visitin' hours over."

Shannon kissed him again, long and hard, not caring that his mother stood watching. "Tomorrow is Sunday, so I will bring Leila by after church. I'll say a prayer for you. I love you."

"I love you. Come back as soon as you can."

"What's wrong now?" Miss Etta asked when he covered his face with his hands. "Did that girl upset you? You want a doctor?"

"No, I don't want a doctor, and I'm not upset. I am lost and confused, Mama. You see, I'll be going home soon, but I don't know where home is." He faced her. "Where do I go when I leave here, Mama?"

"That's a silly question. You come home. I'll get your things from Jeannie and have the room at the back fixed up for ya."

"There's a big problem with what you just said. When I leave here, no matter where I am for the rest of my life, I want Shannon by my side. I want to marry her. I can't offer her much now, but if she's willing to accept me, I'll do my best to make a life with her and our child."

"I know this is hard, but you can't let that ha'pen, Edison. Don't back-peddle 'cause she's but'erin up to you now."

"Shannon was out of my life. She was never out of my heart. She's got every reason to run like hell back to Paris and the life she had there. I gave her every opportunity to do so. Why would she say she wants to stay, to be with me, if she doesn't?"

"Won't be the first time she lied. She just needed a couple of months in Paris, remember? Next thing you know, she's over there shackin' up with that man. They coulda had a fuss for all you know. Maybe he come here to try and make up with her. I'm tellin' you, she'll go back."

"Do you say that because you don't see a reason for her to stay here? You don't think she could love me?"

"Shannon lost her mother. That's bound to humble her some, but that girl's head been in the air since she was born. I don't think she could change if she wanted to."

He was overjoyed when Emmett rapped on the door. "Come in, man. Tell me what's been going on."

He was disappointed to learn there had been no further development in apprehending the dope pushers in Shepherd, but talking to Emmett placed him back in touch with his world.

Leila was asleep when Shannon got home. Miss Brooks was sitting on the sofa, as close to J.P. as she could get. The History Channel was blaring something about post-war Britain. J.P.'s eyes were locked on the screen, but Miss Brooks's eyes were locked on him.

"Is something wrong, Daddy?" She spoke with forceful irritation.

Miss Brooks quickly moved away.

"No, honey. Nothing's wrong at all. Why do you ask?"

Instead of going from the hallway to the kitchen, Shannon walked around the sofa, her face filled with contempt.

"Honey?" J.P. stood beside her. "You asked if anything was wrong, and judging from the tone of your voice and the look on your face, I'm redirecting that question to you. How was your visit to the hospital? Has Edison's condition changed?"

"Edison is physically the same, though he appears to be suffering greatly over his diminished physical abilities." She half smiled. "We had a breakthrough tonight, Daddy. I finally told him how I felt, and he says he never stopped loving me. He even said so in front of his mother."

"That's great. I prayed for this to happen. You and Edison belong together, but something is wrong. I can sense it in your voice."

"Nothing's wrong." She looked down at the sofa and back to her father. "Don't worry about me."

"If you don't want me to worry, you'd better tell me what's wrong. If it isn't Edison, then what is it?"

She was puzzled. He didn't seem to feel that anything was out of place, which meant either he didn't know, or he was pretending. She shook her head. "Nothing, really. Just another run-in with Miss Etta. I'm fine. I'm also tired. I think I'll take a shower and turn in."

"Shannon, I brought some coconut pie for you," Miss Brooks said. "I heard you say it was your favorite."

"Thank you. It is my favorite. My mother made the best coconut pie in the world."

Seeing the disappointment she had caused, she quickly added, "You're a very good cook, so I'm sure I'll enjoy it. Thank you, again. That was very thoughtful of you."

She looked at her father. "I really am tired. I'm going to take a bath, but I'll come back downstairs later."

Once out of sight, she chided herself. *I'm beginning to sound like Etta Page. I don't know why Miss Brooks keeps hanging around, but I know I can trust Daddy. He would never cheat on Mom or her memory.*

Miss Brooks was still there when she returned. Seeing that it was only nine-thirty, she went back to her room and dressed.

"I'm not sleepy, and since Leila is out cold, I think I'll go for a drive." She grabbed a jacket and headed for her brother's house before J.P. could respond. She had to talk to someone who might be able to help her understand.

"I saw that you were upset when she came over before," Donna said. "I didn't say anything because there was so much going on. I was a little shocked when she came in the store today and asked about J.P. She's been in St. Louis helping her sister with their mom. Apparently they had to place their mother in a facility.

I asked why she didn't take her. I wanted to add that she must have a lot of free time, since she's constantly hanging around J.P."

"Okay, you two." John frowned. "You're sounding like two old hens. Daddy would never cheat on Mom. Now that she's gone, I'm not sure how he's feeling. Miss Brooks pampers him. I'm sure he's been missing that, so let's give it the benefit of the doubt."

"Oh, I give him every benefit there is. It's Miss Brooks I'm not sure of. She just keeps bringing food. She knows damn well I can cook. This time she brought me coconut pie. Thankfully, I'm too polite to tell her where to put it."

Seeing that Donna had also noticed and was uncomfortable with the situation, Shannon took her brother's comments into consideration, as well as her father's oblivious or naïve actions. Maybe she was making too much of the situation.

She tried to slip in the back door unnoticed but J.P. called out loudly.

"Shannon! Come in here, please."

"Hey, Dad. I'm tired, so I think I'll turn in."

He hurried to the stairway. "I need you to tell this old fool what's going on here. Do you know why Valerie Brooks keeps bringing food over here all the time? Is that why you seemed so upset when you first got home this evening?"

Startled at his questions and his tone, she frowned and shook her head. "If you're asking whether I knew Miss Brooks has a thing for you, yes, I did. We all did."

"Oh, my God! Why didn't someone tell me? Did you think I was having some kind of relationship with her? Is that what you thought?"

"I knew you would never cheat on Mom. I also know you're vulnerable right now. I thought you needed help to deal with the pain of losing Mom just like I needed Thierry's help to go from married to divorced. Donna's mother said Miss Brooks never married because she's always had a thing for you. John said Donna and I were overreacting and I accepted that."

"So everybody is talking about it? I must be the biggest fool in Shepherd. The whole world. For God's sakes! My wife just died. How could anybody, even Valerie, think I'd be…oh, my God."

"Don't get so upset. I'm sure she didn't mean to be disrespectful. When did you know something was going on?"

He wrung his hands. "When she asked if I thought you were upset about us. I had no idea what she was talking about."

Shannon repressed a smile. "What did you say?"

"I asked what *us* she meant. She…stroked my arm, started unbuttoning my shirt." He made a face of sheer distaste. "I was so shocked, I didn't know what to say. I asked if she was crazy. My wife just died. I was sit-

277

ting on that sofa trying to forget that the woman I love wasn't there beside me. I wasn't even thinking of Valerie as a woman. We've known each other since we were kids. How did I let this happen, and why the hell didn't somebody stop me?"

"Daddy, you asked if she was crazy?"

"Yes, I did. And then I told her she'd better leave. I felt like a fool. Why on earth would I want that old woman?"

"Miss Brooks is not as old as you are."

"Then I'm old. Somebody is old. Your mother certainly didn't look that old."

"I think Miss Brooks is actually younger than Mom. What you don't realize is that your wife was the most beautiful, youthful, gracious lady in these parts. You also don't realize you're quite a handsome dude in your own right."

"Right now, I'm just horrified. At first I thought she was here to visit Mama Lou. I thought they were friends." He looked at Shannon. "How could she think I would consider being with another woman right now? Maybe she is crazy."

"I don't know, Daddy. She started hanging around and you didn't discourage her. She sat there and watched a football game the other day. I'll bet she had no clue as to what was going on. Don't be upset with her."

"I'm sorry I talked to her the way I did. I'd never purposely hurt the woman, but she shocked me. I didn't know what to say. Every second I spent with your mother is with me." He touched his chest. "And will be until I die. Maybe I did subconsciously lead her on. She kept talking about things that happened when we were kids. I'll admit, her conversation was a slight diversion, but that was before I knew her intent. Now it just gives me the creeps. I have to think of a way to apologize. I certainly can't leave it the way it is."

"I would tell you to send flowers, but that might not be the best thing to do. Get some rest. We'll figure it out tomorrow."

Relieved, she went to her room and texted John. "The Valerie Brooks incident is hilarious & sad. Tell you tomorrow."

❧

After promising Leila they would visit Edison later in the day, Shannon went out for some necessary shopping. Hurrying to share her surprise with Edison, she rushed in the door, but stopped when she saw Jeannie sitting on the edge of the bed.

"Oh, hi, Jeannie." She looked at Edison and retained her smile. "I can come back later, if you'd like."

"No, we were just discussing some unfinished business. Come on in. Jeannie was just telling me about

279

a wheelchair she has at…her house. I guess I'll need one of those."

"That's what I came by to tell you. I just bought one. I also bought a wheelchair accessible van. Of course, you won't need it very long, and when you're finished with it, we can donate it to that facility where Mama Lou lives."

"Perfect! You just think of everything."

"She certainly does," Jeannie growled. "I'd better get back to the diner. We can finish discussing those investments some other time."

"Goodbye, Jeannie," Shannon said while smothering her anger. "I'm sure Edison appreciates you stopping by." She didn't look at Edison's face, but continued making small talk to help hide her feelings. "I swear Savannah gets stranger by the day. I went by earlier to get some things for Mama Lou, and that girl was as jumpy as a cat. I know she had some guy there. Either that, or she wears size 11 sneakers."

She watered the plants and continued chatting, though his answers were one-word mumbles. She wondered if he was embarrassed, if Jeannie had said something to upset him, or if she really had walked in on something intimate. Either way, she was not going to let it shake her—at least to the point that he could see. When enough time had passed for her to feel safe, she hugged him and took his water pitcher down the hallway to the ice machine. When she turned the corner in the hallway, she saw Valerie Brooks hurrying away.

"Miss Brooks," she called after her. When she didn't turn around, Shannon followed and called her name again. This time she stopped, but did not turn around.

"Hi, Miss Brooks. I just wanted to thank you for the coconut pie. It is delicious. You're a great cook. Daddy loves the chocolate pie as well. If I didn't keep an eye on him, I think he would eat it for breakfast."

"I'm glad you like it."

Shannon really looked at her for the first time and realized she was quite pretty, though her hairstyle and mannerisms made her appear older than she was. "Are you in a big hurry? Can we talk for a few minutes?"

"Actually, I have—"

"It will only take a minute or two. I just need someone to talk to, if it's okay."

She looked up. "Okay. We can go to the lounge right over here."

"Thank you. I appreciate you taking the time to listen." They sat at a table for two in a corner of the room. Shannon folded the newspaper that someone had left behind and cleared the space between them. "I want to talk to you about my grandmother."

Seeing her face brighten and feeling some of the tension disappear, Shannon felt better. "I'm sure you've heard we had to place Mama Lou in a full-care facility. I'm just sick about it, and so is Daddy. So much has happened recently, and it's all so hard on him."

"I know. He told me how bad he feels about it. I just returned from doing the same thing with my mother in St. Louis. I tried to get her to live with me, but she said she was never coming to Mississippi again. I can't stay in St. Louis."

"Oh, isn't it sad? I hope she adjusts to her new surroundings. Mama Lou is having a tough time. Since you're a nurse, I wanted to ask if you would go out there with me sometimes and give me your observations."

"I'll be happy to go out there. I told J.P. I would visit Miss Louise. I'll make something special for her and take it out there. I know you have your hands full. I heard the sheriff is going to be all right. I'm thankful for that."

"He's doing much better. I'm praying the paralysis isn't permanent, but I'm thankful he made it through surgery. If you don't mind my asking, were you ever married, Miss Brooks?"

She shook her head. "I never married."

"Did you just not meet the right man, or was there someone you really loved and it didn't work out?"

"There was someone. I loved him very much, but I don't think he even knew." She fidgeted in the chair.

"He loved someone else, so it wouldn't have worked out anyway."

"That's painful, isn't it?"

She nodded.

"I guess it happens to all of us at some point in our lives." She stopped talking when she heard a low moan in the middle of the room. Shannon watched the bulky figure sit up on the couch. Miss Etta turned toward them and she wondered if she had kept her presence a secret just to eavesdrop.

"I'll let you get back to your duties, Miss Brooks. Thank you for listening and for that wonderful pie."

She had debated whether to invite her back for dinner, but considering the obvious shyness and recent embarrassment, she thought it best to leave well enough alone.

# Chapter 12

Instead of waking Leila, Shannon stood next to the bed and watched her sleep. So many firsts had happened in her daughter's life, and she had not been there to see them. She wondered if Leila had asked for her, had cried for her at night. She wondered how she could have been so thoughtless.

"Come on, honey. Get up." Shannon gently separated Leila from the warmth of her covers.

"Is Daddy all right? Did something happen?"

"Daddy is going to be all right, but I think he needs some cheering up, and that's where you come in. But I have a big surprise for you as well."

"What is it? Tell me."

The eager excitement of a child drove away the drowsiness and added a glow of sunshine. Their baby really did have the best of both of them.

"It's something you'll have to see once we get to the hospital." Shannon pushed away her concerns of Etta's interference. She did not want anything to dull the wonderful high she got when thinking about the man she loved. It was exciting to know her daughter would get what she desperately wanted—her parents back together.

She was raring to get Edison back on his feet so that she could get him back on his back.

It wasn't just the lovemaking. Intimacy with the man she loved was the one thing that made her feel whole. The best sleep of all had happened afterwards, when Leila was sleeping between them.

Calling ahead, she let Edison know they were coming and bringing a hot breakfast. Everyone brought food, but he was usually at the mercy of hospital meals for breakfast and had expressed his distaste for "cardboard toast." Leila carried the thermos of coffee and Shannon juggled the covered stay-warm dish of scrambled eggs, pancakes, and bacon, thick and crisp, just the way he liked.

"An early morning visit from the two prettiest girls in Shepherd. I know my day is going to be good." Edison smiled and Leila lunged for his neck. "Hi, darling. I'm so glad you came."

He released his daughter and reached for Shannon.

Leila stood by in silence as her parents kissed. Looking from one to the other, she squealed. "You kissed my mommy! You two aren't angry at each other anymore?"

Shannon folded Leila inside her free arm. "This is my big surprise. What do you think?"

"I think I'm glad. Will you be my mommy and daddy together now?"

They both laughed. "I'd like nothing better." Edison's face had brightened considerably. "But right now I need to get well for your mommy and for you."

Shannon saw the pain deep in his eyes. If the paralysis remained, he would never feel the same about himself. Having to face that possibility made facing Miss Etta seem very insignificant.

Edison was making marginal progress, moving his toes and raising his legs slightly. The doctor made a final assessment before releasing him, giving him high marks for his efforts and advising him to keep his therapy appointments and continue working on his own.

Shannon drove the van over for Tito and Miss Etta to see, and to let them know she planned to drive Edison home. "This will make it easy for us to get him to and from his therapy and doctor's appointments. I would like to pick him up tomorrow if you don't mind. The van will stay here so the two of you can easily transport him as well."

"That's sweet of you," Tito said. "We'll wait for you to bring him home."

Etta smiled slightly and nodded, which was more than Shannon expected. She was going to be in Edison's life and wanted very much to keep peace with his mother. She also knew a bumpy road lay ahead. Driving the van to the hospital, she waited with Edison until the doctor signed his discharge papers.

Jackie wheeled Edison to the curb. "Look at this. How many sheriffs do you know who get curb service? You're being treated like the president," Jackie told him before kissing his cheek. "Let me know if he gives you a hard time, Shannon."

He maneuvered the chair onto the ramp, and waved.

"Good job, but don't get too used to this. It's only temporary," Shannon told him. "You'll be walking soon. When that happens I'm going to donate the chair to Shady Meadows in Mama Lou's name."

She saw the apprehension on his face. "Don't worry, sweetheart. It's going to be okay. I love you so much. I refuse to have negative thoughts, and I won't allow you to have them, either. We're in this together and we'll make it work." His weak smile was heart-wrenching, but she maintained her cheerful façade.

His mother cried when Shannon wheeled him into the house, and together, they helped him into his bed. Shannon looked with distaste at the drab blue wallpaper, dated and dark, and the heavy curtains that blocked light and air. She pulled the curtains back and grabbed the pulley on the blind but it would not retract.

"You know Christmas is coming. I think I'll put a tree in here for you. Would you like that?"

He had spoken very little since leaving the hospital. She saw him looking around the room.

"My things are all here. I guess Mama brought them from Jeannie's house. What am I going to do now? What do I do with my days? What do I do with the rest of my life?"

"I honestly don't know, but we'll get through it one day at a time. I'll be here so much you'll get sick of seeing me. I can leave Leila here with you sometimes. She's great company."

His face only grew sadder.

"Oh, honey, I know this is hard for you. I wish to God there was something I could do, but I promise to always be here for you. Please try to look for a rainbow at the end of all of this."

"I'm trying. My life would be different now if I had only listened to you. We should have gone somewhere else and started our family. I should have found a safer job that paid enough to provide for my family. Hell, we could have had at least two more kids by now."

"There's no use looking back. There will be good years for us—lots of good years. We both made choices that may not have been the wisest, but here's no need to sit around and play what if. You know what my grandfather used to say about that."

He tried to smile. "Your mother always said that most of your vocabulary came from your grandfather, but I think I get your meaning."

"If we had waited to get married. If I hadn't started singing. If I hadn't gone to Paris. If you had turned down that deputy position. If, if, if." She hugged him hard. "If I hadn't loved you so much, we wouldn't have married and had the sweetest little girl in the world." Standing back, she looked at his crestfallen face.

"There were problems in our marriage, Edison. Not enough trust on your part and maybe a little too much selfishness on mine. I shouldn't have gone to Paris. I certainly shouldn't have signed those divorce papers. I should have fought for you."

She leaned over and kissed him. "Let's just be thankful you survived the shooting, and we found each other again. Remember what Mama Lou said? Hold on and don't let go."

"I don't deserve you."

"That's true." She kissed him hard. "But since I'm hopelessly in love with you, you're stuck, and there's nothing you can do about it."

She stayed busy, and for that she was very grateful. Between her daughter, working at the store, caring for Edison, and visiting her grandmother, there was little time for regrets. Her father accepted more responsibility at the store because, she suspected, the house held too many memories.

Edison filled her in on some of the things that had happened in Shepherd, including Bobby Joe and Carmen's unfortunate circumstances.

"I still don't want to believe he set me up," he told her while helping choose a wallpaper pattern to replace the dreary one in his bedroom. "No one has seen him since it happened. That's not a good sign."

"Emmett is still wrestling with that drug situation, and I don't think he's any closer to solving it. Look at this." She laid samples of wood finishes on the bed. "I asked your mother if I could install wooden blinds on your windows. She never said no, so tell me which one you like best."

"I'd like for you to stop fussing over me this way, but I do love you for it." He pointed to a walnut finish. "Mama said you wanted to cheer me up by making the room brighter."

"Your daughter and I are planning to put in a tree in that corner, and you can't argue with that. It was her idea."

"Two women fussing over me. How many men are that lucky?"

She knew he was trying to adjust. "I'm the lucky one. I get you all to myself back here in this room."

"Now you're flirting. In case you're wondering, I do have a few working parts."

She wanted him to remember the evening in the hospital. For several reasons, she felt it was important to their future. "I might just have to see how well those parts can function, Sheriff Page."

❧

When the work was completed, she and Leila brought over a small tree and decorated it with twinkling lights and musical Santas.

In her attempts to drive away his sadness, he noticed hers. "You're trying very hard to keep smiling, but I can tell something is wrong. I would never hold you to a commitment knowing that I'm only half a man. If you're having regrets about—"

"Stop it." She laid her head on his chest. "The one thing I'm certain of right now is that having you in my life is the best thing that could happen." She looked at him. "You're right, I'm trying hard, but Edison, I miss my mother so much. This was her favorite time of year. She would decorate…." She struggled against the sobs in her throat.

"Sometimes I can be so dense. I'm sorry, baby. I know how you feel. I miss her, too. I've missed those holidays we had together and missed having your family in my life. I'm just glad I have you and now we both have our baby."

He held her face in his hands. "Let's make a deal, okay? In spite of everything that's wrong in our lives, let's try and look to the future we're going to have with our little girl, and to the happiness we both deserve."

Shannon helped Donna with the holiday rush but found time to spend with Edison until she went over with a bag of Christmas goodies and found Jeannie in his bedroom. Hurt and angry, she spoke politely, excused herself and drove around for hours, thinking and trying to sort out her life. When she returned home her father told her that Edison had called several times. She picked up the phone on his next call.

"I didn't know she was coming by. I hope you're not angry with me. There was nothing going on with Jeannie. I love you and—"

"Edison, hold on. I'm not angry with you and I need no explanation. After all, you and Jeannie were planning to marry, you lived together, and I'm sure there are issues and feelings between you."

J.P. watched her face throughout the conversation, and questioned her after she hung up the phone. "Do you think it's wise to get so involved with Edison right now? This whole thing with Jeannie makes me very nervous, especially since I know Etta wants the two of them together. Edison is sort of at his mother's mercy now. I don't want you to be hurt."

She was hurt, but was also determined not to let it show. "Daddy, I'm not letting that woman come between Edison and me. I'm doing what I should have done all along, fighting for what's mine."

Edison struggled against the numbness in his legs, held onto the chair, and tried to walk. The prescribed exercises left him drained, but also helped him sleep, and he needed that. The dreams that evolved when his consciousness lapsed were the bright spots in his world. In them he was whole, his life was good, and Shannon was by his side.

He did not understand why Jeannie had suddenly developed an interest in him. She apologized and admitted most of her anger was simply jealousy over his feelings for Shannon. When she started to sob, he had wanted to comfort her just as she had done for him when his world fell apart. He weighed his feelings for the two women and knew he could never love any woman the way he loved Shannon, but she was sophisticated beyond his reach, even when he was whole. The questions he asked himself added to his anguish. He kept thinking that he would feel differently if he could walk, and then reminded himself that he had been walking the first time Shannon left.

Shannon smiled through her next visit without mentioning Jeannie. Her life was full. He knew she was there to comfort her father. That also made him wonder if she would leave when J.P.'s suffering eased.

Emmett and Ray were there almost every day. Emmett was now acting sheriff, but still sought Edison's advice on his daily duties. The rest of the family dropped by often, but it was Ray who made him and Shannon smile. Ray had always admired him, especially when he married the prettiest girl in Shepherd.

Shannon planned events with mutual friends, including a dinner party with Jackie, to lighten his loneliness. He had made a fool of himself afterwards. Alcohol had loosened his tongue, and though he knew he was babbling on about wanting and needing her, he could not stop. Whether they were alone or in a crowd, he constantly wondered how he could have ever let her go. His second greatest fear was watching her walk away again.

≈

Christmas was much the same as Thanksgiving for Shannon, except Mama Lou's clarity did not last through the planned two days at home. The staff at the facility had advised Shannon that her episodes were more frequent, and were lasting longer than before. Determined to make her grandmother's holiday as happy as possible, Shannon fussed over her with new gowns and robes and warm slippers.

They all listened to Mama Lou's stories of earlier Christmas holidays, as Shannon taped her tales of yesteryear. Each time her mother's role in those stories was mentioned, Shannon fought to hold her tears.

For Edison's sake, and in deference to the spirit she wanted to feel, Shannon hugged Etta and watched Leila pass out gifts to her grandparents and to her father. Shannon noticed that Edison's spirits were very low. This was typical for a holiday, and in spite of her own pain and sadness, she tried to chase away his.

She talked of the past, and earlier Christmas days when they were so in love and happy together. It didn't help. Even Leila was not able to make him smile. After exhausting all efforts, she helped his mother tuck him into bed and inserted one of the movies she had given him into the DVD player in his bedroom. After Leila said goodnight and started for the car, Shannon returned and whispered in his ear.

"There was one thing missing from my wish list, Mr. Page. You owe me a lot of loving, and sooner or later, I aim to collect." She kissed him deep and long.

This time he managed a faint smile. "You don't want to do that. If you think you're frustrated now, wait until afterwards. You've known excitement that few of us will know, including a French lover."

She refused to take the bait and wondered how he would feel when she told him that the passionate scene from his dream had really happened.

⠀⠀⠀⠀⠀⠀⠀⠀⠀⠀⠀⠀⠀⠀⠀⠀*≈*

When Shannon saw Thierry's number on the caller ID, she assumed it was a simple Merry Christmas call.

"I'm so sorry to do this, but I can't get you released from the New Year's Eve gig. I thought the matter was settled until I took over a contract for the replacement act. It's a long sold-out performance. They're threatening to sue for triple the evening's receipts."

"Thierry, that's less than a week away. How am I supposed to make this happen? I haven't rehearsed, I don't know how quickly I can get flights from here to Paris—"

"It's all arranged," he interrupted. "The only way I could get those people to back off was to set everything in motion right there before them. I had my assistant make your plane reservations to New York City. My jet will be there when you arrive. I've set up rehearsal schedules, and given my personal guarantee that you would be there. If you want, I'll make arrangements to fly your family over for the concert. Edison as well, if he'll come."

She had told Thierry of Edison's mistrust. "You don't know how this will hurt him. He already thinks I'm wishing for my life there, but it's Leila I'm worried about."

"Do you want me to add Leila to your travel plans?"

"No. I don't see how I'm going to prepare for that show as it is. I'll just have to make them understand. When am I leaving Jackson?"

"Two days from now. I know that gives you hardly any time to rehearse, but it's the very earliest I could arrange the connecting flights. You're great, with or without rehearsals."

She hung up, thinking she had to reassure Leila and Edison that she would return. Her father agreed.

"Tell Leila tomorrow morning. If you wait until the last minute, she'll think you're trying to slip away."

"Edison will think that no matter what." She worked the scenario through her mind and came up with a plan. Donna helped her with the final details the next morning.

"Leave Leila back there with the boys and spend some time with Edison this morning. If his parents are home, just get him in the van and leave."

Encouraged, she called and asked Tito to pull the van close to the front gate. The ramp she had installed was next to the steps. She could get Edison out of the house and into the van without their help. He was in the wheel-chair when she arrived.

"Unlock your wheels, my dear. You and I are going for a ride."

"Where are we going?"

"Just sit back and relax, Sheriff Page." She helped him to the van, called to Tito that they were going for a ride, and hoped Miss Etta wouldn't notice until after they left. She watched his face when she turned into the driveway of the house they had shared.

"Okay, tell me what's going on."

"I wanted to spend time alone with my man." She parked under the carport, which was elevated, helped him maneuver the chair down onto the lift and across the threshold. His expression kept changing until they were inside.

"I swore I would never come here again. It hurts to drive by and remember how things were."

"I swore the same thing. I was planning to have our things packed so Mom and Daddy could rent the house, but decided to pay them rent instead. Things are just as you left them, but we're not here to relive the time you spent here after I left."

"Why are we here? You must know this is painful for me."

297

"It's painful for me, too. I came here after you were shot. Memories hit me like a ton of bricks. I could barely drive to Donna's arms."

She locked the door and pushed his chair into the bedroom. "I did come by before I picked you up to make sure the bed had fresh linen." She stroked the stubble on his face and looked into his eyes. "Let's make ourselves comfortable."

He leaned over the bed, used his upper body strength, and pulled himself from the chair. Quickly removing his jacket and shirt, he watched her undress while his chest heaved in excitement. "I don't know where this is going, but I think I might like it."

She took his legs and helped him scoot to the center of the bed, then removed his shoes and socks. "I've been thinking about this all week. I just couldn't figure out a way to be alone with you. This seemed like the perfect spot." She kissed him. "We were happy here, baby."

"I'm happy with you wherever I am, but the time we spent here was the best of my life." His hand found its way under the soft folds of her sweater and touched her nipples. "Dew drops, remember?"

"I remember, and I love hearing you say it now, just as I did then."

"I can't tell you how much I want you right now." His fingers were no longer nimble, but he managed to unhook her bra.

She pulled his sweatpants down in one quick move and stroked his body with both hands. "I shouldn't say this to you, but I don't think any man could ever satisfy me the way you did. Just thinking about those nights after we were married still sends me into a frenzy."

She felt him stiffen. "What's wrong? Are you in pain?"

"Yeah, but not in the way you think. I don't know if I can go through with this. I can't satisfy you now."

"I know everything you do is new to you now. I'm frightened, too, but I want you more than I've ever wanted anything. You can't disappoint me. I love you too much for that."

She removed the rest of her clothing and his. Straddling his body, she took his hands and smoothed them down her body, holding his fingers on her breasts. Throwing her head back, she rotated his hands, feeling his fingers squeeze her nipples.

"I'm sorry." She slid her body down his. "I can't wait."

The explosion was almost immediate—for both of them. As quickly as it ended, they began again. This time she worked his body with her hands and placed hers in easy reach of his mouth. All traces of nervousness melted and lust took over. His response was so violent, she became afraid of causing him pain until she realized his legs were moving under her. Wondering if he knew, she slipped her hands under his head and held his face to her chest. Together they climbed to the top, exploded, and held each other in a slow meltdown.

Still panting, she lay on his chest, careful not to put pressure on his arms.

"I could never get enough of you when we were married." He kissed her forehead. "I still can't."

"Catch your breath and reload, Sheriff. This here shootout has only just begun."

She brought warm towels and cold water, and they lay together in silence. When she felt his hands move, though feebly, over her hips, she rose up on her hands and knees and hovered over him.

"Are you sure? You got a little active the last time. Remember you just had a bullet removed from your head."

"Don't ask me to stop now. Nothing has ever felt this good."

She started slowly, still hovering with her breasts close to his face. His arms closed around her.

"Don't be afraid to love me. You'll only hurt me if you stop."

She felt his knees bend. His thighs closed around her. She wanted to give him as much of her as he needed without stopping, even for a miracle. Afterwards, they lay bound together in a sea of satisfaction. Her breathing finally slowed enough for her to speak. "That was incredible."

"You did all of the work. I just lay here."

"That's a big lie and you know it. Besides, I couldn't work unless I had something wonderful to work with. I love you so much. The only thing better was the night we created Leila."

Shannon anguished over whether to tell Edison that his leg had moved twice. Would it raise false hope?

Miss Etta was waiting when they returned. "I brought you lunch from the diner, Edison. Jeannie knows what you like."

Shannon smiled, nibbled his ear, and whispered, "So do I."

Thierry called her cell several times with updates of his progress in preparing for the concert. Seeing Leila's face when she overheard part of the conversation, Shannon asked her father to help her break the news.

With Leila between them, they explained that she had to return to Paris for a scheduled engagement.

"You said you wouldn't leave." Leila did not cry, but the hurt on her face was crushing to watch.

"I'm not leaving for good, honey. I have to go. I know you don't understand contracts, but they are simply promises made on paper. Each person who signs that contract has an obligation, a legal obligation, meaning if you don't do as you promised, you will be punished. In this case, punishment would mean Thierry and myself paying a lot of money for breaking our promise. He promised a lot of people I would perform there for New Year's Eve, and so did I."

"You said he would fix it so you wouldn't have to go."

"And he did. He fixed all of the promises we made before Thanksgiving. I was planning to come home and stay until right now, after Christmas, so I didn't make any big promises for that time. The concert on New Year's Eve is a big event. It pays a lot of money. That's why we have to pay a lot of money if I don't perform."

"A lot of people bought tickets to see your mother perform on New Year's Eve. Think how disappointed they'll be if she isn't there." J.P. smiled. "She's coming back, honey. That's a promise she's making to you."

Leila looked at Shannon and twisted her head to one side. "Did you tell Daddy?"

"Not yet. Would you do me a big favor and help me tell your daddy? I would never leave him right now, or leave you and Granddaddy if I didn't have to go. Would you help me explain that to Edison?"

Leila nodded. "How long before you come back?"

"I'll be back in a couple of weeks. I need the rest of this week to rehearse. After the concert, I'll pack my things and take care of whatever business I have in Paris, and then I'll come back."

"Bring me another Barbie doll?" She twisted her hands in her hair.

"Since I probably won't be going back to Paris for a long time, I'll bring you two, three, if I can find ones that you don't already have. And in the spring, when it gets warm, maybe you and I can go back together. There are still a lot of places you haven't seen."

They talked until Leila seemed more at ease. After supper, they went to visit Edison.

"He's asleep," Miss Etta said. "He's been 'sleep since you brought him back today. It's time for his medication, but I don't want to wake him up just for that, and I don't think you should neither." She looked at Shannon with a set jaw and flaring nostrils.

Shannon took Leila's hand. "If he does awaken later, please tell him we came by."

She called Donna after Leila had gone to bed. "I'm a little worried. I hope he's okay."

"Okay nothing, the man is in heaven. Quit worrying. This is probably the most relaxed Edison has been since before you went to Paris."

Thierry called again with a list of suggested songs for her performance. He was unable to assemble the usual team of musicians, but he assured her they already knew the material. "I can't tell you how sorry I am that you have to fly back on such short notice, but it will be a great concert. You're a great performer."

She knew the compliments were part of his job, but he did it with unmatched expertise. "Thanks, Thierry. You're a great manager, a great producer, and the best friend I've ever had."

"Friend," he said dryly. "I thought we were more than friends."

"Of course we were. We still are, and will always be."
Her heart broke for him each time they spoke. "I wish
things were different. I'll come back and record or whatever. I'll do concerts, whatever you want. I just can't let
my family down, especially now."

When her plans were finalized, she took Leila to visit
Edison. Miss Etta answered their knock.

"Edison has company right now. He's busy."

Shannon didn't see a car in the driveway other than
Etta's. "I need to speak with him. It's very important."

"Like I said, he has company. Look back there. That
closed door means he don't wanna be disturbed."

Shannon was about to leave, but Leila ran to the back
of the house and banged on the door. "Daddy! Daddy!
Mommy needs to talk to you."

"Chil', didn't you hear me say your father is busy right
now?"

Miss Etta reached for Leila but it was too late. She
had already pushed into the room and was standing still,
staring. Jeannie was sitting on the bed next to Edison and
it was obvious that some form of intimacy had occurred.
Her blouse was opened enough to see her bare breast.

"What is wrong with you? I said your father was busy.
You don't listen!"

Shannon pulled Leila close and used both hands to
cover her ears. "Don't ever yell at my child again, and
don't worry about her not listening because she's not
coming back here, and neither am I."

She stopped when Leila squirmed against her grip and Edison yelled for them to come in. She lifted Leila in her arms and left without looking back. Gunning her father's car out of the driveway, she did not try to hide her anger.

"Why was Jeannie in Daddy's room? She's not supposed to be there, is she?"

"I'm sure they had things to discuss. Don't worry about it, honey. That's something your father will have to fix." Thinking ahead, she cautioned Leila about the future they had discussed. "Honey, sometimes things don't work out the way we had planned. If your father and Jeannie are friends, you should always respect her."

"I don't like her, Mommy. She's not nice to me."

"You don't have to like her or spend time with her. You also shouldn't worry about people who aren't nice. That just means they're unhappy and sometimes just... not everyone is nice, but you don't have to let them bother you." She smiled. "That's exactly why I'm going to hurry back from Paris, and always be around to make sure you don't have to spend time with anyone who isn't nice to you. I'm going to take you to the store. I have a doctor's appointment this afternoon, and I don't want to be late."

"Are you sick?" Leila looked at the blinking red light on Shannon's cell. "Your phone is ringing, Mommy. Are you going to answer it?"

She shook her head. "No, honey. I don't think it's important, and I'm not sick. I'm just going for a checkup."

❧

Donna frowned when she heard what happened. "Don't tell J.P. He's already worried that things may not go well for you and Edison. I think he's also worried that you'll be bored to tears here in Shepherd. I am sometimes, and I'm not a famous performer."

"But you have John and the children. I'll have Leila and the rest of my family." She looked at her phone. "That's him. He's been calling since I left there. I would turn the damn thing off, but I'd hate to miss a call from Thierry. He's giving me blow by blow updates on the concert preparations."

"It will work out, honey. You said Jeannie's car wasn't there, which means Etta probably brought her there to seduce Edison. He can't run away from her, though he probably wishes he could. After all, we know he's not needy."

She returned Donna's chuckle. "That was probably a mistake, but I'm not sorry it happened." She thought of the evening at the hospital. "I'm through being sorry for the things I've done."

After her checkup, she drove the short distance to the nursing home and surprised Mama Lou.

"I had planned to pick you up New Year's Eve so we could get drunk together, but I have to go to Paris."

"You're leaving again?"

She explained the circumstances and Mama Lou smiled.

"I didn't think you'd go away from Leila again. I hope you have a good concert. I'll have these old bats bring me a glass of apple juice and say a toast at midnight." Her eyes dimmed. "Hopefully I'll know when midnight comes."

Shannon assured her grandmother that J.P. would not leave her there over the holidays, kissed her goodbye, and left. Taking her phone from the car seat, she finally answered Edison's call.

"Why did you leave? Bring Leila back. I want to see her."

She could hear the guilt in his voice.

"Some other time, Edison. You seem to be having a scheduling conflict. I guess now that you know you're not impotent, you want to conquer the world."

"We have joint saving accounts and finances that need to be straightened out. It was no big deal. I want you and Leila to come on back so that we can talk."

"No, thank you. If I remember correctly, Jeannie had an attorney send you notification of all matters you two had together. Is there more?"

"Yes. We bought a piece of land out on the highway. Jeannie sold it and deposited the money in our joint account. That's what we were discussing."

"Oh, I see. Are you sure the money was deposited in the bank? I thought it was in her bra, since the top of her blouse was open. Don't play me like this, Edison. Of all things, don't play me. If what we've been to each other lately doesn't mean anything to you, just say so."

"Please come back and bring Leila. We'll discuss everything when you get here."

"I'm not coming back. Besides, you're probably all talked out by now."

"Then you come tomorrow morning, and bring Leila back when she gets out of school."

"I can't do that. I'm going to Paris tomorrow."

Following a long silence, he asked, "Is this your way of punishing me?"

"I hardly think so. I've apologized for my mistakes so many times, I'm sick of hearing myself do it. Because of my mistakes, I've bent over backwards to accommodate you. You don't know the crap I had to wade through when you thought we were married. Since then, I've tried to make you understand how much I love and want you. Your mother yelled at my baby today. I'll be damned if I give her a chance to do it again. Be happy with Jeannie. I can't do this anymore."

"Don't leave things like this. Come back so we can talk. I thought we agreed that you would wait until spring, take Leila to Paris, pack, and come right back."

"Edison, I came to give you the details of my trip, but you were not to be disturbed, as your mother put it. Right now I don't want to discuss anything with you because I'm mad as hell. I don't know if this is your mother's way of getting the two of you back together, but I do know you can and should exert some control over your life. Jeannie shouldn't have been in there with her damn breasts hanging out. I'm hanging up now, and don't try and call me back. I'll be too busy to be disturbed."

She hung up and he called again the following morning before she left for the airport. His first sentence was accusatory. She became angry and cut the conversation short. "I'm running late, Edison, and I can't miss this plane. I hope your progress continues. I'll be thinking of you."

When the airplane landed at Charles de Gaulle, she took a cab to Thierry's house and let herself in. She thought it would be hard, but it wasn't. She didn't belong there. The only problem was that she now felt she did not belong with Edison, either. She walked through rooms of elegant furnishings, art and antiques. It still seemed dreamlike. She had enjoyed the pageantry and applause. She had enjoyed life in Thierry's world, but the people she loved most were a world away.

Thierry arrived, surrounded by an entourage, including two women she did not recognize. He kissed her lightly on the mouth, but his eyes lingered on hers. "I'm glad you're here. We're all set up to rehearse."

He introduced the other musicians, a program organizer, and back-up singers. When they were alone, he asked one simple question. "Here to stay or is this just business?"

"I can't stay. I've got—"

"I've called Jacquette to work on costumes," he interrupted. "We don't have time to make new ones, so she's revamping some old ones for this event. Work with her on that, if you would."

"Sure." She looked at his handsome face. Older, wiser, and seasoned to the fineries of life, he also hid his feelings very well. That was the way of his world.

Love the one you're with.

# Chapter 13

Edison was having a tough time both physically and mentally. She was gone. He called John and Donna, fishing for answers. When all else failed, he asked John to bring Leila by when he knew his mother was not going to be home. After John left, he turned his questioning to her. "I miss your mommy. Do you know when she's coming back?"

"Very soon, but I don't know when. Are you okay, Daddy? You look sad."

"I'm fine, honey. As I said, I miss your mommy."

His mother wasted no time letting him know how she felt.

"What you worried 'bout? You knowed she'd go back to Paris. She's gone right back to that Frenchman, leaving you here lookin' like a sap, just like before."

"Mama, I don't need to hear this. Shannon and I had discussed her return to Paris. Her things are there. Clothes, money, jewelry, everything she has."

"Don't forget to add the Frenchman."

In spite of himself, he was outraged. He was to blame. He wondered just how much of the previous problems, the divorce, had been his fault as well.

Determined to mend their relationship, he called J.P. "Something happened before Shannon left that I'm sure was misunderstood. I need to speak with her as soon as possible."

"There is nothing I would like better than to see the two of you back together, Edison, you know that. She left here quite distraught. She's trying to make up for the past, to be there for you, but you're not helping."

"So she told you about Jeannie being here? What did she say?"

"Actually, your daughter told me. She wasn't too happy about it, either. Shannon will be back soon. Just hang on to whatever you have to say and tell her. You know I love you like a son, but, personally, I feel this has gone far beyond reason. After you got Shannon and Leila excited about the three of you having a life together, you start spending time with Jeannie. Do you blame Shannon and Leila for being upset?"

The frustration he heard in J.P.'s voice made Edison feel even worse. "No, it's my fault. I just need the chance to tell her that."

"Shannon has more options than most people," J.P. reminded him. "She's bright, hardworking, and talented. Having her teaching here in our schools would be a blessing. Having the two of you back together as a family would give me more comfort than just about anything right now, but it will take effort on both sides."

312

He thanked J.P. and apologized again. "I'm so turned around now, I'm just not thinking clearly. I want Shannon back in my life more than I want my legs back."

He called her several times before she answered. "What are you doing? Can you talk for a few minutes?"

"I'm rehearsing. That's why I came here. I have to put on a show in a few days, working with different musicians and a rusty voice."

"I wish I was there to hold you. I remember that you said being in my arms always made everything seem better."

"Your arms are full of Jeannie. I doubt they could do me any good. Look, I've got to go. We're doing full rehearsals and I'm due on the stage in about twenty minutes."

"Before you go, do you mind if Leila spends the night here? John brought her over but they didn't stay long. I miss her so much. I miss you. Us."

"John had to promise not to leave her there before she would agree see you. Your mother screamed at her, Edison. Why don't you ask Ray to drive you to the store and spend time with her there? I've got to go. Take care."

He didn't want to whine, but knew he was. Feeling more than physically pathetic, he called his brother. Before going to the store, they stopped at the courthouse. Edison hoped being in his usual chair would relieve some of the helplessness, but it only made him feel worse. Emmett was discussing the ongoing investigation into drug trafficking and Bobby Joe's disappearance. Edison learned that Junior Vinning was trying to retract his confession on the advice of his attorney, saying it was coerced. He claimed not to have recognized Edison's truck and said he thought his life was in danger.

"Are you saying they might reduce the charges? To what, weapons violation?"

"Over my dead body," Emmett declared. "Half of this state wants his hide. If he gets off lightly, he'd better move."

Edison asked to leave and Ray drove him to Family Supermarket. With Leila in his arms, he tried to imagine how the rest of his life would rate. Without Shannon, he knew it would not amount to much.

❦

Thierry was gone most of the time, leaving Shannon alone with the staff and various roving entertainers. Henri asked if she had reconciled with her ex-husband. She explained how the loss of her mother had weighed in her decision to return home.

Thierry was backstage at the concert, as usual. He praised her performance and told her he was leaving for Luxemburg. "Are you sure…I mean about staying in Mississippi?"

"There's nothing else I can do right now. I can't take Leila away from her father and from my father. I can't leave her there with no one to care for her."

He stroked her face with the back of his hand. "I will miss you."

Tears welled in her eyes. "I'll miss you, too."

After two days of closing bank accounts, emptying safety deposit boxes, and packing her belongings, she wrote a long and tearful letter of goodbye. She thanked Thierry for making her dream come true, for bringing joy into her life, and showing her a world she would always remember. She didn't assert or deny her feeling for him, but promised to keep him in her heart forever. She wasn't sure if his trip was necessity or personal, but she understood.

J.P. had told her about Edison's call. "Honey, he's freaking out again. He knows you have reason to be angry and he thinks you'll punish him by not coming back or by coming back for Leila."

She thought of Edison every second. "He obviously had something with Jeannie or he wouldn't have thought of marrying her," she told her father. "Even after she denied his child, he's still willing to let her come between us."

"Are you having second thoughts, about just Edison, or about leaving Paris?"

"Dad, that decision was pretty much made when Mom died. I can't leave Leila and I can't take her away from her family. I've written Thierry a note telling him I will honor my contract and record or perform just as I did this time. I could never let him down, but I have no intention of staying here. I hope to bring Leila here often when she's older. There's so much I want her to learn, but taking her away from her family would hurt her, and I can't do that."

She called Thierry on her way to the airport. "I'll miss you. Will you call me sometimes, just to say hi?"

"I will, but I'm not sure you'll want me to when you and Edison reconcile. You're special, *agneau*. I'll find ways to keep your career going. My office in New York is growing. I'll see you often."

She rented a car to keep her father from having to drive to the airport late at night. She arrived in Shepherd just as she knew her father and Leila would be finishing breakfast. Rushing through the door with four Barbie dolls in a bag, she was not prepared for the look on her father's face.

"Edison is back in the hospital. He started having some kind of involuntary movements in his legs, jerks, like someone having a seizure. They're going to do another surgery. The news is not all bad. Jackie said this surgery could restore the use of his legs. A doctor from Houston has developed a new technique to stimulate re-growth and rejuvenation to damaged nerve endings. I don't know what the risks are, but Doctor Welch is waiting to speak with you."

"Thanks for telling me, Dad, but I'm no longer part of Edison's little menagerie. I'm sure Miss Etta and Jeannie are there."

"I understand he upset you, but you have to go to him. He's refusing to have the surgery unless you're there with him."

"I don't think Edison knows what he wants, or, more precisely, who. I want him to recover, but I'm tired of being on this seesaw."

Leila had overheard talk of her father's surgery and clung to her mother.

"What's going to happen to Daddy now? Is he going to die?"

"No, baby. I'll give you the complete story once I speak to the doctors, and in the meantime, I don't want you to worry."

Still angry, but willing to help if she was needed, she spotted Jackie as she entered the all-too-familiar surgical wing.

"Shannon. Over here. Girl, I'm so glad to see you. Edison needs immediate surgery to relieve the pressure on those damaged nerves, but he won't consent. The doctor just called me in and asked if I knew how to contact you."

She followed Jackie into Edison's room. His face was more distorted then before, his eyes fixed on the ceiling. She knew he was heavily medicated, though tousled bedcovers indicated he was also restless. His arms were flung lifelessly across the bed. One look and Shannon's anger melted away.

"I'm going to find Doctor Welch." Jackie gave her a push. "Go to him."

She took deep breaths and fought against panic that was more crippling than standing in the center of a large crowd. He was groaning softly, almost like an infant. She wanted to help him recover, but knew each time they were together, it became harder to pull away. She touched his arm and smiled as he turned his head.

"I'm sorry for the way things turned out. Are you in pain?"

"Not anymore." He squeezed her hand. "I kept thinking I'd driven you back to Thierry. Please don't be angry with me, Shannon. I love you more than life. It's no good unless you're by my side."

Her smile was weak and uncertain, but she forced the words from her lips. "I love you, too."

"You're still angry. I can tell. I won't agree to this surgery until we've cleared the air." His eyes were pleadingly wet. "Talk to me. Let me know where I stand, and don't hold back because of my condition. The one thing I ask of you, and everyone else in my life, is to treat me the same as you would if I were healthy."

"I thought that's what I was doing." She spoke softly and calmly. "Love isn't all of it, Edison. Our relationship shouldn't be constantly plagued with doubt—on either side. You say you love me, but I find you and Jeannie behind closed door one time too many. I say I love you and that I'm staying here in Shepherd, but you question my truthfulness. You're right; I'm angry and hurt. I thought the two of us had reached an understanding. I know you have issues to settle with Jeannie and I can respect that, but behind closed doors while I'm told you can't be disturbed is a bit much. I'm no better at sharing than you are."

"I didn't want to say all of this over the phone and you wouldn't come back so I could explain in person. Jeannie and I had several business issues to settle. I told you about the piece of land. We also purchased a car together, and both of us have too much at stake to allow our credit rating to erode."

"That's not the explanation I need."

"I'm telling you everything. Jeannie came over twice. We had concluded our business long before you arrived. She started to tell me that we could work things out. She wanted to have sex, which is the reason the door was closed. I didn't know what she was up to until she opened her top.

"Honestly, I have no desire to be with her. If you were not a part of my life I would still feel the same way. I don't understand her motives. It's like she's playing some game where she doesn't want me, but she keeps finding ways to hang on."

"Maybe you don't understand, but I do. With your mother's help, Jeannie has successfully run her little game on you. I don't know why she wouldn't come to you before, but she's making it clear that she wants you now. I'll be here for you, Edison, because that's where I want to be. There's more going on than you know. I have to get my head on straight no matter what. I'm not going to allow your mother to insult me or yell at my daughter anymore. I'm not coming there to see you anymore. When you leave the hospital, whether you're in a wheelchair or walking, you're coming home with me."

"Don't you see? That was the reason I wanted to get things settled with my finances. I do have a little money saved. Probably not much by your standards, but I can afford to marry you."

Shannon's eyebrows arched quizzically. "Did you tell this to Jeannie?"

"Truth is, Mama brought Jeannie over there. I don't know what she was told, but I got tears, promises, and offers I had no problems refusing. I just wanted to get everything settled between us and move on. I touched her when she started crying and she accepted that as my approval for her to disrobe. I was trying not to hurt her feelings. I was simply getting things in order for us to be together."

"I was thinking the same way. Daddy wouldn't sell me the land our house is on, but said he would deed it to us, along with the two acres that is his share of Mama Lou's estate. We can have another house built, a swimming pool, everything Leila needs. I've spoken with an architect in Jackson. If it were just the three of us, we could stay with Daddy, but…" She stopped, and smiled. "I thought maybe…"

"You want more children with me? Where's that doctor? Let's get this over with. I've got a marriage coming up, babies to make."

"Fine, let's get married right now."

"Don't you think I want that more than anything? But I can't make that kind of commitment until I know what I'm asking you to commit to. I don't know if I'll be a husband or a dependent."

"You're not the first man to lose use of his legs, and you won't be the last. I'm willing to take the risk because I know that unless you allow this affliction to affect you mentally, there's nothing we can't overcome."

He gave her his broadest smile. "I love you so much."

Doctor Welch arrived on cue, accompanied by another physician, both with smiles. "Mrs. Page. I'm so glad you're here. This is Doctor Myles Sorenson from Houston. I presented Edison's case at a medical convention and he offered to determine if Edison met the criteria for a new procedure he developed two years ago. When Edison's condition worsened, I called him and he agreed to come here and perform the surgery. This could restore the use of Edison's legs."

"Hello, Doctor Sorenson." Shannon gripped his hand to try to control her tremors. "Now let's have the other side."

Doctor Welch moved closer to her. "Pardon?"

"I know there are some risks. There have to be."

"Yes." He stroked the white beard around his chin. "I'll let Doctor Sorenson give you the details."

"I'll give you the statistics to date. I've performed this procedure six times with four successes and two failures. One of the failures died from complications, one saw no improvement in his condition. The other four regained all or part of their motor functions, and all but one is still improving."

"Given Edison's medical profile, what's the prognosis for his recovery?" Shannon asked, wanting Edison to hear.

"I would have to say that given his age, physical condition, and the damage sustained, his chances are excellent." He went on to explain that the surgery would entail minimal intrusion and a brief recovery period, provided there were no complications. The worst-case scenario was full paralysis of the back as well as the legs.

"So I could walk or become completely paralyzed?" Edison asked.

"Yes. I have not experienced complete paralysis with any of the other patients, but it is a medical possibility."

Doctor Welch moved forward. "Doctor Sorenson's innovative techniques and his experience have given us something we didn't have before. He's also brought along his assistant, Doctor Raj. Together they make an unbeatable team."

After Edison agreed to the surgery, Shannon followed the doctors out of the room. "I have a lot of concerns. Edison underwent serious depression when he realized he was not able to walk. I'm not afraid of the surgery, but I'm frightened of his emotional reaction if it fails."

"I know, Mrs. Page," Doctor Welch answered. "I am, too."

She spent most of the night awake, praying and planning. If Edison's condition worsened after surgery, she would get a list of the most prominent neurosurgeons in the world. She did have money, much more than she'd confided to Edison, and she would use it. Hiding her concern from her daughter, she went to the hospital early and sat with Edison. J.P. was there for her when they wheeled him away.

"How's Leila doing? Do you think we should have sent her to day school?"

"Yes. I think she's better off there," J.P. answered. "Hopefully the activities of the day will create enough of a diversion to keep her from worrying. How about you, honey? You look drained."

When he put his arms around her. She melted against him. "I've never been so scared in my life. If he dies, I don't know how I'll get through this. If he's a cripple, I don't know how he'll get through it."

"Do the only thing you can do." He stroked her brow. "Pray."

The waiting room began to overflow with family and friends. Emmett and one of the new deputies were there, along with most of Edison's family. John took the day off from school and joined them.

In the pandemonium that followed the attack on Edison's life, Shannon had forgotten about the man who pulled the trigger. "What happened to that Junior Vinning, Emmett? Is he in jail?"

"His attorney made a nice plea for bond. The judge took one look at Junior's rap sheet, and asked the attorney if he was delusional. There's a movement going on among area lawmen. We plan to storm that courtroom and let the jurors know where we stand. It's hard enough getting them behind bars, but when they've tried to murder the essence of the law, they can't win leniency."

She agreed, but could not waste emotions on hatred.

The little groups in the waiting room took turns going for coffee, and the smokers kept disappearing down the hall. As people moved in and out, Shannon somehow missed Jeannie's entrance until she was standing next to her.

"You didn't waste any time moving in on him, did you?"

Shannon stared for a second and then smiled. "No, I didn't. The year we've been apart is enough time wasted."

"He asked me to marry him and I'm going to hold him to our agreement. What do you think of that?"

"Not very much. Actually, if you want the truth, I think you're a conniving bitch. You really didn't want Edison because of his condition, and now that there's a chance he'll recover, here you are. I never imagined you were such pond scum. Edison Page is mine, with or without mobility. I love him and I'm not letting him out of my life, ever again."

Not waiting for a reply, she joined her father, brother, and Emmett. They were talking about Bobby Joe. She listened, her mind going over everything she had seen and heard. When she finally focused, she had an idea but decided to keep it to herself.

She began to fidget and pace. Drinking coffee made it worse. Her father and Jackie kept telling her to calm down, and John kept embracing her and smiling.

"I see Jeannie is here," John said. "Do you think she'll pose a problem for you and Edison?"

"If Edison walks out of here, I'll deal with any problem that arises from Jeannie to Miss Etta and beyond. As a matter of fact, John, other than worrying about Edison's condition, I'm totally at peace. I do feel very badly about Thierry. I love him, personally and professionally. I never want to minimize the contributions he made to my life. I owe him big time."

"Is this guilt or gratitude?"

"A little of both, I suppose. Regardless, I'm not going to allow anything to stand in the way of my happiness. I look at Mama Lou, holding on to each moment of lucidity, savoring every good day as if it were the last. Life is too short to settle for anything less than happiness." She looked around for Jeannie and found her standing alone by the candy machine.

"Damn Jeannie and Miss Etta. I love Edison and he loves me. Things are different now."

Both Doctor Welch and Doctor Raj were smiling as they headed down the hall. Shannon's heart leaped into her throat. "How did it go? How is he?"

Doctor Welch spoke first. "We don't want to jump the gun on this, but all indications are that the surgery was a success. I think Edison will walk again." As everyone started to cheer, he held his hand in the air. "Don't forget he will need recovery time, and nothing is certain at this point. He's very strong and in great physical condition."

"Thank you," Shannon said. "Both of you and Doctor Sorenson. Thank you from the bottom of my heart."

# Chapter 14

After grabbing lunch with J.P. and John, Shannon realized she was not going to sleep. Something was nagging her and she couldn't put it out of her mind. She drove the short distance to Mama Lou's house. When she was young, they had pretended their grandparents' house was a fortress because it sat high on a hill. She was not surprised that Savannah's car was there, but the blinds were drawn and no sound came from the living room.

She knocked and waited. "Savannah! Open up." She could smell cigarette smoke. "I need to get something for Mama Lou. Open the door."

Instead of waiting, she hopped off the side of the porch and hurried around to the back door. "And where the hell do you think you're going?" She held up her hands. "I never thought I'd be as disappointed with anyone as I am with you, Bobby Joe. How could you do that to Edison? He loved you like a brother."

Bobby Joe finished stuffing his shirt in his jeans. "I wouldn't hurt Edison. You've got to believe that. How could I know that crazy Vinning boy was going to shoot him?"

"I'm not sure, but I will be before I leave here. You're going to tell me everything you know, and don't think you can shit me. I'm not nearly as nice as Edison. Come on out of there, Savannah! I see you peeping through the window." She had been only partially listening when Savannah said Bobby Joe was clean. She did remember that the man at Carmen's house definitely wasn't Bobby Joe. She also remembered Mama Lou mentioning "that boy who hangs all over Savannah."

"Don't stand there." She looked up at her cousin. "Come on out here. If you've got anybody else in there, you'd better get them out here, too. I've already told Emmett I suspected the two of you. He went to get backup just in case there was trouble, but I couldn't make myself feel afraid of you. See, Edison isn't the only one who loved you like a brother."

"He didn't do anything to Edison." Savannah's eyes were filled with tears. "We knew everyone would think that, and they did. That's why he's been out here with me."

"You know, when we were kids, you would tell Mama Lou the biggest lie, and do it with a straight face and water in your eyes. I don't believe a damn thing you just said. I want the truth, Bobby Joe, and I want you to tell me."

"I didn't set Edison up. I swear."

"Okay, then tell me everything you know about the drugs coming into Shepherd and everything else. Tell me who's behind it. Edison is going to be out of that hospital and back on the job before you know it. I will not have him coming back to something that you can put an end to right now. Your mother and father didn't raise you this way. Now, your sister is a different story. She must have been raised by wolves."

Bobby Joe sat on the edge of the elevated porch, his legs dangling. Shannon remembered the happy times when they would sit there, drink sodas and talk for most of the night. She and Edison. Carmen and Bobby Joe. Jackie and Fred. Life had been so simple back then.

She took her cell phone from her purse. "I'd better let Emmett know what's going on."

"Shannon, I'm in big trouble." Bobby Joe scratched his beard. "I can't let anybody know I'm here. They'll kill me."

"Who will kill you?"

"Shannon, if you say I told you, I'll deny it. He's already looking for me. Maybe he won't kill me, but I do know he'll mess me up pretty bad. I was the bagman for Marcus Lewis."

"Marcus?" She had a vision of the handsome face of the man she once considered the best-looking guy in Shepherd.

"It's not a big operation. I pick up the stuff. That's all I do. Everybody knows me, and no one suspected me— until now. I make the drop wherever Marcus tells me."

"What do you drop?"

"Weed. Crack. I didn't know they were selling to minors at first. I swear. I just bring it in. I don't distribute it. Mel Harris does that. Something happened about a month ago. Some guy jumped me over at Carmen's house. He took the stuff. Now, Marcus thinks I double-crossed him. That's why I've been hiding out."

"So what about that stuff you fed Edison?"

"I lied. They did use Boise Creek at first. Kids out there making out. Wanting to get high. I honestly don't know what they do now, but if Emmett wants to stop the flow, I can tell him who to arrest. He already had Mel in jail, but couldn't hold him."

"Okay, we'll do it this way. You can't hide out here for the rest of your life." She looked from one to the other. "If Mama Lou knew what was going on here, she'd…"

Savannah sobbed and Bobby Joe tried to console her. Shannon knew they had done bad things, but they weren't bad people. Instead of condemning them, she knew she had to help.

"There's one other thing I have to tell you," Bobby Joe said. "It's about my sister."

⁓

Shannon returned to the hospital, refusing to go home even after Doctor Welch advised her that Edison would sleep through the night.

"Can I just sit next to him? I want to be here when he wakes up. It's very important."

"Stay, by all means." He patted her shoulder. "He's a lucky man. I must say, I found his personal situation rather distressing at first, but it's very clear now that he has someone in his life who will love him regardless of his condition."

Doctor Welch had confided during one of Shannon's earlier pretend sessions with Edison that his memory lapse was unique. "I've never seen a patient so clear about everything else, but unable to find the correct spot on his timeline. This might be pretend, but his feelings are very real, at least to him."

Shannon watched Edison sleep. He stirred once during the night, but did not awaken. She sat next to the bed, occasionally wiping his face and kissing his forehead until exhaustion overcame her and she fell asleep. She was awakened by movement in the room and looked up to see Edison's parents in the corner.

"Good morning," she whispered. "He slept all night."

"The doctors said he would. I thought you'd go home and get some rest, too," Miss Etta said. "It ain't good to lose sleep this way."

Shannon smiled and nodded. Words of concern from Miss Etta were rare. "I went home. I just couldn't sleep."

They waited together. When the doctor arrived, Miss Etta further surprised Shannon by voluntarily leaving them alone.

"I'm gonna go down the hall for some coffee and leave you here for him when he wakes up."

Happy for the lack of animosity, but unsure of the reason, Shannon stepped out to make room for Doctor Welch and the nurse, but remained next to the door. Doctor Welch motioned for her as he lifted the sheet from Edison's legs.

"Look at this." He grasped Edison's foot and pulled his leg into an eighty-degree angle. Within a few seconds the leg returned to an elongated position. "He has motion. I doubt that he will be able to get up and run out of here, but he can move his leg."

Shannon wept.

"Why are you crying?" Edison's asked as he awoke. His voice was low and strained. He raised his head and tried to sit up. "It's bad, isn't it?

Shannon ran to the bed. "No, baby. You can move your legs. Go ahead. Try."

Hesitating for a moment, he bent his left leg, slowly at first, and then both legs. When he was able to speak, he took Doctor Welch's hand. "How can I ever repay you?"

"By keeping us safe, the way you've been doing. The ones you need to thank are Doctor Sorenson and Doctor Raj. Unfortunately, Doctor Sorenson had to return to Houston this morning, but I'll be happy to give you his address. His daddy was some sort of lawman, which increased his interest in your case. He wanted very much for this operation to be successful."

When Edison drifted off again, Shannon went home to spread the good news and rest. She returned later to find him alert and having a rowdy chat with Jackie.

"Hi, you two. Sounds like a party in here. Can I join?"

"Yes, you can. In fact, the party's in your honor. Edison was just telling me about a wedding in the very near future."

"A wedding?" She feigned surprise. "Who, pray tell?"

"All I'm allowed to say is that it's a serious case of love." Jackie laughed. "I'll leave you two lovebirds alone. Don't do anything I wouldn't do." She looked over her shoulder and winked.

"You're looking wonderful. How do you feel?" She kissed his forehead and gently rested her head on his shoulder.

"Like I've been hit by a truck. A big truck. I suppose it's partly the medication. I can't tell you how great it is just to wiggle my toes. I've been lying here wiggling them and thanking God. I'm very lucky." He kissed her cheek. "In more ways than one. I don't know…" He turned away.

"Come on in, Mama." He looked past Shannon as his mother and father came through the door. "I want you to know what's going on. I doubt I'll have your blessings, but Shannon and I are getting married." He took Shannon's hand.

"And this time, it will work. If she needs to go to Paris to complete her obligations, she's free to do so. I don't know Thierry well enough to trust him, but I do trust Shannon. We haven't worked out all the details yet, but we love each other. We never stopped. We'll raise our daughter together and deal with whatever comes at us as a team."

His voice was strong in affirmation. Shannon braced herself for Miss Etta's comeback when she walked closer to the bed.

"Well, the way I see it, you can wait 'til you walk out of here and have a ceremony, or Shannon can go see Judge Rhodes and git that license so the minister can come here 'n do it."

Edison's grip tightened on Shannon's hand. Both of them waited for the fireworks.

"So, which is it? I talked to the judge. He said ain't nothin' stoppin' you from doing it right now if that's what you both want." She glanced sideways at Edison. "Besides, that baby'll need a name when he's born."

Shock waves rushed though Shannon, but Edison's astonishment was greater.

"Mama, what are you talking about?"

When Miss Etta looked surprised, he turned to Shannon. "What's she talking about?"

"I'm so sorry." Miss Etta went to the other side of the bed and patted Edison's shoulder. "I didn't mean to run off at the mouth. I thought she'd told you and that's why you was talkin' 'bout getting married. I didn't know. I'm sorry."

"Shannon?" He wrung his hand from hers. "What the hell is Mama talking about? You're pregnant? How would she know that, and why would she think it's mine?"

"Don't go fussin' at her. She's pregnant, and it's yours."

Shannon moved away from the bed. She had kept the secret much too long, even from her family. "I'm pregnant. I was about to tell you when Miss Etta came in. I don't even know if you remember when…it happened. I have no idea how your mother knows, or why she feels certain you're the father, but you are."

"I'll answer that." Miss Etta half-smiled. "I went to that restroom down the hall the day Edison was shot. You had just come out of the stall. You left signs that it was that time of the month. I saw you take some of the pills you take for cramps and saw you doubled over next to Edison's bed, holding your stomach. I even know when it happened."

Shannon dropped her head.

"Well, you know more than I know," Edison said. "What happened between us just took place just before Shannon left for Paris. There's no way this baby is mine."

"To hell it ain't." Miss Etta tugged at Tito's sleeve. "Tell him. We both heard you in here beggin' one night, back when you thought Shannon was still your wife."

His expression changed. "That actually happened? It keeps coming back to me, but I thought…it really happened." He looked at Shannon. "We are having a baby? Seriously? One time?"

"One time is all it takes," Miss Etta told him. "And in case you two forgot, this is a small town. Them nurses down at Doctor McCutchen's office all just like wore out 'frigerators. They can't keep nothin'. I went over there for my feet yesterday and old Marva Hilliard asked me if I knowed Shannon was pregnant with that Frenchman's child. I told her she's tellin' a damn lie. That baby is my grandchild. Even if somethin' hap'ned when the Frenchman came here, ain't no way she'd be that far along."

The door cracked behind them.

"Come on in here." Miss Etta invited J.P. and John in with a big wave of her hand. "I got somethin' to say, and I wanna do it just one time."

John frowned.

J.P. followed him into the room with Leila in his arms. "What's going on here?" he asked.

"I'll tell you part of it, and they can tell you the rest." She reached for Leila. "I wanna hold my grandchild, if she'll let me. I need to 'pologize to a lot of people, but I wanna start with her."

She took Leila from J.P.'s arms. "Honey, your granny was wrong." She shook her head. "Your mama is a good person and you good as gold. Now, I still say it would be better if she sang in church, instead of on some stage, but her heart is pure. God knows that. Now I know it, too."

J.P.'s eyes bulged. "I don't understand. What…Etta? You'd better tell me something quick. Do we need a doctor in here? Last rites or something?"

"Don't be sassin' me, J.P. Travers. I'm sayin' I was wrong. I was." She looked at John, who seemed too awed to speak. "I was wrong 'bout you, too. You a good husband. Good man."

"Thank you," he stammered. "Forgive me, but I still don't know what's going on."

"For starters, Shannon and I are getting married." Edison laughed when Leila squealed and Miss Etta placed her on the bed. "Sweetheart, your mother and I are getting married. We'll be a family, just the way it should be. We'll live together. If your mother has to go to Paris or anywhere else for business, she'll always come back to us."

Shannon beamed and joined their hug. "There's another bit of news we have to share." Feeling her face flush in embarrassment, she looked at Edison. "During the week Edison thought we were married, and I had to pretend, we exceeded all expectations. I'm pregnant."

They looked at her stomach.

Leila frowned. "That means you're having a little baby?" she asked.

"Yes. We're having a baby," Edison added. "You're going to have a little sister or brother. Isn't that great?"

J.P. pulled a chair from the back of the room, sat down, and looked from one to the other. "Let me get this straight. You're pregnant and this happened when Edison was...confused?"

Shannon nodded.

"You're getting married and Etta approves?" His voice heightened as he cast a suspicious glance around the room. "Now I'm confused, especially about the last part."

"Ain't no fool like a old fool," Miss Etta said. "I done made my share of mistakes, and I ain't too proud to say so. The only fool worse than me is that one Edison was 'bout to marry."

This time, they all gasped in unison.

"I been wrong, but I ain't all the way blind. I saw how she kept seesawin'. First she loved Edison so much, but she didn't want to get married. She didn't get mad 'cause Edison got confused. A man from the state come by and offered her a pretty penny for that place her daddy left out on Buffalo Creek where they planned to build that penitent'ry. She didn't need no husband then, and she was scared she'd have to share that money. That's why she didn't want to marry."

Edison finished the explanation. "People out that way put up so much fuss, the planning committee decided to build the prison on the other side of the county. It happened right after my first surgery. That's when Jeannie started coming over to the house. The mayor told me about it the other day. He thought I knew. I didn't confront her. It was no longer important."

Bobby Joe had said as much to Shannon. She was still shocked.

"You might not be seein' her 'round no more," Miss Etta told him. "She said Shannon had come by the diner to throw it in her face 'bout Edison thinkin' they was still married. Three people, one of 'um was her helper, said she was lying. They say Shannon asked her to visit Edison. Shannon told her Edison wasn't confused no mo' and needed her. She said she wasn't going nowhere to see him."

Shannon kissed her father. "I guess miracles really do happen."

"I keeps my ears open," Miss Etta said to Shannon. "I heard what you said to Valer'y Brooks. Everybody in town knows she been sweet on J.P. all her life. I knowed how much you loved your mother, but you treated her kindly. Right there I thought I'd been wrong, but it took a while to get the devil outta my head."

"Wow. This is some revelation," John said. "Thank you for everything you just said, Miss Etta. It takes a big person to admit they're wrong."

"I don't mind 'pologizing when I'm wrong." Miss Etta dusted her hands down her arms as if brushing away something foul. "I sho' was wrong 'bout Jeannie and I 'pologized for it."

"You apologized to Jeannie for what?" Edison asked.

"'Cause I thought wrong o' her, too. I thought she was a Christian. She ain't nothin' but a hellion."

Emmett walked in during their laughter.

"Come on in, man," Edison said. "Now I've got my whole family around me."

"I'll come back. I just wanted to ease you mind about the drug thing. We know how they got in. We got three people in custody here in Shepherd. They got a whole bunch in jail over in Jackson."

"You don't know how good that makes me feel." Edison reached for Emmett's hand. "I'm glad you figured it out."

"I didn't." Emmett shrugged, pointing to Shannon. "She did."

Stories were shared until Edison began to yawn.

J.P. harrumphed. "Say goodnight to your father, Leila. We need to let him get some rest." He looked at Miss Etta. "I never thought I'd say this, but after all this time, I'm proud to say you're family, Etta. I just wish..." He glanced upward.

"I wouldn't worry 'bout that." Miss Etta patted his shoulder. "I 'spect she knows."

With a full heart, Shannon looked at the faces around her and wiped a tear from her cheek. "I've done a lot of thinking these past few weeks, and even more when I learned I was pregnant. After seeing all of the boarded windows in Shepherd and learning of the crime and drugs, I wasn't sure I would be able to stay here, even for a little while. After Edison was shot, I was sure I didn't want to be here any longer than I felt necessary, but I see things differently now."

She took Edison's hand in her hers. "The people I love most are here. Dad hasn't given up and neither has John. Edison, Emmett, and the others are placing their lives on the line to protect the town and its citizens. Maybe I can help, too."

She looked at Miss Etta, who was holding Leila. "Thank you, Miss Etta. Thanks for everything you just said. Edison and I are going to have another child, and maybe another after that. It's good to know that our babies will never suffer for affection."

Everyone came closer in a circle, uniting in love. Shannon felt the glow of happiness shining around them. It was strong and mighty, she thought. The glitter of Paris could never compare.

# About the Author

Joan Early has enjoyed a long career in mortgage banking and now works as a realtor, but her first love is writing. She also enjoys reading, especially Lee Child and Stephen L. Carter. Joan lives in the Houston suburb of Kingwood with her husband, Dale.

## 2011 Mass Market Titles

### January

From This Moment
Sean Young
ISBN-13: 978-1-58571-383-7
ISBN-10: 1-58571-383-X
$6.99

Nihon Nights
Trisha/Monica Haddad
ISBN-13: 978-1-58571-382-0
ISBN-10: 1-58571-382-1
$6.99

### February

The Davis Years
Nicole Green
ISBN-13: 978-1-58571-390-5
ISBN-10: 1-58571-390-2
$6.99

Allegro
Adora Bennett
ISBN-13: 978-158571-391-2
ISBN-10: 1-58571-391-0
$6.99

### March

Lies in Disguise
Bernice Layton
ISBN-13: 978-1-58571-392-9
ISBN-10: 1-58571-392-9
$6.99

Steady
Ruthie Robinson
ISBN-13: 978-1-58571-393-6
ISBN-10: 1-58571-393-7
$6.99

### April

The Right Maneuver
LaShell Stratton-Childers
ISBN-13: 978-1-58571-394-3
ISBN-10: 1-58571-394-5
$6.99

Riding the Corporate Ladder
Keith Walker
ISBN-13: 978-1-58571-395-0
ISBN-10: 1-58571-395-3
$6.99

### May

Separate Dreams
Joan Early
ISBN-13: 978-1-58571-434-6
ISBN-10: 1-58571-434-8
$6.99

I Take This Woman
Chamein Canton
ISBN-13: 978-1-58571-435-3
ISBN-10: 1-58571-435-6
$6.99

### June

Inside Out
Grayson Cole
ISBN-13: 978-1-58571-437-7
ISBN-10: 1-58571-437-2
$6.99

## 2011 Mass Market Titles (continued)

### July

The Other Side of the
Mountain
Janice Angelique
ISBN-13: 978-1-58571-442-1
ISBN-10: 1-58571-442-9
$6.99

Holding Her Breath
Nicole Green
ISBN-13: 978-1-58571-439-1
ISBN-10: 1-58571-439-9
$6.99

### August

The Sea of Aaron
Kymberly Hunt
ISBN-13: 978-1-58571-440-7
ISBN-10: 1-58571-440-2
$6.99

The Finley Sisters' Oath of
Romance
Keith Thomas Walker
ISBN-13: 978-1-58571-441-4
ISBN-10: 1-58571-441-0
$6.99

### September

Except on Sunday
Regena Bryant
ISBN-13: 978-1-58571-443-8
ISBN-10: 1-58571-443-7
$6.99

Light's Out
Ruthie Robinson
ISBN-13: 978-1-58571-445-2
ISBN-10: 1-58571-445-3
$6.99

### October

The Heart Knows
Renee Wynn
ISBN-13: 978-1-58571-444-5
ISBN-10: 1-58571-444-5
$6.99

Best Friends; Better Lovers
Celya Bowers
ISBN-13: 978-1-58571-455-1
ISBN-10: 1-58571-455-0
$6.99

### November

Caress
Grayson Cole
ISBN-13: 978-1-58571-454-4
ISBN-10: 1-58571-454-2
$6.99

A Love Built to Last
L. S. Childers
ISBN-13: 978-1-58571-448-3
ISBN-10: 1-58571-448-8
$6.99

### December

Fractured
Wendy Byrne
ISBN-13: 978-1-58571-449-0
ISBN-10: 1-58571-449-6
$6.99

Everything in Between
Crystal Hubbard
ISBN-13: 978-1-58571-396-7
ISBN-10: 1-58571-396-1
$6.99

## Other Genesis Press, Inc. Titles

## Other Genesis Press, Inc. Titles (continued)

## Other Genesis Press, Inc. Titles (continued)

## Other Genesis Press, Inc. Titles (continued)

## Other Genesis Press, Inc. Titles (continued)

| | | |
|---|---|---|
| Mae's Promise | Melody Walcott | $8.95 |
| Magnolia Sunset | Giselle Carmichael | $8.95 |
| Many Shades of Gray | Dyanne Davis | $6.99 |
| Matters of Life and Death | Lesego Malepe, Ph.D. | $15.95 |
| Meant to Be | Jeanne Sumerix | $8.95 |
| Midnight Clear | Leslie Esdaile | $10.95 |
| (Anthology) | Gwynne Forster | |
| | Carmen Green | |
| | Monica Jackson | |
| Midnight Magic | Gwynne Forster | $8.95 |
| Midnight Peril | Vicki Andrews | $10.95 |
| Misconceptions | Pamela Leigh Starr | $9.95 |
| Mixed Reality | Chamein Canton | $6.99 |
| Moments of Clarity | Michele Cameron | $6.99 |
| Montgomery's Children | Richard Perry | $14.95 |
| Mr. Fix-It | Crystal Hubbard | $6.99 |
| My Buffalo Soldier | Barbara B.K. Reeves | $8.95 |
| Naked Soul | Gwynne Forster | $8.95 |
| Never Say Never | Michele Cameron | $6.99 |
| Next to Last Chance | Louisa Dixon | $24.95 |
| No Apologies | Seressia Glass | $8.95 |
| No Commitment Required | Seressia Glass | $8.95 |
| No Regrets | Mildred E. Riley | $8.95 |
| Not His Type | Chamein Canton | $6.99 |
| Not Quite Right | Tammy Williams | $6.99 |
| Nowhere to Run | Gay G. Gunn | $10.95 |
| O Bed! O Breakfast! | Rob Kuehnle | $14.95 |
| Oak Bluffs | Joan Early | $6.99 |
| Object of His Desire | A.C. Arthur | $8.95 |
| Office Policy | A.C. Arthur | $9.95 |
| Once in a Blue Moon | Dorianne Cole | $9.95 |
| One Day at a Time | Bella McFarland | $8.95 |
| One of These Days | Michele Sudler | $9.95 |
| Outside Chance | Louisa Dixon | $24.95 |
| Passion | T.T. Henderson | $10.95 |
| Passion's Blood | Cherif Fortin | $22.95 |
| Passion's Furies | AlTonya Washington | $6.99 |
| Passion's Journey | Wanda Y. Thomas | $8.95 |
| Past Promises | Jahmel West | $8.95 |
| Path of Fire | T.T. Henderson | $8.95 |

## Other Genesis Press, Inc. Titles (continued)

## Other Genesis Press, Inc. Titles (continued)

## Other Genesis Press, Inc. Titles (continued)

# *ESCAPE WITH INDIGO !!!!*

Join Indigo Book Club©
It's simple, easy and secure.

Sign up and receive the new
releases
every month + Free shipping
and
20% off the cover price.

Visit us online at
www.genesis-press.com or
call 1-888-INDIGO-1

# Order Form

**Mail to: Genesis Press, Inc.**
**P.O. Box 101**
**Columbus, MS 39703**

Name _____

Address _____

City/State _____ Zip _____

Telephone _____

*Ship to (if different from above)*

Name _____

Address _____

City/State _____ Zip _____

Telephone _____

*Credit Card Information*

Credit Card # _____ ☐ Visa   ☐ Mastercard

Expiration Date (mm/yy) _____ ☐ AmEx   ☐ Discover

| Qty. | Author | Title | Price | Total |
|------|--------|-------|-------|-------|
|      |        |       |       |       |
|      |        |       |       |       |
|      |        |       |       |       |
|      |        |       |       |       |
|      |        |       |       |       |
|      |        |       |       |       |
|      |        |       |       |       |
|      |        |       |       |       |
|      |        |       |       |       |
|      |        |       |       |       |

Use this order
form, or call
1-888-INDIGO-1

**Total for books** _____

**Shipping and handling:**
**$5 first two books,**
**$1 each additional book** _____

**Total S & H** _____

**Total amount enclosed** _____

*Mississippi residents add 7% sales tax*